The Long Road

D1251455

Daniel Oliver

Black Rose Writing | Texas

The final approval for this literary material is granted by the author.

First printing

This is a work of fiction. Names, characters, businesses, places, events and incidents are either the products of the author's imagination or used in a fictitious manner. Any resemblance to actual persons, living or dead, or actual events is purely coincidental.

ISBN: 978-1-68433-008-9
PUBLISHED BY BLACK ROSE WRITING
www.blackrosewriting.com

Library of Congress Control Number: 2017962669

Printed in the United States of America
Suggested Retail Price (SRP) $18.95

The Long Road is printed in Adobe Garamond Pro

Bridges: The Science and Art of the World's Most Inspiring Structures by Blockley (2010) 125w from pp. 85-86, 174-175, 178
By permission of Oxford University Press

I give many thanks to fellow authors who helped me edit this novel. Its completion would not have been possible without them. Also, I thank Black Rose Writing for offering the opportunity to publish this story.

The Long Road

1.

I struggled to keep my white Audi close to the speed limit. My rearview mirror showed no headlights in the distance. *Relief.* I merged onto California's 101 South near Novato and headed to San Francisco. My phone, sitting on the passenger seat, lit up with an incoming call. *Is it Tom?* I risked a glance. No. An unknown caller—maybe my neighbor, the one with the gun.

My hands tightened on the steering wheel as if it were my lifeline, as if I were hanging off the side of a building. Now cars approached from behind on the larger freeway. At a half-mile stretch of hills, a rusted sedan with only one headlight edged up beside me. I imagined the driver—a rough-looking man with sideburns and a drawn collar of a trench coat—pointing a pistol at me. To confirm my suspicions, I stole a glance. But the driver was a middle-aged woman, who bobbed up and down to her music. *More relief!*

I neared the Golden Gate Bridge. The last thing I needed was an accident, since I hadn't bothered to change out of my pajama bottoms and slippers. The bridge, its dark-orange towers shrouded in an early-spring fog and its narrow lanes largely empty, was all that lay between the city and me. I squeezed the steering wheel even tighter. In a hurry, I avoided the toll lanes and illegally cruised through a lane dedicated to FasTrak. An alarm startled me, but I kept on.

Finally, I made it to the city. As I turned onto Van Ness from Lombard, a cop cruiser sped by, its sirens wailing and lights flashing. I ducked in a pathetic attempt not to be spotted. The cop continued on. I strained my eyes for the entrance ramp to 101, which picked up again as a freeway beyond downtown. San Francisco wasn't my destination. Tom lived in San Jose, farther south.

Unsure of my exact location, I exited 101 somewhere near San Jose. Though I'd been to Tom's apartment during my drive out West, I didn't have his address. *Why doesn't he call?* The glowing green clock on my radio display read 2:32 a.m. The prospect of driving aimlessly at this hour daunted me. I passed an Exxon, a McDonald's, and an IHOP before spotting the gold circular logo of a Sunset Inn. I whisked into the parking lot and skidded to a stop.

I caught a glimpse of my six-foot frame in the darkened window of the front door of the hotel as I approached. My long, thick brown hair stood up in thick clumps that refused to stay down despite my modest efforts. Light reflected off the lenses of my thin-rimmed glasses. My overgrown beard needed clipping. I looked like a scientist who had been stranded in the jungle for weeks.

The hotel clerk, a young Latino dressed in a white shirt, stood behind the gleaming front desk and gave me a disapproving eye roll but proceeded to check me in anyway. Luckily, I had my wallet with me, along with my passport and a plastic bottle of water.

"Your name, sir?"

I looked around before answering. No one within earshot. Keeping my voice low, I said, "Hank Galloway."

The last thing I wanted was to draw unnecessary attention to myself, yet dressed in pajamas and carrying no baggage, I was anything but inconspicuous. A man in the same white shirt and black slacks as the clerk came whistling down the hallway. He nodded, and I grabbed my hotel key and bolted.

The hotel rooms were stacked in two-story rows parallel to one another, organized like a barracks. My room was on the second story. After triple-checking the lock and closing the curtain, I started for the bed, then figured I'd better try Tom one last time. I left another message, my fifth. My mind continued to race.

Starving, I found a menu and dialed room service. With the phone cradled against my shoulder, I peeked through the blinds. The boulevard was dead. After placing my order, I turned on ESPN, more as a distraction than anything else.

My ham sandwich arrived ten minutes later, but I managed only a few bites. I tossed the uneaten portion into the trashcan by the desk. I was pacing back and forth by the window when my phone rang, and I hit my shin on the bed frame in my rush to get to it.

"Hey, buddy. What's up?"

I sighed with relief at the sound of Tom's groggy voice. "I've been trying to reach you for hours."

"Sorry. It is the middle of the night. So what's going on?"

"I'm in Santa Clara."

6

"Santa Clara?"

"Yeah. The Sunset Inn. Listen, Tom, something's happened and I need you to come get me."

There was a moment of silence and then, "Sure. OK. What intersection?"

I searched my memory for street names, but my mind was mush.

"Hank, I'll come get you, but I need an intersection."

I glanced at a brochure on the desk. "Great America Parkway."

"Great. Hang tight. I'll meet you outside the hotel in twenty minutes."

I waited until the last possible moment, then headed out to the street. My teeth chattered partly from the chill and my lack of clothing but mainly because I was terrified to be this out in the open. I was an easy target outside my hotel room. When Tom's black Dodge pulled up to the curb, I couldn't get into the car fast enough.

Tom did a double take. "What's going on? You look like crap."

I did a quick scan of the street, which to my relief was empty.

"Seriously, bro. What gives?" His sandy blond hair was rustled, his deep-set hazel eyes showed that he'd recently woken up, and his high cheekbones revealed faint whiskers.

"I'm in trouble. Big trouble."

Tom's concern seemed genuine. "In trouble? What kind of trouble?"

Anxious to get going, I gestured toward the dashboard. Tom obliged. Once we were in motion, I tried to explain what had happened. I told Tom about my neighbor, a biker who lived in the apartment next door. I'd always suspected he was bad news from the smell of marijuana coming from his place. But yesterday I parked in his spot because a delivery truck was in mine. He literally exploded, pounding on my door and screaming for me to get my wimpy ass outside. He reamed me out for the better part of twenty minutes, first claiming I'd run over his wife's flowers—which I had, though completely by accident—then berating me for parking my rich-kid car in his spot. It would have continued if our neighbor hadn't threatened to call the cops if we didn't quiet down. The guy was mental.

"Trust me, Tom. This guy was out of control. He was going to shoot me. I'm not kidding."

Tom, who had been listening intently, turned, a look of shock on his face. "Holy shit! Your neighbor pulled a gun on you?"

7

"Well, he didn't actually pull it on me."

"But he had a gun?"

"Sort of."

"Wait. What do you mean 'sort of'?"

"I didn't actually see the gun, but I know he has one."

"But I thought you just said..." Tom rubbed his chin. I could see he was struggling with my explanation. "Listen, Hank. I don't know how to break this to you, but even if your neighbor owns a gun, that doesn't mean he intended to use it on you. Lots of people own guns, and they don't just go around shooting people who piss them off."

"Dude, you weren't there. This guy wanted to shoot me. You think I'm making this up?"

Tom braked at a stoplight. He pivoted in his seat so that he was looking directly at me. "No. No. Of course I don't think you're making this up. It's just...I mean, I hope you don't take this the wrong way, but this whole story of yours...It's a little unbelievable."

"My neighbor was going to shoot me." I said this slowly so it would hopefully sink in.

"Because you parked in his spot?"

"And ran over his flowers."

The light changed, and the Dodge eased forward. "But why?" he asked, his voice almost pleading. "It doesn't make much sense." Clearly frustrated, he cupped a hand over his mouth and exhaled. Neither of us spoke for several minutes. "Stress," he said almost as much to himself as me. "I bet you're just stressed out...you know, from school. You *are* making out all right in your classes, aren't you?"

"Classes? Sure. Yeah. Classes are fine. I mean, I *have* been having difficulty sleeping lately, but that's—"

His eyes darted over me. "Drugs! I should've known. You're taking drugs."

"Drugs? No! You know I don't do drugs. Heck, I've had two beers in the last two weeks."

"You sure?"

"Of course I'm sure." I waited for his expression to soften. I thought Tom knew me better. "You don't believe me, do you?" I said, somewhat disheartened by his lack of faith. "You think I'm lying."

Tom shook his head. "Come on, man. This…this story of yours. It's…well…it's a little strange, don't ya think?" I sensed he wanted to believe me. "I'm sorry. I honestly don't know what to say. But you've got to put yourself in my position. I mean, have you looked at yourself in the mirror? You're a mess. And then you tell me that you drove here in the middle of the night, all because you and your neighbor argued over a parking spot and some flowers. I don't know about you, but to me it sounds like you're doing drugs."

"Tom," I said, my voice even more emphatic. "I'm not taking drugs."

"Then what the hell is going on?"

A flicker of light drew my attention to the side-view mirror where I saw an approaching car. I slumped down in the seat. "Don't look now but I think we're being followed."

"What?"

"There's a car behind us."

Tom glanced at the rear-view mirror, then turned as if to confirm what he'd seen.

"Shit! I told you not to look."

For the first time since the conversation had started, Tom seemed genuinely angry. "It's a car. You know, those big mechanical contraptions that drive on roads…roads like this."

I glanced in the side-view mirror again and panicked when I saw the car gaining on us. "Please. We've got to get out of here."

Tom seemed as if he were about to say something but stayed quiet.

Perspiration broke out on my forehead. I gripped the door handle on one side and the armrest on the other, stared straight ahead, and went rigid. We sped along the freeway, the white lane markers streaming by on either side of us, and the rhythmic bumps in the asphalt prodding us along. I didn't care where we went as long as it was fast.

2.

The sky was still black when we arrived at the Bay Area Hospital.

"Hospital?" I stared at Tom. "Why are we at a hospital?"

Tom pulled into the multilevel parking garage. "To get you some help."

"Help? But I'm not sick."

"You're acting strange. I think its best we get you checked out."

I thought about protesting, but I'd seen that stoic expression before, many times. Tom had made up his mind, which meant that any resistance was useless. The last time we'd had an argument was in high school. It was over who was a better basketball player, so he challenged me to a one-on-one in the gym after school and beat me handily. I'd always hesitated to challenge him since. His take-charge style made him a leader of our pack, and I wasn't in any mood to argue now. Plus, maybe if he had me checked out, he'd finally accept that I wasn't on drugs. Either way, I was too tired to protest. I would have preferred the couch at Tom's apartment, but for now a hospital gurney would have to do.

A receptionist with a grim face greeted Tom while I sat.

"My friend," Tom started in a normal tone, then made an effort to lower his voice. "He's acting strange."

Confident that Tom's idea to go to the hospital was a mistake, I said nothing. That was when a tall man walked behind me, and I flinched, certain he was about to attack me. I went to the floor in a fetal position with my arms covering my head. When he passed without incident, I looked up from my crouched position. Tom and the receptionist were staring at me.

Maybe I do need to see a doctor after all. I shook my head in frustration and disbelief that I'd let someone scare me so much and returned to my seat.

The receptionist handed Tom some paperwork to fill out, and he sat down next to me.

Despite the early-morning hour, the large waiting area was a place of hustle and bustle. The phones rang constantly. Across from me sat a young Latino woman, her face pale and eyes full of apprehension. She cradled an infant draped in a shawl and drew the bundle closer to her chest when she noticed me looking. To my right, a tired-looking couple slumped against each other, their eyes focused ahead in a vacant stare. Beside them was a heavy-set black woman wearing a 49ers sweatshirt. Her head tilted back against the wall, and her eyes fluttered open and closed as she faded in and out of sleep.

"Can you give me the phone of someone in your family?" asked Tom. "I should probably let them know where you are."

I really didn't want to involve my parents, but Tom insisted. I started reciting my parents' number and then decided that was probably a bad idea and opted for my brother Zach's number instead.

Tom returned the paperwork to the receptionist. He sat back down, adjusted his black sweatpants, and pushed up the sleeves of his orange Princeton sweatshirt. He didn't say much. Not that I blamed him. Neither of us was in the mood for talking. I sat with hands clasped.

"Hank, just relax," Tom said. He nodded toward my foot tapping nervously against the linoleum.

Sure, it was easy for him to be calm. He wasn't a sitting duck in danger of being murdered by his neighbor. *Could he have followed me all this way?* I couldn't help but think he might have.

Still, for Tom's sake, I stopped. I glanced up to meet the stare of a gray-haired, wrinkled Asian man with a pale face that had about as much animation and color as a corpse, and I quickly looked away.

A half hour passed before a slim, middle-aged nurse called my name.

Tom nudged me with his elbow but stayed seated. That's when I realized he wasn't coming back with me, and I hesitated. "Don't worry," he said. "I'll be right here. I promise."

I walked through the double doors and sat down in the triage room. The nurse, who wore a standard white lab coat over baggie maroon scrubs, introduced herself. She directed me to a chair positioned adjacent to a plastic desk. Glass jars filled with cotton swabs, Band-Aids, and alcohol were pushed back in the corner of the table. On the wall in front of me hung a blood pressure cuff and next to it a poster of a smiling nurse in blue scrubs that read, *Have you had your flu shot today?*

"Are you taking any medications?" asked the triage nurse curtly.

"No."

Her fingers zipped across the keyboard, and I wondered what in the world she could be typing on the desktop computer in front of her.

"Any medical conditions?"

"None."

"What about alcohol? When's the last time you had a drink?"

"Maybe a week ago."

"Any drug use?"

I answered with a confident no wishing Tom was around to hear me.

"What do you do for work?"

"I'm studying at Dewey State."

"At twenty-six?"

"I switched careers."

"Your friend…" She paused.

"Tom," I offered.

"He wrote here that you drove all the way from Sonoma County, in the middle of the night, because you believed your neighbor had a gun he intended to use on you."

I didn't really feel like going through this again. I leaned back in my chair, my hands clasped behind my head, and stared up at the ceiling.

"Mr. Galloway," the nurse prompted to me, and I exhaled forcefully through pursed lips.

If it will get me out of here, then I'll do it. So I went through my story again. I described the argument with my neighbor, his explosive temper, and the shouting. When asked about the gun, I told her exactly what I'd told Tom, that I'd never seen it, but I was sure he had one. She occasionally offered a nod or um-hum to acknowledge my responses, the whole time her fingers tapping away at the keyboard. Once I'd finished answering all her questions, she explained that I would be called back into the emergency room shortly.

She walked me back to the general waiting area, and I ambled over to where Tom sat thumbing through an outdated issue of *Sports Illustrated*.

"So how did it go?" he asked.

"It went," I said. "They'll come for me as soon as they can see me."

He nodded that he understood. "You feeling OK?"

"I'm tired."

"Don't worry. It will all be over soon."

I picked up a *Better Homes and Gardens* from the table in front of me and flipped through the pages, though I was only superficially aware of the magazine's contents. Mostly I thought about Tom's suggestion that I wasn't well. We'd been friends forever, and I'd thought he knew me better than that.

Finally, a Filipino nurse escorted me back. As we entered the heart of the ER, the sterile odor of a hospital reached me. Alarms from monitoring devices sounded off. Nurses and doctors called to one another. Technicians rushed about with their electrocardiogram machines and blood-drawing paraphernalia.

For God's sake, it's the middle of the night!

"Right here," the nurse said as we arrived at our destination. She reached into a cabinet and withdrew a gown and plastic cup. "For a urine sample," she said, handing me the cup.

She gave me some privacy, and leaving on my pajama bottoms, I slipped on the gown. Next, I urinated in the cup and left the sample on the countertop as I had been told. When I was finished, I sat on the gurney. Otherwise, drawn curtains surrounded me.

I hadn't the faintest idea how I ended up in an emergency department. I was positive I'd end up on Tom's couch when I met him at the hotel. Part of me seethed that I'd trusted him with what had happened with my neighbor. *Is this some sort of cruel joke that he is playing on me? Is this how friends really treat each other?* Or maybe he had turned on me and wasn't my friend anymore. Maybe he was cleaning his hands of the situation and just wanted to be done with me. Dump me in the hospital and go on with his life.

Several minutes passed before the young Filipino nurse drew some blood. As she pricked my arm, the patient next door made a deep guttural groan that caused me to cringe. After filling a few vials, the nurse returned with a yellow pill and a cup of water. I eyed the pill suspiciously. "What's this?"

"It's something that'll calm you down and help you sleep."

"What else could happen if I take it?"

"Please, don't worry. Just take it."

I hesitated and finally washed the pill down. The nurse left briskly.

I second-guessed the medicine, since I had no idea what the nurse had given me. On top of that, the staff was in such a rush that I wondered if they really wanted to help or not. It seemed I was a bother to them if anything else.

Done with this whole thing, I began to climb off the gurney when an older female nurse with bifocals saw me and said in an authoritative tone, "What are you doing? Please get back on the gurney."

"I just wanted to see my friend in the waiting room."

"You can't leave the gurney. Please stay in it."

I obeyed and climbed back on.

A couple of minutes later, a security guard wearing his navy-blue uniform and standing tall and erect appeared. I was surprised to see him. His arms folded across each other, he looked at me as if I were a troublemaker.

I waited, tapping my hands on the rails of the gurney and hoping the patient next to me didn't gasp his last breath. I was too young and freaked out already for a fellow patient to die right next to me.

After about an hour, three orderlies dressed in all-white scrubs arrived and mentioned a head scan. They were Latino and spoke to one another in Spanish. All three of them carried on as though they were catching up on the latest funny story.

"Could you speak English?" I asked them.

They ignored me. My temper rose. My face flushed. The whole night was terrible and getting worse each moment.

"Hey, assholes, speak English!"

A conversation in the adjacent bay went silent. The security guard shook his head and pursed his lips. A black woman in a gown who walked with a urine bag in her hand in front of my open bay said, "Mmm…mmm."

"Speak in English?" said a short one with a mole on his cheek. "OK, *amigo.*" Then he turned to one of the tall ones, said something in Spanish to him, and nodded in my direction. The laughter continued.

They wheeled me to a room with a big circular machine. Without my glasses, I could still see a narrow surface for a patient to lie on with one end close to a doughnutlike structure. They guided me off the gurney and onto the thin, firm bench, which was covered with white sheets.

A technician appeared and took over. He strapped me onto the bench and then sat in an office at the controls. The giant machine revved up and made a spinning noise.

Is this really a head scan or something else? I had no clue.

The machine revved down. The orderlies, still chatting in Spanish, reappeared, unstrapped me, and told me, in English, to get back onto the gurney.

They wheeled me back outside the room and down a long corridor. We turned down another hallway, one that I didn't recognize. It was empty. The gurney went faster and then stopped.

The two tall orderlies pinned me down. One grabbed hold of my ankles while the other held down my shoulders. I immediately struggled but couldn't move except with my arms, which flailed but didn't connect with anything. The one with a mole on his cheek grabbed my forearms.

I screamed, "Get the fuck away! Let me go!" but no one else was in the corridor. The orderlies said nothing more, although they continued to pin me down as we started back to where we'd come from. I still struggled against them as we arrived at the ER.

Back in the bay, the security guard took up his post. The orderlies began strapping me with restraints. One of the tall ones said in English in a raised voice to no one in particular, "He bit me."

"I didn't bite anyone!" I said, shocked.

The security guard, who was the only other one in the room, wore no expression. The orderlies left, and I waited.

My original nurse brushed the curtains aside and entered the bay to check on me.

"The orderlies pinned me down in the empty hallway!" I exclaimed.

"Sure they did," she replied.

I wasn't so sure by the tone of her voice that she believed me. "Look at my arms—how red they are!"

Largely ignoring me, she began writing in my chart.

I thought of Tom and changed my tactics. "Can my friend come back here?"

"Not right now," she said.

"Why not?"

"We want to stabilize you a bit more before he's allowed to see you." Her face was all business, and she didn't make eye contact with me as she continued writing and then walked away.

Still in restraints, I grew tired and concentrated solely on my breathing. The guard rubbed his forehead with his hand as if he, too, were weary. Time dragged. I tried to read a clock posted on the far wall but couldn't make out the hands with my limited vision. My eyeglasses rested on a metal tray not within reach. Was it 4:00 a.m.? Five? Impossible to tell.

Finally, a woman in scrubs appeared. I thought she was another nurse. "How are you feeling?" she asked. She leaned over my gurney and studied me.

"Not too good," I said.

She asked me some of the same questions that the triage nurse had asked. I answered them again. "Is there anybody in the area that you can go to—any family?" she asked.

"No."

"Where is your family? Where are your parents?"

"In Georgia."

"Do you want to go to your parents in Georgia?"

"No!"

"Then we're going to send you to a psychiatric hospital."

"A psychiatric hospital?" Now I knew that she was a physician and not a nurse.

"You need to spend some time under direct medical observation to make sure you adjust well enough to the medicine we gave you."

"What about my friend?" I asked.

"We sent him home," said the Filipino nurse. "He said he'd see you tomorrow."

"Tomorrow?" I tried to conjure some argument for an immediate discharge instead, but the physician and nurse left abruptly.

Fuck. Just when things couldn't get any worse, they did.

3.

Being locked up in a hospital where most patients didn't speak English and acted unpredictably made me uneasy, even at night when I was supposed to be sleeping. I was always on edge, expecting the worst. Even while passing the time walking the long hallway that served to connect offices, the common room, sleeping room, and nurses' station, I held my breath and averted my eyes when passing other patients.

Will they attack me?

The shock of being admitted to the hospital still held strong. I'd never been to one for any reason. I was a model of good health—went to the gym, drank only once in a while, didn't do drugs, and now this.

Zach, my brother, visited only a short time. He flew up and then returned to Los Angeles the same day. His wife and infant occupied his life outside working at a bank, so he didn't stay in town until my discharge. I was embarrassed that he took a whole day to travel and come see me. I was usually so self-sufficient with my life that an emergency visit such as this one had never been necessary.

The medication lines at the nurses' station, the group sessions with a staff member, and the daily meetings with the psychiatrist—they were all degrading experiences. It was as if the place were an institution and the stoic patients all just went through the motions. It scared me to think I would be there for three days when the female psychiatrist first told me my discharge date. I immediately wondered if I could hack it that long. Some patients came and went during my stay, while others, who looked like they *really* needed the hospital, were present when I arrived and remained after I left.

An old man who did speak English asked me to help him open a cardboard carton of milk for his breakfast the first morning. He wheezed, and his gnarled hands couldn't quite tear open the container. After I assisted him, he said, "Thank you." That was the first interaction I had with another patient.

The following day, in a group session, the elderly man stopped breathing altogether! No one noticed but me until I alerted the group leader, who then called for help while I began chest compressions. All of a sudden, four staff members surrounded the man, who was on the floor. They did CPR and took him away, off the floor, and the rest of the patients and I never saw him again. Even though I asked one of the nurses the next day if the patient survived, she told me out of privacy concerns that she couldn't give me his status. I wondered if the poor guy made it.

Performing CPR on someone, even for just the short time, scared me further. It made me think of my own mortality and added to the strangeness of the psych ward, with the vacant stares of the patients and the strained eyes of the staff, as if they were overworked.

The sleeping arrangements shocked me the most. The sleeping room consisted of beige recliners bunched together. Private rooms were nonexistent.

How can that be?

Every recliner was occupied. A few patients snored, and I struggled to sleep in the close quarters. Eventually I dozed off due to the medicine, but my sleep was fitful, full of strange dreams and interruptions when the staff entered the room to check on us.

It was hard enough speaking with Tom when he visited the day after my admission, though I greatly appreciated seeing a familiar face. I mumbled some words of thanks for his visit while I tried to deal with the shock of my hospital stay. He looked tired from the events of the night before and didn't stay long.

The psychiatrist seemed particularly uninterested in my upcoming calculus exam at my university. Despite my persuasion for an early discharge, she held firm to my three-day stay. Nerves settled in while I milled about in the psych ward in anticipation of discharge and my return to my studies. Doing poorly on any exam hurt my chances of getting into a mechanical engineering program and ultimately working for NASA.

I didn't want to complain to anybody, though, since doing so might anger the psychiatrist, and angering the psychiatrist might prolong my stay. At least that was my reasoning.

Despite some lingering doubts, I was convinced that the whole idea of going to a psychiatric hospital was a mistake; I was too normal to be mentally ill. But I didn't take out my anger over what happened with the Latino orderlies, nor with being locked in a hospital, on Tom—that was over and done with. I valued our friendship too much.

. . . . .

After discharge from Bellevue, the psychiatric hospital, I climbed into the front seat of Tom's Dodge wearing a T-shirt that Tom had brought, my pajama bottoms, and my slippers. The discharge plan was for me to spend the night at Tom's apartment and drive back to Halifax, my town in Sonoma County, the next morning.

Nicole, Tom's fiancée, her curly black hair still wet from a shower, sat in the back. She worked as a kindergarten teacher and always exuded cheer. She and Tom had met at Princeton and moved to California after graduation.

After breathing in the stale air of the dim, aging psych ward, I sucked in fresh air and squinted in the sunlight. My thought process crawled, due to the medicine from what the psychiatrist told me, but my overall relief at leaving drowned out all other emotions. Upon discharge, my nerves were frayed, but seeing my two old friends heightened my spirits instantly.

Three days in the hospital had allowed me to reflect on my rendezvous with Tom. He was right. I had never seen my neighbor with a gun. I looked a mess after driving half the night. Maybe if the roles were reversed, I'd have brought him to the hospital, too. Anyway, I was out of the ward and allowed to return home, though I still had some reservations about a future run-in with my neighbor.

"It's good to see you," Nicole chirped. "Finally, you're out of that place. It looks like a dump from the outside."

"It was a dump on the inside, too," I stammered. My relief was so great that a lump was in my throat.

"Really?" Nicole asked.

"The paint was cracking on the walls and the wooden floors creaked in the psychiatrist's office. The whole place had a stale smell, as if it hadn't been aired out in years. It must be a low-budget operation," I concluded.

"Tom said most of the other patients looked catatonic when he visited you," continued Nicole.

"Yeah..." I didn't know what to say. Blood rushed to my face in embarrassment that she knew about my hospital stay.

For the first time, I felt bad that I'd put Tom and Nicole through all this, especially Tom. The phone calls in the middle of the night, the waiting in the emergency department, and the visit to the hospital. I wondered if they thought I was a lunatic, if our relationship would change going forward, or if they'd even associate with me anymore when I got back to Halifax.

After Tom paid the parking attendant, I let out another deep breath but remained speechless. I tried to think of something to say but thought of nothing.

As Tom merged his Dodge onto 101, its rhythmic bumps reminded me of the night that he drove me to the emergency department. Four days later, the event seemed a dream, a nightmare to be more precise. The bumps made it more real, as if my environment wouldn't let me forget.

"Did your brother visit you?" Tom asked while we cruised south to San Jose.

"Yeah. The day after you did." I scanned the rolling hills, the low-level buildings lining the freeway, and the occasional billboard. "He got a chance to talk with the psychiatrist. She said it's too early to give a diagnosis. My new psychiatrist that I'm meeting Wednesday will have to figure it out."

"That's understandable," said Tom.

"Did you talk to your parents? Tom said they didn't make the trip out to see you," chimed Nicole.

"It's a long way for them, I guess. My mother worried about me over the phone, mentioning something about recovering and taking the rest of the semester off."

"It might be something to consider, you know? How about your dad? What did he say?" Tom asked.

"He...he was playing golf when I called. Couldn't talk." My father was retired and played golf three or four times a week at his country club. I wasn't surprised when my mother told me that he wasn't around when I talked to her from the hospital phone. Only now, when I told Tom and Nicole, did it occur to me that it was strange that my father played golf while I was in a hospital.

An uncomfortable silence ensued. I gripped my hands together, noticing the whites of my knuckles, and then fixed my gaze on the car in front of us.

"We've got a frozen pizza for dinner. I hope that's all right," said Nicole.

"Fine...just fine," I stammered. The lump was still in my throat. Anything was better than the slop served to the rest of the patients and me.

"We'll get you food and a good night's rest. Your car is good. I checked on it right before we picked you up," Tom said.

"Thanks, Tom." For some reason, I felt like crying, but I held back. The shock of my hospitalization almost spilled over. Thankfully, silence ensued again. I was grateful Tom and Nicole didn't delve further into my hospital stay.

Today was Sunday, giving me Monday to get back to school in time for a review session with some classmates in the afternoon and my calculus exam on Tuesday morning.

"I hope you'll be comfortable on the futon," Nicole said. "Tom, did you put the sheets in the dryer?"

"They'll be ready by the time we get home."

"Remember, next weekend we have to decide on a band for the reception. If we don't book one now we'll have to settle on a second-rate group."

"Don't worry. We'll take care of it."

The couple chattered on about more wedding preparations. I willed my eyes to stay open and tried to accustom myself to life's fast pace outside the hospital.

4.

The morning of my calculus exam, I deliberately avoided my classmates. I studied until the last moment in the library and then went straight to my seat in our classroom, knowing that interacting with them would sap my energy and make me even more nervous. Our study session the day before had helped minimally, as fatigue had set in my brain and I'd excused myself to go home early.

With the exam in front of me, I brainstormed, trying to come up with derivatives. How were coefficients involved with them? I jotted down total guesses, and my confidence sank. I was lost again doing the word problem at the end; my mind was all fuzzy, my heart raced, and beads of sweat ran down my sides. I hunched over my exam with my hands clenched in fists, pencil in my right hand.

When I finished, I placed the packet in front of the professor, walked out of the classroom, and let the metal door bang shut. Suddenly, after I'd gotten solid grades for the majority of my first year of studying prerequisites, my hopes of getting into a high-quality engineering program dimmed.

A math major, Rob Hernandez, who sat next to me in class, approached from a group of students waiting outside. We always discussed the exams after we finished them. His black hair spiked in front, and the sleeves of his bright red rugby shirt were pushed up on his forearms. "How'd you do?"

"I think I failed it." I put on my green jacket and looked away from his intent eyes and down the hallway.

"You failed it? You always get decent grades."

I frowned. "This time I don't think it'll happen. How did you do?"

"I got most everything except for the word problem at the end. Just couldn't figure it out." I sensed Rob sizing me up. "You still look out of it. Didn't you get enough sleep last night? Everything all right?"

"I came down with the flu last week. Still a little weak." I continued to avoid eye contact.

He backed away from me with a look of concern, as if I had the plague. "Oh…are you better?"

"I'm recovering."

"Maybe that's why you didn't do well."

"Probably." Though I considered Rob a friend, I didn't reveal the real reason for my poor performance—my hospitalization. Word would spread fast if I told him about it.

We joined a group also discussing the exam. When we dispersed, Rob asked me, "Are you coming to the cafeteria with us? Or are you going to be antisocial?"

"Not antisocial. Just wiped out." Angry and disappointed, I walked alongside him out of the building and across the main plaza, which teemed with students. Some of them lay on the grass, soaking in the early spring sun. A light breeze kicked up, and the sky was a deep blue.

"You better grab some coffee or something. We've got finals coming up in a couple weeks. What are your hardest ones?" asked Rob.

"Biology and chemistry, along with calculus."

"Good luck with those. I heard chemistry is hella hard. You sure picked the wrong time to get sick."

Worry crept into my psyche again. *Can I handle finals feeling like I do now? Probably not. My energy level has to go up a couple notches or else I'm really in trouble.* Calculus, biology, and chemistry were prerequisites to begin a mechanical engineering program. I needed a solid performance in all of them. My grade point average had been great before this exam, but if I'd failed the calculus exam, there was no telling what my chances would be going forward.

I loafed to the cafeteria with my head down, lost in thought.

"Hey, man. Cheer up. Finals are two weeks away. You'll be in tip-top shape," continued Rob.

Tracy Owens, a junior I knew from my Spanish class, approached us. I'd had my eye on her since the first week of the semester. Well-proportioned, with straight, long black hair that fell to her shoulders, she smiled at Rob and me.

"Hank, how are you?" she asked, her green eyes glowing.

I forced a smile. "Good. How's it going?"

"We just got out of a calculus exam. Hank thinks he failed it," interjected Rob before Tracy could answer.

"You're kidding! He always does well on his exams," Tracy said.

"He took forever to finish it. And yesterday he ducked out of our study session early because he was tired. Imagine that."

"I don't believe it!" Tracy turned toward me, as if waiting for a confirmation.

My faint smile faded. I looked straight ahead, solemn.

"Hank, who usually stays behind after the study session to review everything one more time by himself, left early?"

"He was so pissed off he let the door slam while the rest finished," said Rob. He chuckled.

"What's with you?" asked Tracy, continuing to study me. "Has the southern gentleman lost his manners?"

"I was upset. Still am," I said, my mind swirling with emotions. Tracy's arrival was bad timing. Usually I was laying on the charm while talking to her, but now I just wanted to sulk. Maybe watch a movie. After lunch I still had two more lectures, so going home seemed far off at the moment.

"Hey, you weren't in class on Wednesday or Friday last week," said Tracy.

"I was sick," I said gruffly.

"We have to write a two-hundred-word essay on Cervantes. It's due on Friday. Better get to it," she said.

"Thanks for the warning," I said, trying to muster up some enthusiasm, though it was impossible. The shock of my hospitalization still weighed heavily on my mind, and my medicine still prevented me from having my usual amount of energy. "Anything else I missed?" With the calc exam looming, I hadn't given my other classes even a thought.

"We reviewed our homework on Wednesday and watched a movie on Friday."

As we neared the cafeteria, Tracy peeled off in the opposite direction. "I'm off. I've got a yoga class at one. I'll see you in class, Hank?" she called.

I turned my head to her. "Yeah. See ya."

After Tracy was out of earshot, Rob nudged me with his elbow. "I thought you wanted to ask her out? She's into you."

"Not today."

"Don't worry. We've got the final still. That counts as thirty-five percent of our final grade. Come on, man. One day you'll be at NASA, and all of this will be just a memory." He grinned. "I thought for sure you were going to ask Tracy out just now. You've been talking about her all semester!"

Finally, I turned to him, looked down on his short frame, and smiled. "I'll get around to it. Just don't get any ideas for yourself."

"She's all yours."

5.

The next day I went to see my first psychiatrist, Dr. Allen. His office was in Petaluma—close to Halifax. Luckily he had an opening for me soon after my discharge. Other patients weren't so lucky, from what one of the nurses had told me in the hospital.

I doubted that I needed further care. I wasn't like some of the other patients in the hospital—drooling, staring out the window, mumbling to themselves.

I made it to the office in a large, four-story complex with a spacious parking lot painted with fresh white markings. A few stairways from the parking lot level led to exterior balcony corridors where entrance doors to many of the offices were. I looked over the directory, wandered around, and pulled open the heavy glass door with his name, among those of other psychologists and psychiatrists, on it.

I took off my jacket and sat down alone in the waiting room. A couple of circular white-noise machines made the sound of wind blowing, and a basket full of magazines sat next to a green-cushioned wicker chair. Feeling tense, I stared ahead of me and passed up on a magazine. Instead, I waited for the doctor himself to appear.

I tried to imagine how I should act but was not sure what to say or do. I was at a loss, since I'd never met with a psychiatrist, except for the woman in Bellevue. During my interviews there, I only struggled to stay awake, not to answer the questions she had asked me.

Ten minutes after my scheduled appointment, the door opened, and Dr. Allen emerged. I towered over him by at least a few inches. He had a broad forehead and curly black hair. His body frame was thin, almost frail.

After we formally met and shook hands, he motioned me into his office. A coffee table of clear circular glass sat in front of a long brown leather couch. A dark-colored throw rug covered a large portion of the wooden floor. On the walls were modern paintings whose shapes and colors went together in a fashion that made me think of Picasso. Opposite the couch, on the other side of the coffee table, were two lounge chairs; we both sat down. I rested my hands flat on my thighs after settling in.

"So," he said, "how've you been doing since your discharge from Bellevue?" I noticed a stuffy nasal quality to his voice, as if he had a cold.

"Good," I said, trying to sound upbeat, though I really wasn't. "No big problems, besides being tired all the time."

"That's a common side effect of your medicine, Connect. What about your neighbor? Any concerns?" Dr. Allen leaned forward in his chair, attentive to my answers.

"No. I've spoken to him since I returned to Halifax. We're on good terms again." I had seen my neighbor in passing the evening of my return from San Jose. He said hi and shook my hand. I was afraid of what he might do because it was the first time we'd crossed paths since the argument. He mentioned not seeing me for the time when I was in the hospital, but I brushed it off, saying that I was visiting my brother in Los Angeles.

"That's good to hear," said the shrink. He crossed his legs, looked down at my chart, and flipped it. "The psychiatrist who saw you gave a diagnosis of psychosis not otherwise specified, which is rather vague." He read some more. "Remind me how much Connect you're taking right now."

"Fifteen milligrams."

"At night, right?"

"Yes." My nightly pill was a drag. Taking it gave me the impression that I was sick. But I still took it.

"How much are you sleeping?"

"About eleven hours a night, and sometimes I take a nap in the afternoon for an hour."

"Ah, yes. That is quite a bit," he said. "Any other changes since you've started the medicine?"

"Uhh…Not that I know of."

"Any constipation, headache, or dizziness?"

"No." Uncomfortable at the thought of more side effects, I shifted in my seat.

He continued. "What about your family? Anybody suffer from mental illness?"

"I think my grandfather was bipolar. My mother has depression."

"Which grandfather? On your mother's or father's side?"

"My father's side."

"Do you have any idea what medicines he took?"

"I have no idea." I glanced away from his stare. His questions were making me uneasy, since I'd never talked to anyone about mental illness in my family. My family and I brushed such issues under the rug.

"Now, just to get to know you a little better. Your parents are back in Georgia, correct?"

"Yes. And Zach, my brother, lives in Los Angeles. Chrissy, my sister, goes to college in Georgia."

"Your brother lives in Los Angeles," he repeated after me, as if reflecting deeply on that fact. "And do you have any other siblings?"

"No. Just Zach and Chrissy."

"Are your parents still together?"

"Yes." Images of my parents squabbling in their mansion came to mind. Their marriage wasn't a happy one—it never had been as long as I could remember, though I didn't relate any of this to Dr. Allen.

"And what brought you to Sonoma County? I mean…you have no family here."

"I've always been fascinated with California, especially the Bay Area, since I visited my friend, Tom, right after he moved here. The people, the surfing, San Francisco…it's where I want to be."

"Ah…I see. Do you plan on staying here?" He smiled.

"Yes. At least until I'm accepted into an engineering program, but I'd like to live here after my studies are complete and work at NASA."

Dr. Allen's eyebrows rose. "NASA, eh? That's a lofty goal. What made you decide on that?"

"I've always been interested in rockets. It started with going to see commercial fireworks on the Fourth of July and watching space shuttle launches on TV."

"Any backup plans in case that doesn't work out? I'm not trying to discourage you, but engineering is a tough profession to get into and stay in— even for someone without mental health issues."

My blood boiled when he insinuated that I had mental health issues, but I answered calmly, "I can do it."

"Of course," said Dr. Allen. He settled back into his chair. "Now getting back to your hospitalization. What was going on in the days and weeks prior to your admission?"

Memories came up—the lack of sleep, wondering if someone was out to get me, and the distrust of my friends. I didn't go into all that, though. "I just couldn't fall asleep about a week before it happened."

"Was there anything going on in your life that caused this?"

I fidgeted with my hands as I thought about my stress and hours of lying in bed. "I am taking some difficult courses, but I can't say for sure what caused me to stay awake so many nights in a row. I've always taken hard classes, even when I studied finance in college—you know? But I never lost so much sleep before."

"You studied finance, but now you're studying to enter engineering school?"

"I made a career change. I was working in a bank in North Carolina and then decided to pursue engineering."

"So that's why you're a bit older?" pursued the doctor.

"Yes."

There was a pause. "Getting back to your symptoms. Any strained relationships or other stressors in your life at that time?"

"None."

"I see. And how are your classes going now?"

"My last exam in calculus wasn't so easy for me. I think I failed it because it came two days after my discharge. And I was so tired. Up until that exam, I was doing very well."

Dr. Allen nodded. "As I already mentioned, the medicine is causing all of this sedation. We should probably change it, considering your family history and this side effect. We won't make the change just yet because I want to make sure that you're stable, but I think a different regimen could be more effective. How does that sound?"

"Fine," I said, although the fact that he wanted to keep me on any medicine disappointed me.

"This was your first admission to a psychiatric hospital, right?"

My voice dropped, and I avoided his small circular eyeglasses and beady eyes. "Right." I felt an impulse to explain to him how I thought the admission was a mistake, but again, I kept quiet.

"And you never had trouble with your sleep before?"

"No…never."

"You could have a chemical imbalance that you inherited from your mother. It's very possible that this condition is manifesting at this point in your life. That's why I want to make the medicine change."

"The new medicine is for depression then?"

"Exactly."

"I see." I stroked my now-clipped beard while I processed this information.

"What do you do in your free time?" continued Dr. Allen.

"I like to surf." This time I put some enthusiasm in my voice.

"You like to surf? Where did you learn to surf growing up in Georgia?"

"I spent summers with my grandparents along the South Carolina coast. There *are* beaches with waves. My grandfather taught my siblings and me."

"Were you close with him?"

"Very much. He encouraged me to follow my passions in life, like rockets." All of a sudden, talking about surfing, my grandfather, and rockets made me calm and content.

"Your mother's father?"

"Yes. He passed away a few years ago."

"I see." Dr. Allen rested the side of his head in his hand. "What about a girlfriend? Are you dating anyone?"

"Not at the moment. I'm hoping to in the near future."

"Relationships are always tricky." He paused after this small talk. "Do you get back to Georgia to see your family often?"

I gulped. I couldn't help feeling anxious about seeing my parents after my hospitalization. Over the phone, my mother sounded worried and my father tepid at best, very businesslike as usual. "Yes. I'm going back after the semester is over in a couple weeks."

"Ah, good. I'm sure they'll want to see you." He gathered up my chart and closed it. Though we made an appointment for the following week, just the thought of returning was a downer.

After we rose from our chairs, he gave me a quirky smile, the same kind of forced smile that he had given me when he first met me, and followed me to the door.

I walked back to my car in a sullen mood. Weekly sessions with a shrink weren't my idea of fun, but at this point, there wasn't any way around them. Just like my medicine. I still had to take it, even though I didn't think I needed it. I resolved to cooperate with my treatment plan.

6.

That weekend, Tom and I decided to go surfing. We made the trek to Bodega Bay, a spot located off the cliffs that jutted up from the sandy beaches along the coastline. The wind whipped my thick hair, but the sun had burned through the morning clouds and shone, glimmering off the ocean and mildly warming the air.

We parked along the scenic Highway 1. Below, when we looked down from the cliff that separated the road from the beach, waves struck boulders emerging from the sea, spewing water high into the air. A dog chased its owner's Frisbee into the foamy water, and farther inland toward the cliff, little children played in the sand. Those on the beach wore long pants and sweatshirts. The air smelled of the sea.

Tom and I put on our wetsuits at his truck, touched up the surfboards with coconut-scented wax, and set down the narrow, dusty path to the beach. We waited at the shoreline for a calm in the ocean. When we saw a smooth horizon to the west, Tom shouted, "Let's go," and led the way into the chilly waters.

As we paddled out through the ever-present kelp to the other surfers, smaller breaking waves crashed in front of us. Feeling the cold water in my face when I dived under the approaching surf woke me from my medicine-induced stupor and invigorated me. Blood pumped through my body for what seemed like the first time in weeks. My full-body wetsuit inhibited my movement somewhat and forced me to strain my shoulders while I paddled alongside Tom. Finally, we reached beyond the crashing waves, an area called the lineup, and waited, sitting on our boards. A couple of surfers chatted with one another, but mostly the only sound was the waves breaking behind us.

While we waited, my thoughts drifted to when I surfed as a boy with Grandpa Joe, my mother's father, during the summers in South Carolina. He was gentle, never chiding anybody except when someone tried to cross him. He taught Zach, Chrissy, and me how to catch a wave. "Paddle hard!" he'd urge us. "Don't get up until you're sure you've caught it!" He showed us how to wax our boards until our skin held tight while we paddled and stood up, gripping and maneuvering with our shifting weight along the open face of the wave. He waited with us in the breaking surf and coached us as small knee- to waist-high waves approached. I still heard his voice as we stood on our boards and turned them right or left. "Excellent! You've got it now." He was different from our father, who, with his beatings and yelling, was anything but gentle.

Grandpa Joe taught us more than surfing. I remembered his words when he encouraged us to follow our interests and passions in life. "Only doing what you believe is your calling will bring you peace with God and happiness," he said. "Many lose their way along the path."

Four years before his death, I had lost my way while in college. My father sat me down in his study right before my sophomore year, the year when I had to choose a major, and gave me a long speech about working in banking and the importance of choosing a respectable profession. I bought into his pitch.

After I graduated and settled in a bank in Charlotte, my salary gave me a comfortable lifestyle—a nice apartment in a fancy part of town. I had no student loans or car payment. My father paid for my college tuition, and my Audi was a graduation present, also from my father.

But after a couple of years I knew something was missing. Being unhappy with my work gnawed at me until I finally quit my job and pursued engineering. I had been eyeing California. Far away from my father, I could make a clean break from his influences.

My attention returned to the lineup. A set of waves rose from a distance, and I paddled toward the beach to build momentum. The first wave carried me, and I felt the sudden acceleration of going down the steep face, or sloped portion, of the swell. I hopped to my feet and glided, making a distinct track up and down the face, before falling into the whitewash portion. After gathering my board, I headed back toward Tom.

As I paddled back to the lineup, reflecting on my late grandfather still, a wave with a barrel, or tubular portion, broke ahead to my right. I paddled hard to avoid being crushed when out of the tube popped another surfer. He bore down on me full speed, and I blocked his way. It was too late to maneuver out of the way, and he rammed the side of my board with the tip of his. The wave crunched the boards, the other surfer, and me, spitting us out into the whitewash as it moved farther toward the beach and left us in its wake.

When I surfaced, the other surfer, as skinny as a rail but tall with long, stringy hair down to his shoulders glared and approached me while he waded through the chest-high seawater. "Hey, asshole. Look at my board." He pointed to the chopped-off tip of his bright green shortboard. Mine was gashed in the side from the collision and revealed its inner core.

"Sorry, man. I didn't see you in the tube," I said in between breaths; the wave had held me down for a while.

"Sorry! Is that all you can say?" He came closer, wading through the whitewash. "Where are you from anyway, you country hick? You shouldn't be on this beach. It's for locals only!"

I tried to explain that I'd surfed at Bodega Bay every week since I'd lived in California but froze instead. *This guy's gonna beat me into a pulp.* My mouth opened, but nothing came out. Instead, another wave crashed into us. By the time we surfaced, the guy had moved within close range, his right arm cocked with a fist, his mouth set, partly open showing his teeth. He hovered over me.

"Hey!" I heard Tom shout from about ten yards away. He closed fast by riding a wave that had already broken and lying on his board like a missile.

I stood helpless. I couldn't spur myself to action. *Why am I a wimp, like when my neighbor reamed me out?*

The angry surfer let his right go, but Tom got to him just in time from behind and kept him from connecting on my chin. Then Tom grabbed the surfer's head in a headlock.

"Let go, fucker!" wailed the surfer. He thrashed like a shark attacking its prey until Tom set him free. By then I had moved out of striking distance.

"What's with you?" Tom asked the surfer.

"This hick got in my way. He shouldn't be here." The guy pointed to his board. "He's paying for this!" He started toward me again, but Tom lunged to tackle him in the midst of the whitewash from another wave that had broken. When the two of them surfaced, Tom had him in a headlock again.

Tom yelled to me. "Go to shore."

I obeyed and headed to the beach with my gashed board still attached to my ankle with the leash.

Tom stayed with the guy for a minute or two, and then they both made their way in. By the time I reached Tom's pickup, the angry surfer had peeled off in the opposite direction along Highway 1 to head to his ride, I supposed.

"That dude was pissed off. Why didn't you get out of the way?" asked Tom as he caught up with me.

"It was too late. I didn't see him until he came out of the barrel."

"Didn't you see him take off on the wave?"

"No. I was sort of…lost in thought. Wasn't looking."

Tom shook his head and looked away. "First he's psychotic. Now he's daydreaming," he said under his breath.

I hung my head in disappointment. "I'm sorry. That's the first time something like that has happened."

"Do have any cash to pay the guy to fix his board?"

I gave Tom all the cash in my wallet. When he returned from paying the angry surfer, he continued. "I'm just worried about you. I'm not always going to be around to save your ass, you know."

"I can take care of myself." I didn't say this with much conviction and wondered if Tom noticed.

"If you're gonna get through an engineering program and work at NASA, you need to."

Back at Tom's truck, we took off our wetsuits, toweled off, and dressed. When we were on our way south on the curvy Highway 1, Tom asked about my appointment with the psychiatrist. His question was another downer to the day.

"It was OK," I said. "We didn't exactly become best friends."

"You can change doctors, you know. There are others out there."

I had no idea where to find another psychiatrist, but Tom's suggestion made sense.

Tom continued. "What about your family? Is your father supporting you?" He was hitting all the sore spots.

"I spoke to him briefly after I was in the hospital. He asked how I was doing and when I was coming to visit, but that's about it." I scanned the Pacific Ocean from the passenger seat of the pickup.

"Maybe he doesn't know how to react."

"Maybe."

"Try not to take it personally, Hank. I remember him as being stern when I talked to him at our high school graduation. He wasn't the sensitive type."

"I'm not looking forward to seeing him. Last time I visited, he insisted I move back to Georgia and take up banking again. When I declined, he threw a fit and yelled at me, calling me ungrateful after he paid for my college and car. That was the night before I left to return to California. Then the next morning, he left for his country club without saying goodbye."

"How was he over the phone, before your hospital stay?"

"No temper tantrums but he was distant. I don't know…I just don't have a good feeling about my visit next month."

Tom's direct manner when speaking about some of my issues made me uncomfortable, but at the end of the ride when he dropped me off, I actually felt much better. Better than I had after seeing my shrink, who had had no skill in getting to the bottom of my issues so far.

7.

After passing my final exams satisfactorily in May, it was on to Atlanta, the capital of Georgia. As the plane neared approach, I spotted the familiar red clay where the ground lay bare and construction of house subdivisions took place, contrasting with the green forests. The gleaming skyscrapers of downtown and the treeless Stone Mountain brought back memories of growing up.

My parents met me at a largely empty subway station in the affluent suburb of Peachville, north of downtown. They drove up in their black Lexus as I waited at the curb in a blast of heat and humidity. Evelyn, my mother, wearing blue jeans and a white button-down shirt, greeted me with a kiss on my cheek and a hug. She had the same baby-blue eyes I had. Brent, my father, stayed in the car.

My mother's forehead wrinkled into a furrow, and our eyes met. Her straight brown hair showed streaks of gray.

Has it grayed more since my hospitalization?

My father greeted me as I climbed into the back seat. "Hi, Hank," he said sternly, as if addressing someone beneath his rank in the military. He didn't bother to turn to me.

"Hi, Dad." I caught a glimpse of his freckled, somewhat bloated face from where I sat. It reminded me of a wrinkled pumpkin. A circle of pale, hardened skin the size of a pencil eraser stood out on his cheek. His receding hairline was combed neatly to one side.

I gazed out the window as we drove through familiar roads and saw the Waffle House where my friends and I had gathered late at night, the dog park, and the movie theater. My parents kept quiet as did I, none of us knowing what to say. Our family wasn't the kind to fill emptiness with idle conversation, but now the silence seemed to draw attention to itself, as if what needed to be said was being purposely avoided. The car ride stifled my initial excitement of being home. Instead, frustration grew inside, though I couldn't put my finger on the exact reason.

We arrived at the mansion, its columns standing on either side of the double doors that served as the front entrance. Its bricks were painted white, and an American flag hung from a pole off to one side of the entrance. Set back from the road with an expansive, treeless front lawn, the mansion reflected what sunlight was left at the late hour. I glanced at my upstairs bedroom window, in the upper corner of the second floor, as my father drove up to the three-car garage.

Jocelyn, our maid, greeted us as we entered the kitchen. She was almost middle-aged and plump. When she smiled, like she did when I arrived, her full set of white teeth contrasted with her black skin but matched her all-white uniform. She dusted her hands off on her apron and hugged me. The granite countertops were free of clutter and wiped down. The kitchen table had a single placemat and set of silverware on it.

"Welcome home, Hank. I cooked your favorite meal—chicken casserole. You just sit down, and I'll bring you a plate. You must be hungry!"

I sat down at the table while my father went to the living room and turned on the television.

After heating a plate of casserole in the microwave, Jocelyn handed me the plate of steaming food. Its odors filled the air as I picked up a forkful and let it cool. My mother joined me at the table while Jocelyn prepared to leave to go home.

"We were so worried about you while you were in that hospital," my mother said. "You look like your old self, though. A little tired…"

"I had a long plane ride, Mom."

"You're right." She patted my arm from her seat at the long table. "You rebounded well from being sick, going right back to school and passing all of your classes. Your father and I were afraid you might…well, not be able to continue at your university."

"I'm all right, Mom," I said matter-of-factly. "I just lost a lot of sleep and let my fatigue get the best of me. It was a matter of catching up on rest."

"But, Hank. Some of what you did wasn't…" She paused, searching for the word, I supposed. "Rational."

"Mom, don't worry. I was just super tired."

"Are you taking your medicine?"

"Yes."

"That's good. Your medicine is very important, from what the psychiatrist at Bellevue told your father and me." I had given the physician permission to speak with my parents. Now I wondered if it was a bad idea. I hadn't given permission for Dr. Allen to do so.

I shoveled in some casserole.

"What was the hospital like? You didn't sound like yourself over the phone when you called from there. Zach said you looked out of it."

"The medicine they gave me made me real drowsy. That's why my voice was different over the phone." I didn't go into how I was scared out of my wits at being locked up like a caged animal.

My mother continued. "So you're here for only a week? Why so short a visit?"

"I'm on the schedule for my summer job at the deli already. I have to get back." I couldn't stand visiting more than a week anyway. Listening to my parents bicker after a few days grated on my nerves, so I'd learned to make my appearances short.

"Oh…" My mother slouched back and looked out the window as if she were disappointed.

My father walked into the room with a cocktail in hand. "How's the casserole? It's good to eat some of Jocelyn's cooking, huh?"

"Yeah," I said. I labored to get the word out, feeling my frustration rise again.

"How'd your finals go?"

"Fine. I passed all of them."

"What about calculus? Weren't you having some trouble in that?"

"Don't worry, Dad." I stopped eating.

"And this psychiatrist you're seeing? What's his name?"

"Dr. Allen."

"Right. How do you like him?" My father took a gulp of his drink. The ice rang against the bottom of the glass after he brought it away from his mouth.

"He's all right."

"Does he think you can complete your studies?" He put his glass down on the counter with a clink.

"Yeah, he's optimistic." I exaggerated because I didn't want my father to know that my shrink had his doubts as well.

"That should be a concern—whether you can handle your studies and the stresses of being an engineer."

"He's optimistic, Dad." There was measured tension in my voice.

"OK, Hank. I just don't want you to go after something that's not possible for you to accomplish. That's all. You don't have to get upset."

I had lost my appetite by now and sat back in my chair, staring out the window while my parents studied me.

"You can always live with us and work in a deli here," my father continued. "There's no shame in that."

Memories of listening to my parents squabble while I sat in their midst at the dinner table, particularly of my father badgering my mother, ran through my mind. I had gone eight years without this environment and had already promised myself never to return. I struggled to keep my composure, but my anger rose.

"Have you thought of what you might do in case your plans don't work out?" asked my father.

"Why wouldn't they work out?" I asked.

"Engineering's a tough field. And those schools that you're interested in—which ones are they? MIT and Stanford? Those are hard programs, Hank. I mean, I applaud you for trying, but lots of applicants get rejected."

"A couple of lower-ranked programs are on my list as well."

"And your hospitalization—that can't help matters."

"What do you mean?"

"Your illness, son. Don't you think you're being overly optimistic, especially considering you have one?"

"It's nothing serious. Going to the hospital was a one-time thing. It won't happen again."

"Won't happen again, eh?" My father's lips tightened. He squinted, and his face reddened—his signature stern look. My mother's eyes showed fear. My father left the kitchen and returned to the living room.

My mother rested a hand on my forearm. "Hank, all we're saying is for you to take care of yourself—go to your appointments and take your medicine. That's all. We're not saying you should quit your studies. If you want to be an engineer, then go for it." She forced a smile and took my plate away. I wasn't so confident after her false encouragement, and my frustration at my father almost sent me into a tirade of my own.

I grabbed my suitcase and went to my room, the one that I had used before I moved out to college, to cool down. My parents had redecorated it. Gone were the posters of my sports heroes, replaced by two paintings, one of a barn in a meadow and another a stately portrait of an unknown aristocratic woman, each of which hung over a separate bed. The two full bedroom windows had blue cloth drapes instead of the familiar white blinds. A plush cream carpet softened my steps as I slowly walked around the room. Nothing differed from my Christmas visit five months ago, but only now, after my hospital stay, did I fully notice all of the changes. It was a strange feeling being there, as if I didn't belong in it anymore.

As I lay in bed that night, I thought about the car ride home. How no one mentioned my hospitalization until my mother did at dinner, when my father was away. Apparently no one wanted to acknowledge the elephant in the room. I supposed that was how it would be from now on.

Will Chrissy react differently when I see her? She studies pre-med, so she should have more compassion, right?

During the rest of my stay, all I could think of was returning to my own place in Halifax. I played a round of golf with my father at his country club, but I let him do most of the talking since we played with two of his buddies. Spending time there was more torturous than anything else. Those elitist country club attitudes, which I couldn't stand, came out on the course and afterward in the clubhouse, after my father and his buddies had a cocktail. I could've declined the invitation to spend any time there at all, but staying in the mansion all day with my mother wasn't my idea of fun, either.

8.

I returned to California, and the summer progressed. Tourists, eager to visit the wineries close to Halifax and the quaint town itself, flocked from San Francisco and beyond. I spent the majority of my time in the local supermarket deli, hauling meats and cheeses from the cooler out onto the slicers and then returning them to their correct spot.

On my days off, I surfed at Bodega Bay despite my apprehension about other surfers since my accident; I was careful to stay out of their way. I didn't see the surfer who rammed me and wouldn't even know what to do if I did encounter him.

Will he attack me if he sees Tom isn't around? Probably. I found myself scanning the cars and trucks parked along Highway 1 and the lineup while waiting for waves, watching for him.

In July, I finally set up a date with Tracy. By chance, she came to the deli one day to order bologna. I seized the opportunity to ask her for her number and called her two nights later to arrange something. We decided on dinner that Saturday at a Mexican restaurant in Santa Rosa, an old cow town that was quickly becoming a lively northern suburb of San Francisco along Highway 101. Tracy was spending the summer at her parents' house there, so that's where I picked her up.

She must have seen me drive up because, before I could get out of my car, she walked out of the house and settled in the passenger side. She wore sandals and a cream-colored summer dress that hugged her body. Her hair fell down her bare shoulders, and a hint of makeup accentuated her lips and cheeks. The air around her smelled of perfume.

"I couldn't wait to leave the house for a while. My parents are driving me crazy!" Tracy gave me a peck on the cheek as I put the Audi in gear.

"I know exactly what you mean," I replied.

She smiled. "You look nice, dressed like a southern gentleman."

"Thanks. You look good, too."

The day was sunny and hot. I blasted the air-conditioning. Tracy hummed along to a pop tune on the radio during the short drive to the restaurant downtown. Her buoyant personality heightened my spirits during an otherwise uneventful summer.

At the restaurant, we settled into a booth, sitting on opposite sides. Typical Mexican Norteña music played on the speakers. The characteristic ump-pa-pa beat and multiple singers singing in Spanish, combined with the service staff racing here and there, trying to keep up with a full restaurant, made a lively atmosphere.

My new medicine, Boost, which I'd been taking for six weeks, didn't make me so groggy, so I felt energetic and upbeat for a change. I tapped my fingers on the table to the music as we perused the menu.

Tracy broke the silence. "You look well rested. Toward the end of our semester you were run-down. I guess finals took a lot out of you."

I shifted in my seat and ceased the tapping. "They did."

"How's the deli?"

"It's not bad. Better than just hanging around my apartment, you know?"

"Isn't it hard work, though? Lugging all those blocks of meats and cheeses all day long?"

"It isn't something I'd do for the rest of my life."

"I think it's funny that you drive an Audi and work at a deli. I bet most of your coworkers take the bus."

"Some of them do. They're nice to me, though. It's only for the summer. Maybe I'll go back during winter break."

The server came and took our order. After she left, Tracy and I resumed our conversation.

"So your parents drive you crazy, too?" I asked her.

Tracy rolled her eyes. "I try to stay busy. My lifeguarding job at the YMCA is good. I babysit the kids while the moms play on their cell phones. Otherwise, I just watch the swimmers. I can't wait for school to begin again. We've already decided on a back-to-school party the weekend before classes begin. It'll be crazy!" Now her face filled with enthusiasm, her eyes sparkling, her perfect teeth showing in a wide smile. She was irresistible.

I smiled back. My past episode was easier to forget now. Being with a beautiful young woman did the trick, especially if she invited me to the party at her dorm.

Without warning, she covered one of my hands with hers. "Thanks for taking me out. This is nice." Her eyes continued to twinkle.

"My pleasure." I turned my hand so that our palms met and gave a quick squeeze. She blushed.

Our food came, and Tracy and I ate ravenously because the food was so delicious.

After she finished an enchilada, she said, "I've always had a thing for surfers, you know."

"Really? Even surfers from Georgia?"

She laughed. "I can't imagine there are many of them. How did you get into surfing anyway if you're from landlocked Atlanta?"

"I spent summers in South Carolina with my grandparents. They had a small house near Charleston and took my brother and sister and me surfing."

"That makes sense. I bet the waves here are bigger than the ones in South Carolina. You're so brave to be out there in the cold water and among all those locals! Some of them scare me, the way they act toward visitors."

The angry surfer who tried to clock me came to mind, but I steered away from talking about that incident. "I try to keep my distance from them."

"I would, too." Tracy took a sip of her margarita through a straw. "And you worked in a bank in North Carolina before moving here?" she asked. "You mentioned that in Spanish class once."

"Yeah. I got fed up with it, though. Decided it wasn't my thing."

"So you said 'to hell with banking' and moved to Sonoma County to surf and study for engineering school? That's so cool!"

"I want to work for NASA here in the Bay Area eventually."

"I'm sure a mechanical engineer could get a job there."

"That's one of the reasons why I'm studying prerequisites out here, to get into Stanford's program and then onto NASA. There are other programs on my list that have strong reputations, too."

"Why do you want to work for NASA?"

"I love rocket flight. Ever since I was eight-years-old, I was crazy about commercial fireworks. Launching rockets into space is what I want to work on someday." I paused. "What about you? What do you want to do with your art degree?"

"I want to work at the art gallery in downtown San Francisco and eventually show my work in an exhibition there."

"What about New York? Doesn't the art world congregate there instead?"

"Of course. But my whole family lives in the Bay Area. I want to stay close. Plus, I hate snow."

We finished our meal, filling the conversation with talk about our next Spanish class in the fall. Señor Ortiz was the teacher. I'd heard from other students that his class challenged students and relayed this to Tracy.

"We'll survive," she said. "Just like last semester, right?"

"I'm nervous about my other classes, too," I admitted. "Calculus-based physics is going to be tough. I struggled with high school physics."

"You can do it. You're one of the most conscientious students that I know."

Our eyes met again, and I smiled.

We left the restaurant and walked in the downtown strip. Then we headed back to the car. On the way, Tracy asked, "So what do your parents think of you changing careers?"

I froze inside. I hadn't expected that question and didn't want to open a big can of worms with a truthful answer. I racked my brain. *Quick!* "Umm…they aren't as enthusiastic as I'd like them to be."

"Really? They aren't proud to have a son that's pursuing NASA?"

Instead of closing the door on the conversation, my answer had produced more questions. I had to think of another neutral answer that wouldn't reveal the strife between my parents and me. It was too embarrassing to talk about.

"My father was a finance guy. He prefers banking to engineering. My mother thinks the same."

"Oh. Too bad."

I was relieved that the questions stopped at that point. More of them might've even spoiled the date for me.

When we arrived at the house, my date leaned over from the passenger seat and kissed me full on the mouth, eyes closed. She smiled at me when the kiss ended and headed for the front door. Content, I headed back to Halifax. My date had been the highlight of the summer thus far and made me forget my shrink, my parents, and the local surfer who almost beat me to a pulp.

9.

Three days later, I raced to the airport to pick up my younger sister, Chrissy. She was on summer break from the University of Georgia, about an hour and a half's drive from Atlanta, where she studied biology and was beginning her senior year in September. This visit was her second since I'd moved to California; she was the only one in my family who visited me, besides Zach when I was hospitalized. I pulled to the curb at baggage claim after I spotted her straight brown hair and medium-height frame.

"How are Mom and Dad doing since I visited them?" I asked her as I pulled out to exit the airport.

Chrissy saw my parents on the weekends usually. "They're worried about you, especially Mom."

I knew my mother felt badly. I wondered about my father. "Dad's worried about me?"

"Mostly because you're so far away. 'If Hank had been closer and working at his old job, all this stress of living far away and studying so much wouldn't have got to him' is what he said at dinner last night." Her voice grumbled like my father's when she impersonated him.

"I'm not going back to my old job."

"I know. Try telling that to Dad, though."

Chrissy and I knew him well. The day I told him I'd quit my job and was moving to California, his mouth had dropped open. Then he'd frowned and furrowed his brow like he always did when he exploded. The tirade that ensued made my blood boil, even though I had listened to hundreds of them at the dinner table with my siblings while growing up. Most of them weren't directed at me. So this one had hurt and surprised me, even though I saw it coming.

I'd shouted, "Stay out of my life," to which he'd replied that I was throwing away a perfectly good life already.

Chrissy had been at the table, too, though she hadn't said much. When Jocelyn found out the next day she put her hand on my forearm and said softly, "You sure did make your parents upset with your plans to go west. Your father's about to have a heart attack." Then she'd continued on her way out the door to catch the bus.

Stopped in traffic on 101, I turned my head to Chrissy. "You've gotta choose your own way. You chose to be a doctor. I tried out banking, but it didn't keep my interest. So now I'm finally doing what I want. Even though I went to the hospital, I am happy, you know."

"As long as you're happy. Just don't stress out so much."

"I thought I was handling my stress well. I never thought I'd have to…"

"Go to a psych ward?"

I turned away. "Yeah."

"Why are you taking all of these courses anyway? Can't you just start an engineering program without them?"

"Uh, no. I need these classes to get into a good program. Also, they're prerequisites that I've never taken before. I was a finance major in my former life. Remember?"

"How much are you paying for them? They must be draining your savings."

"I get in-state tuition, since I was here for over a year when I started last fall. It's a public university, so the courses aren't *that* expensive. I'm being careful. Don't worry."

"I'm not. But Dad is."

"I know. I do have some money coming in."

"From where?"

"At a deli in a supermarket."

"In a deli? Like what you did when you were in high school?"

"It's better than nothing."

I saw Chrissy smiling out of the corner of my eye while I concentrated on the eighteen-wheeler in front of me. "What?" I asked her.

"You're really going through with this mechanical engineering thing?"

"I'm working for NASA someday."

"I know. Mom told me."

"They have a headquarters in San Jose. That's where I want to work."

47

"You always were fascinated by fireworks."

Fourth of July was my favorite day of the year because of the displays given on Stone Mountain, east of downtown Atlanta. Despite the mountain's infamous history of being a meeting spot for the Ku Klux Klan in the twentieth century and a place where the South's famous Civil War icons showed on its north face, many still attended the Fourth of July fireworks. That was where I fell in love with the basic concepts of rocket launching. Now that I would learn about the flight of rockets in physics, part of the foundation of mechanical engineering, next semester, I teemed with excitement.

I had already told my parents about working for NASA, but they'd blown off the idea. My father had told me I was in a "dreamland," while my mother had warned me about "chasing unattainable goals." I'd returned to my room upstairs in the mansion deflated that my parents didn't support my new career. The next day, I left for California in my Audi, determined to make my new career a reality.

Tom and Nicole supported me at least. And Chrissy. She knew I wasn't happy at the bank in Charlotte. The day she found out I quit, she called to congratulate me, unlike my father.

As traffic lightened and we neared Halifax, I couldn't help wondering if Chrissy visited me out of sympathy for me being in the hospital or for a vacation like she'd said over the phone. Or was she checking up on me for my father's sake? No. She wouldn't do that. My heart accelerated when I realized my thoughts.

Stop being paranoid, Hank. That's what led you to the hospital...

. . . . .

The next day, a Saturday, we joined a throng of tourists at the John Crush winery for a tour. Chrissy made me uncomfortable, the way she downed the tastings. I abstained because I was driving. Her cheeks flushed, and she slurred her speech as she almost stumbled down the stairs of the main building of the winery after the tour ended.

My cheeks flushed because she was making such a scene. I steadied her arm after she stumbled. A guy who was a little too forward with his earlier flirtations, and tipsy himself, held her other arm. The three of us headed to the Audi.

Chrissy was on vacation, but this drunkenness was too much for me.

We got to the Audi, and I reached around to steady Chrissy's other arm, so that I stood behind her at the passenger-side door. "Thanks buddy, we've got it from here," I said to the guy who'd helped us.

"Sure. No problem. Hey, my friend and I are going to another tasting just down the road. It starts in half an hour. You and your sister can join us." He gave a nod and a smile. His eyes were glazed over after having had too many.

"Yeah, Hank. Let's go to another tasting!" Chrissy's drunk enthusiasm was evident.

"I don't think so. I'm taking you back home." I'd had enough of this guy hitting on my sister.

"Come on, Hank. Listen to your sister. She's on vacation!" The dude reached for Chrissy's shoulder but reached too far and ended up grabbing her breast instead.

"Hey, creep," shouted Chrissy. Now she obviously wasn't interested in the guy.

I cocked my right arm and landed a punch on the guy's chin and sent him to the ground.

His sidekick saw the whole thing and came running over to help the drunkard back to his feet. "What's the matter with you?" he asked me.

"Your friend grabbed my sister in a place she doesn't want to be grabbed, pal."

"I should call the cops on you!"

"Your friend started it. The blame's on him."

I shut the passenger door with Chrissy safely inside, bumped into the drunk guy, though I would've liked to have steamrolled him, walked round the front of the car, and opened the driver's side.

I reversed out of the parking spot while the drunk guy knocked on Chrissy's window, trying to get her to open it, and peeled out of the parking lot to the exit of the winery.

"That was great. Getting piss drunk at a tasting." Now I was almost sure she'd come to California to have fun. I accelerated back onto the main two-lane highway.

"You're such a downer. I could've gone to another tasting." She ran her hand through her long brown hair and viewed the vineyard.

"And I'd have to witness that guy slobbering over you. No thanks. I'll make you dinner back at my place instead."

Chrissy propped her elbow on the door panel and rested her head on her hand. She turned and smiled. "You always take good care of me. Even when we were young and Mom and Dad fought. It was you who protected me, not Zach."

"Always have. Always will."

"I was shocked when you went to that hospital. I thought I'd be taking care of you."

I kept my eyes on the road. "No way. I take good care of myself."

10.

A month after my first date with Tracy, in August, I rapped on her dorm suite. Inside, I heard the bass of hip-hop thumping and laughter. It was the weekend before classes began, and, like Tracy had promised, she and her roommates threw a party to kick off the semester.

She and I were hanging out a lot—to dinner, the movies, and lunch dates while she was on break from her lifeguarding—but hadn't made love yet.

Will this be the night?

I hadn't told her about my hospitalization. The thought that at some point I'd have to tell her had crossed my mind, but I didn't think it was the right time tonight. Plus, going to the psych ward had been an isolated incident. It wouldn't happen again. Maybe there was no need to inform her at all.

I knocked again. This time a young woman opened the door and squinted at me with glazed eyes.

"Who are you?" she asked.

"I'm Hank. Tracy invited me."

She continued to squint as if my words didn't register a single thought, but then her eyes widened and she broke out smiling. "Oh, Hank. Yes. Tracy's told us about you. Come in! She's in the living room."

The scene was raucous. Everybody spoke in loud voices above the music. A keg stood in the kitchen. Little groups of three and four stood holding plastic cups filled with beer and other drinks. A couple made out on the couch. Tracy and her roommates were indeed celebrating their dorm suite.

"Hank," Tracy yelled from near one of the windows of the living room. She broke away from her group and ran to me, threw her arms around my neck, and kissed me.

Good start to the night.

"Welcome!" she said as she broke away. "Let me get you a drink." She held my hand and led me to the kitchen.

Pretty soon I was on my third beer from the keg, smiling and nodding at Tracy and her friends in our group and teetering from foot to foot while my head swam.

Get a grip on yourself! Stay sober enough to stay on your feet!

I had never been a big drinker. I *really* needed to limit myself, especially with the medicine I was taking. It didn't mix well with alcohol from what my shrink had told me. But Tracy and her friends kept refilling my plastic cup. Despite being in such a festive atmosphere, my anxiety rose. My palms became sweaty. My heart pounded, and I withdrew from the conversation that our group had. Tracy asked me if I was OK. I told her I was fine.

The night went on. I had a full beer in each hand now but barely sipped on them. I'd never felt this way after having drunk a few, but then again this was the first time I'd been in this situation since I started Boost or my previous medicine for that matter.

Finally the sweat dissipated, the living room cleared out for the most part, and Tracy and I ended up in her dorm room alone. My full beers, warm and flat, sat on a worn coffee table in the living room.

Tracy's tour of her room didn't last long, and soon we sat kissing on her bed. Back came the anxiety—performance anxiety this time. I was sure she wanted to make love by the way she unzipped my pants and undressed herself.

Am I too drunk to have sex? Or will my medicine screw things up down below?

Reading the whole list of side effects, which included sexual dysfunction, had shaken me.

Tracy must have sensed my angst because she stopped kissing me, opened her eyes and asked, "Are you OK?"

"What?"

"You seem nervous, that's all. Is this your first time?"

Quick! Think fast! The truth won't do at this particular time. I broke eye contact and went for another angle instead. "It's my first time in a while. That's all," I said. That was the truth, too, though not the whole story.

She broke into a smile. "Aww…it's all right." She studied me with that lingering joy in her face.

"I just want to make it good for you." Now I really was hamming it up, but Tracy gave a careless laugh, the kind that made me want to be with her, and proceeded to do things that made me forget my medicine, hospitalization, and psychiatrist again and finally enjoy the night instead.

We both slept deeply afterward.

The next morning, I realized I hadn't taken my dose of medicine as usual the night before. The single pill lay in a sandwich bag, which slightly protruded from one of the front pockets of my jeans. I slithered out of bed, careful not to wake Tracy, and stuffed the baggie deep into the pocket and out of sight.

. . . . .

Two weeks later, Tracy and I trekked to Santa Cruz to join Tom and Nicole for a beach outing. Santa Cruz was a surfing hot spot an hour and a half south of San Francisco by car. Usually the beach and main drag were quiet during the week, but today was a Saturday. After the sun had burned through the morning fog, these two locations teemed with tourists.

We met Tom and Nicole on the beach. I introduced Tracy to them for the first time. I wondered what the couple, especially Tom, would think of her.

Despite the sunny skies, most of those on the beach wore shirts and shorts, including the four of us; the air maintained a chill with the help of a stiff breeze. Some even wore hooded sweatshirts.

Tom and I declined to bring our surfing gear. Instead, we watched the surfers in their black wetsuits bob up and down in the lineup while sitting on their boards, waiting for a good wave. They looked like a group of seals from afar, poking their torsos out of the water. Occasionally one or two caught a wave and carved it up.

"Do you have any siblings, Tracy?" asked Nicole.

"I'm an only child. But I have cousins in Santa Rosa."

"And Hank tells us you're an art major. Who's your favorite painter?" continued Nicole.

"Monet. Some of the other impressionists of the period interest me, too, but I like Monet's style the most."

I remembered the whacked-out paintings in my psychiatrist's office and thought of Picasso but didn't comment. Tracy was still unaware that I saw a shrink. I had debated telling her about my visits and my hospitalization but decided against it. Knowing this, I coached Tom and Nicole not to say anything about them, either, during our outing. They seemed to understand.

"Tracy has a mini studio set up in her dorm room. She does some painting of her own," I said.

"Cool!" said Tom.

"I've seen some of her work." I turned toward Tracy. "What is it you do, watercolors?"

"That's my specialty. Landscapes. The coastline is my favorite place to paint."

"I'd like to see your paintings," said Nicole.

"My goal is to sell them at some point. Maybe set up an exhibition at a museum," said Tracy. "What about you two? What do you do for work?"

"I teach at a kindergarten, and Tom works for Google as a software engineer."

"Wow! Google. That's a great job."

"It has its fair amount of stress. But I like it," said Tom. "I'm doing what I want to do, so that's important."

My mind turned to my pursuit of working for NASA. Tom's words rang true to me. Ever since high school, he had had his sights set on Google. He set his goals and achieved them. I hoped I could achieve mine.

"And Hank tells me you two just got married?"

"Last June. In Nicole's hometown—Santa Barbara."

"That's a nice place. Hank, did you go?"

"Of course! I wouldn't have missed my best friend's wedding." A great career. A new wife. Tom had it all together. It seemed he had the perfect life.

"Were you in the wedding?" continued Tracy.

"I was one of the groomsmen."

"I can't imagine what it was like," said Tracy.

I was puzzled. "What do you mean? You've been to Santa Barbara before, right?"

"Yeah. But all you Georgians must have felt out of place in Santa Barbara. I mean with your accents. Didn't people make fun of you?"

Tom hated when someone made comments about his accent. Especially when it happened in California. Most Californians regarded those from the Deep South to be backward, uncultured. Some motorists had even yelled at me to go back to Georgia when I had my Georgia license plate on my Audi when I first moved to California.

Tom became serious and clenched his jaw. He turned from watching the surfers and directed his attention fully to Tracy. Tracy didn't know what was coming, but I did.

I tried to prevent an argument. "Oh no one said anything." That was a lie. Several of Nicole's cousins from Southern California snickered about Tom and the rest of us with southern drawls.

"You Californians are so elitist!" Tom exclaimed. "God forbid anyone should come from another state and live here to ruin your pristine paradise."

"Tom, stop it," said Nicole.

"I was just saying your accent must have drawn some attention," said Tracy, apparently standing her ground. "It wasn't an attack."

But Tom wasn't finished. "It doesn't matter how educated you are. A southern accent is viewed with contempt everywhere else in the country. I don't laugh at Boston accents, do I? They're strange, too. But no. Everyone has to make fun of Southerners. Like they're stupid or something."

"Tom. Take it easy." Nicole put her hand on Tom's arm.

It was true. I got a lot of comments from Tracy and other students about my accent. Not all of them were flattery. Tom got angry, whereas I tried to brush them off. They bothered me, too, but Tom was better at standing up for himself than I was. And his temper was quicker.

Tom and Nicole stood and went for a walk on the main drag of the surf town so that Nicole could calm her husband down, I guessed.

After they left, Tracy commented, "Tom's not as much a gentleman as you."

When they returned a half hour later, Tom's joviality had surfaced again. He had visited a surf shop and had an idea of which surfboard he wanted to buy next. The four of us steered clear of talking about southern accents from then on and tried to enjoy the remainder of the afternoon.

11.

The rainy season returned to Halifax in November, reminding me of my hospitalization. On a Wednesday morning, as the drops pelted the window, I sat leaning forward in Dr. Allen's waiting room with my hands clasped and recalled all that had happened—the busy emergency room, the psychiatric hospital, and my foggy brain in the weeks after my discharge. Even though the past was slowly becoming a memory, I couldn't help playing it over and over in my mind. I took a deep breath.

Though my doctor rarely brought up what he described as my psychosis, it still weighed on me. By now, I coined what happened as a nervous breakdown, like what writers and parents who had lost their children suffered. I could live with that. Maybe I'd been putting too much pressure on myself with my schoolwork at the time. But now everything was fine. I was sleeping, getting good grades, hanging out with Tom and Tracy. My breakdown was a blip on the radar—nothing more. I was my old self again.

Another patient waited with me. The guy's eyes darted this way and that, like he was afraid of something. He kept clearing his throat. His face was unshaven, his skin was leathery from too much sun, and he wore a short-sleeved Hawaiian button-down shirt, untucked, and faded blue jeans with brown sandals.

"Hey, man," he finally said to me, although I had avoided eye contact with him, "how you doing?"

I studied him briefly. "All right."

"That's good, man. What are you seeing the doc for?"

"Uh...I'd rather not discuss it."

"That's cool, man. That's cool." He leaned back in his chair and stroked his whiskers, contemplating what I had just said, I supposed.

Then a door opened from an office other than my psychiatrist's. "Hi, Jimmy," said the woman who emerged. She looked like a therapist or psychiatrist.

"Oh, hi, how are you?" said my waiting room companion, abruptly getting up from his chair and walking into the office. "See you, man," he said, looking over his shoulder at me.

"See you." I unclasped my hands, leaned back, and laid my palms down on my thighs.

Dr. Allen emerged. He wore his standard khaki pants and tieless button-down dress shirt.

"So," he said after we settled into our usual seats in his office. "How're finals shaping up for you?"

"I'm struggling in physics. I'm hoping studying for the final over Thanksgiving break will bring my grade up."

"You're not going back to Georgia?"

"No. I'm going for Christmas and New Year's with Tracy."

"I see. It's a long trip to go twice in a short period." He flipped open my chart. "Are you in danger of failing physics?"

"No. I have a C plus average now. Trying to bring it up to a B minus."

"That's a respectable grade. I'm sure an engineering program wouldn't look badly on it."

I relaxed and settled back into my chair after my psychiatrist said this.

"How about the rest of your courses?" Dr. Allen asked.

"All As and Bs."

"Well, I'm glad it's going more smoothly than last spring. I think the medication switch was a good one—it took away all of that sedation." He paused. "You're continuing at Dewey State next semester?"

"Yes. Over Thanksgiving I'm doing applications for my programs and sending them off before I leave for the semester break. If all goes well, I'll start at an engineering school next fall."

"Oh, good!" He crossed his legs and studied me. "How is your financial situation?"

"Fortunately I still have money saved from my banking job." Despite my hospital bills, I calculated that I could still make it through Dewey State with some money left over, though not nearly enough to pay the tuition at a high-profile engineering school. Student loans would have to pay that, as well as my living costs, until I graduated. I told him this.

After expressing his satisfaction with my plans, Dr. Allen switched gears. "How has your mood been with the medicine?"

"Good," I said. "My energy level is high during the day when I go to class, and I'm doing all of the activities that I usually do in my free time—surfing and spending time with friends, dating." Besides not wanting to nap all the time since my change of medication, I hadn't noticed any difference. My mood was the same, but I was sure the doctor didn't want to hear that!

"Good!" he said enthusiastically, leaning forward in his chair and looking at me with bug eyes through his glasses. "Is your sleep OK?"

"Eight hours a night."

"You've been on Boost for six months with no side effects and no symptoms of what led you to the hospital back in April. Since you're doing so well, I'll start taking you off the medicine."

"Really?" I met his eyes and straightened up in the lounge chair.

"I think the problem that you had was a one-time episode, and I don't think you need to be on medication any longer."

"OK," I said, trying to stifle my enthusiasm and not say anything that would jeopardize this turn of events, though I couldn't help letting a smile come to my lips.

He also smiled, as if he gained some satisfaction giving me the good news.

"I'll begin tapering the medicine after the holidays. In March you'll begin visiting me every three months or so. You've done well, Hank. Congratulations." He switched topics. "Any concerns about visiting your family—your father in particular?"

My father came up frequently during our sessions, though the image he and I had of him were different. My psychiatrist had no doubt my father, an accomplished retired banker who had sent his sons to private prep schools, loved me very much. I wasn't so sure. He still didn't know about the tirades, insults, and physical abuse.

My father hadn't had anything very interesting to say over the phone since I'd last seen him—just the same distant coldness. My smile disappeared, but I answered, as I had done on many other occasions, to the doctor's satisfaction. I didn't want to ruin this change of events and end up staying on the medicine. "No. We've been on good terms."

"Excellent!"

Dr. Allen gave me instructions on how to taper my medicine. I listened attentively, as if I were on the last question of an exam on which I knew I had done well. All I had to do was finish it and turn it in. Most of the answers I had given the doctor over the seven months that I'd visited him were apparently correct, though at times not entirely accurate. I justified my exaggerations and omissions with the fact that I hadn't belonged in the hospital in the first place. I deserved the doctor's decision to take me off the medicine.

I shouldn't have been on it.

I would be medicine-free in a few months—a new man! After my appointment, I walked with a lighter step to my car and accelerated with a bit more pressure on the gas pedal as I exited the office complex. Going past the vineyards and back to my apartment on that gray, raw November morning, I hummed along to a classical music station.

That evening, I rang Tom and told him the news.

"He what?" asked Tom.

His tone took me by surprise, but I repeated what had happened. "My psychiatrist is taking me off my medicine."

"Why would he do that?"

Again, I was taken aback but continued to answer his questions, though my heart accelerated. "He decided I was stable enough to go off it or something..."

"Are you sure you're OK with that? I mean, you don't want to go through what happened last spring again, right?"

"Of course not." My voice sounded defensive. I wasn't quite sure why, but it did.

A few seconds of silence. *Why am I craving Tom's approval so much? Does he think I need to be on medicine permanently to prevent a relapse?* I tried to put these questions out of my mind.

"Listen. If you begin to feel like you did that night, call me. I always have my phone on."

"It was a one-time thing, Tom. It won't happen again." My grip on my phone tightened. Another few seconds of silence. I exhaled a deep breath. "OK. I'll call if you insist."

"Great. And memorize my number, too. Just in case."

After ending the call, instead of rejoicing in the good news, I slouched on my couch, watched a movie, and got drunk off a six-pack of Coors Light. As the night got into a late hour, I became depressed.

12.

Tracy and I visited Atlanta during our semester break in December. I finished my fall semester with a B minus in physics. Tracy looked forward to getting to know my family and my city. The two of us had spent Thanksgiving with her family in Santa Rosa, so now it was my family's turn to host. She still wasn't aware of my hospitalization, and now that my psychiatrist was taking me off my medicine, I decided to let the whole incident blow over and never tell her of it.

Zach; his wife, Jenny; and baby, Michaela, and Chrissy had all traveled to the mansion as well, but what should have been a joyous occasion was once again stressful for me. I cringed at the thought of Tracy meeting my father in particular. Would the two of them collide when they discovered they were on opposite ends of the spectrum in terms of personality? I tried not to imagine a blow up. Tracy was so carefree, though. This fact served to allay my fears. Perhaps she would steer clear of any arguments. I had my doubts, though, after her encounter with Tom.

My parents picked us up at the train station again after we'd flown in. Tracy and Evelyn dominated the conversation during the short car ride. Brent cursed a slow driver in front under his breath but stayed silent throughout for the most part.

"We're glad to finally meet you," said my mother. "Is this your first time to the South?"

"Yes. It is. I love your accent, Mrs. Galloway," said Tracy. "It's just like Hank's."

"We all talk like that here, sugar!" replied my mother. "I bet Hank's like a fish out of water when he speaks in California."

"All of us at the university are getting use to it," replied Tracy, smiling at me.

On we went, until we pulled into the driveway. I turned my head to see

Tracy's jaw drop, and she exclaimed, "Wow," in a soft utterance.

"Welcome to our home!" my mother said. "I hope you'll be comfortable in the guest room. Hank's staying in his old room. Can't have a couple that's not married yet sleep in the same room, now can we?"

Tracy's and my eyes met. We both frowned.

Over the next few days, I showed Tracy Atlanta. We hit all the points of interest, the World of Coca-Cola, the aquarium, and the Varsity, the oldest fast food restaurant in the country. Tracy enjoyed the tour, and I was more relaxed than before the trip began.

Then Christmas day arrived, and we all sat around the dining room table, eating turkey with all the sides. Zach and Jenny doted over Michaela, who lay in a rocker on the floor between them. Chrissy, Tracy, my parents, and I rounded out the attendees. Jocelyn took the day off.

My father wolfed down his meal and talked money with my brother.

"Interest rates went up. It's good you financed your house when you did. What did you say your mortgage was?"

Zach, whose receding hairline was more pronounced than when he visited me at the hospital, told him.

"I could've got a lower rate if I handled the matter myself. But that's a fair one," said my father. He continued. "I think you'll be satisfied with the rising property values in that part of town if you decide to sell for a bigger house in ten years or so. You having any problems with you supervisor at work?"

"He's satisfied with my performance," Zach said. "My bonus wasn't as big as I expected this year. That's how management is."

"Those cheap bastards," said my father.

"Brent—the baby," exclaimed my mother.

"Oh, Evelyn. She doesn't know any better. She's asleep anyhow." Now finished with his meal, he leaned forward and put both forearms on the table. "Anyway. When's that promotion you were talking about coming?"

On and on they went. Chrissy, Tracy, and I sat in silence, concentrating on our food. Finally a short silence ensued, followed by my mother asking a question. "Are you taking your medicine, Hank?"

"What?" I asked, with my mouth half-open and full of sweet potato.

"Your medicine. Are you taking it every night?" repeated my mother.

I almost choked on my food before Tracy asked me, "What medicine?"

I racked my brain, trying to minimize the damage of my mother's question but couldn't think of anything to say before my mother said, "Oh my…you don't know what happened?"

Tracy studied me with a quizzical look.

Once again I was speechless. I glanced around the table. Everyone had stopped eating and fixed their gaze upon me.

Finally my father put his silverware down on his plate in dramatic fashion and spoke. "Hank, you haven't told her about going to the hospital?"

"What hospital?" Then Tracy studied everyone's face. She knew there was something she didn't know.

Now I was really in damage control mode. My anxiety was through the roof. The visit had gone so well up until this point but was going downhill fast. *What can I do?* I managed to swallow my food, take Tracy's arm, and guide her into the kitchen adjacent to the dining room.

Tracy's eyes narrowed, her hands in fists as if she were ready to lay a punch on me.

I broke eye contact, glanced at the carpet, and said, "Tracy, I'm sorry I didn't tell you—"

"Didn't tell me what? Everyone seems to know except me." She placed her fists on her hips. "You better tell me…now!"

"I was in a hospital last spring for a nervous breakdown. But I'm doing fine now. I take a medicine, which my psychiatrist is taking me off soon. I'm OK."

"But you decided to hide it from me! I'm disappointed in you. I thought you were more mature than that."

Aside from silverware clinking on dishes, no sound came from the dining room, as if my family were listening to the whole discussion.

I maintained a sort of dumbfounded silence, stuck in a speechless stupor. I had been caught with my pants down.

"I'm going to a hotel," continued Tracy. She headed for the guest room.

Caught off guard, I had never seen her this angry. "Tracy…"

She raised her middle finger and didn't even turn around, keeping on to the bedroom. Then she slammed the door.

I remained fixed in the same spot. I wanted to follow Tracy but figured I wasn't welcome to do so. Returning to the dinner table wasn't too inviting, either. I wrung my hands. Then my niece began crying, breaking the silence in the kitchen.

While Jenny tried to soothe the baby, I remained in the kitchen. Finally Tracy emerged with suitcase in one hand and her phone in the other and headed to the front door.

She is really serious and angry.

"Let me help you with your bag at least," I said.

"I've got it. I'm going to a hotel and flying back tomorrow."

"You don't even want to wait for our flight?"

"I'd rather not." She didn't make eye contact and shut the heavy front door behind her.

"Damn," I said under my breath. I never thought keeping my hospitalization a secret would blow up in my face like that.

I stomped back to the kitchen and approached my mother. "Why did you ask me about my medicine at Christmas dinner?" I shouted. "I hadn't told Tracy about it yet!"

"Hank, I'm sorry. I—"

"Now she's gone, Mom! Thanks for nothing!"

"Wait a minute," said my father coolly. "Whose fault is it that she's gone?"

My mother began sobbing, and Zach and Jenny shuffled out of the room with the baby. Chrissy remained.

I stopped my tantrum. Usually my father did the yelling, so his cool demeanor caught me off guard.

"It's Mom's fault," I said.

"I disagree," continued my father, his voice rising in a crescendo. "If anyone's at fault, it's you for not telling her about your illness!"

"First of all, I'm not sick! Second, Tracy wouldn't have known if Mom hadn't brought it up!"

"You should've told her a long time ago! It's not Mom's fault. It's yours. And yelling at your mother is only making it worse. Look at her."

My mother had her head on the table, resting on one arm. She continued to sob. Chrissy moved to pat her on the shoulder.

All of a sudden, I felt guilty for yelling at my mother. The sight of her broken down made me want to apologize. But before I could utter another word, my father gained momentum. "Hank, you've ruined Christmas. All because of this impossible dream that you're following. If you'd stayed at the bank, like I recommended, none of this would've happened—your hospitalization—none of it!"

"Dad, it has nothing to do with me pursuing a different career."

"Yeah? I think everything has to do with it! And I don't want you coming here and ruining things when you visit, either. So don't come back!"

I stood silent. My father had never kicked me out and told me not to return.

He continued. "You can stay until your flight leaves, but I don't want to see you again after that until you decide to return to banking. You have to learn about throwing away a good life that your parents made for you!" He made his way to the living room to smoke his cigar for the evening.

I left my mother at the dinner table with Chrissy and slowly climbed the steps to my bedroom, still in shock about what just happened.

My last days with my parents were an uncomfortable experience. I insisted on continuing my studies at dinner the evening before my flight and promised that I would make it to NASA. My father didn't say a word and left the kitchen as soon as he finished eating. My mother cried and mumbled about me ending up destitute. The next morning, I rose after my father left for a function at his country club. My mother's eyes were bleary and tired when she came to my door and told me it was time to leave for the train station. Chrissy and Jocelyn said goodbye softly. I stayed calm throughout and kissed my mother on the cheek before heading downstairs to the platform to catch my train to the airport, though inside my heart wept. No one knew when I'd be back.

13.

The start of a new semester was only a few days away. I had picked up some hours at the deli for the last couple weeks of my vacation, after I had returned from Atlanta. I apologized to Tracy, but she didn't accept. She largely ignored my calls and texts. Finally, I took her out to her favorite Italian restaurant near campus to try to patch things up.

"Will you tell me if you're feeling sick again?" she asked with her arms folded across each other at the opposite side of the booth.

"Tracy, I won't get sick again. I promise. What happened was because I wasn't taking care of myself—not sleeping well, getting stressed out. I'm better now. My doctor is even taking me off my medicine."

"Are you sure that's a good idea?"

Again, someone doubts whether I should be off my medicine! "That's how well I'm doing. I didn't tell you about my hospitalization because I thought it was a minor event. My doctor even thinks so."

Tracy seemed to think over this last fact. We sat in silence, and I felt like now was the time she'd either forgive me or break it off entirely. I let her speak first.

"You still should have told me. In the future, if you care about me and our relationship, I don't want to hear your personal history from your mother at Christmas dinner first."

"I made a mistake. It won't happen again." I looked out the window that we were seated by. Then I met her eyes again. "Will you please forgive me?"

Another silence!

"How are we going to live in the same city away from our families while you're in engineering school if you hide shit from me?"

"It won't happen again," I repeated.

"All right. But if anything like this comes up, like another breakdown, I want to be the first to know."

. . . . .

By now, Dr. Allen had begun taking me off Boost. I was satisfied. The past week or so I hadn't slept much, but I attributed that to nerves because of my situation with Tracy and the upcoming semester.

In my one-bedroom apartment in Halifax, I lay on my queen-size bed. I listened to drops of rain falling from the tree leaves because it had rained earlier in the night. It must have been about 2:00 a.m. All was quiet otherwise.

Then the revelation hit me. *My father is trying to poison me!* That was why he and my mother were so insistent on me taking my medicine. He wanted to do away with me once and for all. The pills weren't meant to help me but rather harm me. There wasn't any other explanation for his conviction in the matter.

It was lucky I had figured out his plan. Maybe if I'd taken the full dose instead of following my doctor's instructions, I'd be dead at this point! I turned my head toward the bathroom, where the circular container with my leftover Boost stood in the medicine cabinet. There must be someway to prove the pills were poisonous.

Maybe some test that the police can do? Yes, that's it. I'll call the police right now and get them involved.

I grabbed my cell phone from the night table and dialed 911. A woman answered and asked about my emergency. I said, "My father is trying to poison me." The woman asked for my address. I told her. She told me help was on the way, so I hung up and waited, trembling.

In a few minutes, I heard a car pull up on my street and a knock at my door. I peeked through the peephole to see two cops standing outside.

I opened the door. My apartment was still pitch black.

"What's going on?" asked one of the cops, a tall one with a mustache and his head thrust forward.

"My father's trying to poison me by making me take some pills," I said. My eyes went from one face to the next—neither of them looked sympathetic.

"Where's your father?" asked the other cop, a short man with a crew cut.

"He's in Atlanta." I saw complete confusion come to their faces. The one with his head thrust forward furrowed his brow and squinted. He looked at his partner. The two cops' eyes met.

The short one turned back to me and continued. "Your father is trying to poison you, and he lives in Atlanta? Atlanta, Georgia?" He didn't bother to lower his voice; I feared my neighbors would hear.

"Yes, I mean…" I started to realize how far-fetched my story was but held on to my belief. "Could you check my pills for poison?" I asked, almost in a whisper.

"What do you take them for?" asked the tall cop.

"The pills? I was in the hospital last year for a nervous breakdown or something—"

"Are you taking them?" continued the same cop.

"My doctor is weaning me off them. I'm taking half the dose from usual."

"Are you sure you're not supposed to be taking the full dose?" he continued. Then he leaned toward me and shined his flashlight directly into my face. "Are you feeling all right?"

Suddenly, I was on the defensive. *The cops want to take me to another emergency department!* I brainstormed and said, "I'm tired. I think I just need rest."

"Are you sure?" asked the short one. "We can call an ambulance and take you to the hospital."

No way! "I'm fine. I think I'll go back to bed."

The short one lowered his light to the floor and looked at his partner. The tall one shrugged his shoulders and frowned. The short one said, "You get some rest now." He turned and, with his partner, walked back down the hallway and out of the building.

"Thanks," I whispered and closed the door. My plan had failed! The cops left, and I was alone again, which scared me. I stood in my dark apartment for a moment. *Did my neighbor the biker hear the cops and me talking?* I hoped not.

I paced my apartment. I thought of calling 911 again but didn't act. The cops didn't believe me. They wouldn't understand if I tried to explain myself a second time. They might just force me to a hospital.

I lay down and closed my eyes. Drops continued to fall from leaf to leaf on the trees outside. Everything else was quiet.

The next thing I knew I woke up to daylight and the sound of my neighbor revving his motorcycle outside. I immediately checked the clock—8:02. I had slept five hours.

One of my upstairs neighbors' kids made a pitter-patter sound as he raced across the kitchen floor. It seemed like just another day, except the feeling that I was in certain danger remained. I remembered all that happened the previous night, and my heart began pounding.

Is my medicine really poisoned? Is my father really intending to murder me?

I had nothing planned for the day besides running a few errands. I moved to the medicine cabinet and took out my Boost. Looking over the pills, I tossed them into the trash.

After my father finds out I'm still alive, he'll come after me in some other manner. Maybe the police, an ambulance, or possibly even my neighbor!

My best bet was to get out of town for a few days. Lay low. Let this whole situation blow over. I needed a place to stay but not a hotel. Tom was on vacation. No dice there. I thought of those I knew farther away. Zach and Jenny, who were eight hours away by car, with some luck. That was a possibility!

The more I pondered my next course of action, the more I knew I should head to Zach's place. Hopefully he'd understand my predicament, unlike the police. I thrust some belongings—my night kit, a change of clothes—into a bag and changed into jeans, a T-shirt, and sweater. After scurrying safely to my car, I locked all the doors immediately, called Zach's phone, and left a message saying I was coming down to visit for a few days.

I felt a great relief as I pulled onto the main highway because I had foiled my father's plans. I was safe. My escape had been just in the nick of time. Zach's house was a haven for me now. All I had to do was get there…

I took 101 South and hit traffic heading into San Francisco. Then an accident near San Jose slowed my progress. After finally leaving the Bay Area, I leaned forward to concentrate on the road, driving through the arid, sparsely populated Central Valley in the winter gloom. Traffic was lighter now on the two lanes heading south. At lunch hour I took a break at a Burger King along I-5 to wolf down a burger and fries. An overweight man with a beard down to his chest fixed his eyes on me. I thought of yelling at him to ask him why he stared but then realized I hadn't showered that morning and had a over a week's growth of beard—reasons for him to give me a peculiar look. I ignored him and tried to act natural.

Causing a scene will be trouble for me.

Zach called as I stepped back into my Audi around 12:30 p.m.

"Why are you coming down today? It's a bit short notice," he said.

"I'm sorry. I had a rough night last night."

"A rough night?" He sounded puzzled. "Are you feeling all right?"

"Yeah. I just realized I've got to stay away from my pills," I blurted.

"Stay away from your pills? What are you talking about?" A pause. "Hank, are you sure you're all right? You sound weird."

Uh-oh. I'd heard those words before from Tom when he brought me to the emergency room. Warning signals flashed in my mind. I knew a trip to the hospital couldn't be far off if I didn't do some damage control. "Um…Don't worry. I'm fine," I stammered. "I just thought I'd visit before my semester begins."

"Get down here as soon as you can. We'll be waiting for you."

14.

Back on the highway, I neared a sign for Los Angeles, still 246 miles away. I increased my speed past the limit to seventy-five. A patrol car set up in a trap came into view, and I slowed to a legal limit just before reaching it, then sped back up.

My cell phone rang. It was my parents. I let it go to voice mail and hoped that my brother hadn't told my parents of my call to him. My gut reaction told me otherwise.

I began wondering if my plan to go to Zach's house would work. I stopped at a rest area and listened to the message. It was my mother who'd called, and she sounded worried. "Hank, this is your mother. Um…we got a call from Zach saying you called him and were on your way to his house already. He said…he said you were worried about your pills or something like that. So I was calling to make sure that you're OK. Please stay safe, Hank, and get down to Zach's. He's waiting for you."

I'd rarely heard my mother sound that desperate. It reminded me of how she sounded when I was in the hospital last year. I paced back and forth beside my Audi.

My parents knew that I was going to Los Angeles. Surely they'd have some appointment with a psychiatrist set up for me there, or even have Zach bring me to an emergency room straight off.

I drove off from the rest stop, but instead of going south, I went north on the 5, back toward Halifax. Day turned to night, but I pressed on, determined to make it back home. I strained my eyes to see the highway, and the hum of the engine and the tires on the pavement lulled me into a kind of trance, which made my eyelids heavy. My fear that my father was trying to poison me still held strong. I was convinced that if I went to Zach's place, he'd bring me to a hospital or, now that he was in touch with my parents, he'd be the one to poison me—maybe through food or drink!

.　.　.　.　.

I awoke to the terrible sound of crumpling metal, and my body jerked forward with all of the momentum that I carried only to be restrained with the seatbelt and airbag. My car had drifted onto the shoulder of the freeway, having been stopped in its tracks by a parked eighteen-wheeler.

The car is going to catch on fire. I have to escape the wreckage fast! Yelling, I climbed out as quickly as possible through the driver's door, which fortunately still worked. At first, no one responded.

I hopped around in pain on the side of the highway. My right shin throbbed, so I couldn't put any weight on it. I clasped my left wrist with my right hand, trying to ease the sting.

Then the truck driver of the eighteen-wheeler calmly walked up to me. He was of medium height and stout with a gray beard. He adjusted his overalls and took his cap off his head and then put it back on. His eyes were stern.

"What happened?" he demanded.

"I fell asleep," I said, amid my limping around and my gasps of pain.

I expected some sympathy from the man, but the opposite was true. There was growing anger in his voice. "Are you drunk or on drugs?" he asked.

"No." I continued limping around in a circle on the shoulder of the freeway.

He surveyed the back end of his truck, which had caved in from the impact of my Audi. "Look at what you did! Who's going to pay for this damage?"

I said nothing and tried to focus on his blurry face by squinting, since my glasses were somewhere in the wreckage. His mouth was open as if he were about to say something more, but he kept quiet.

The police, fire department, and emergency medical technicians showed up. I was the center of attention, which made me uneasy. EMTs swarmed about me. I stopped limping and glanced from face to face. *I am not going to another emergency department—not after what happened the last time I was in one.* A few cars slowly rolled by, taking in the scene and avoiding my Audi, which was sitting, half smashed and unrecognizable, in the right-hand lane.

The EMTs immediately tried to get me into the ambulance, but I refused. They made me recite the address on my driver's license and asked me some other simple questions. I stayed calm and answered all of them, although inside a state of shock grew.

"Are you sure you don't want to go to a hospital?" asked a red-haired female EMT, looking me over. "You've just had an awful wreck."

"I'm OK," I insisted.

They backed off slowly. The red-haired woman even took a few steps backward, with her eyes still on me.

"That boy's been smoking marijuana. Look into his eyes," the old trucker told the police officer. The cop was tall and massive, his chest and arms full of muscles. He had high jawbone lines.

He peered into my eyes. "What happened?"

"I fell asleep," I said meekly.

"I'm giving you a ticket for reckless driving." He began writing on his pad.

I stayed quiet.

The officer continued talking to the trucker while I stood off about ten feet away. They largely ignored me and finished up their conversation. The old man rolled the eighteen-wheeler onto the freeway and drove off.

A tow truck driver, a rough-looking fellow with a scraggly beard and a chewed-up baseball cap, had also arrived. The cop walked past me without as much as a glance and began speaking to him. The tow truck driver gave me a once-over while talking to the officer, which frightened me. I trusted neither him nor the cop. My shock and fear of the unknown grew by the second.

After the EMTs and trucker left, the only ones left were the police officer, the tow truck driver, and me. The cop approached me and again leaned down toward my face, saying, "You need to get off the freeway. Get a ride with the tow truck driver to the nearest hotel."

I obeyed, walked gingerly to the tow truck like a lame dog, and reluctantly climbed into the passenger side. I brought my right leg into the cab, wincing as I bent it after sitting down. I sat as still as possible, with measured breathing. The driver climbed in to check for something and gave a menacing look. I shuddered. Careful not to move my left arm from the side of my body, I slid out of his truck and stood on the shoulder once more. I just couldn't trust the man!

The officer and the tow truck driver finished their conversation, and the driver pulled away with the remains of my Audi. The cop said to me again, "You need to get off the freeway."

I remained quiet, standing on a slope next to the shoulder and still trying to shake off the pain from my shin and wrist. The cop acted too much like a bully for me to believe he would help me in any way. Besides, I had no idea what to do now.

The cop filled out paperwork. I inched my way toward him, hesitating.

"Look," he said, "you either get off this freeway, or I'm going to arrest you for disobeying an officer."

"How am I supposed to leave without a car?"

Ignoring my question, the officer kept writing.

Finally, I said, "I guess you're going to have to take me to jail."

The cop turned toward me with a scowl and told me to turn around, so I faced the side of his cruiser. He patted me down, placed my wrists together behind me, and forcefully put me in handcuffs, which dug into my skin. The pain from my left wrist shot all the way up my arm. I flinched but remained silent. The officer opened the back door of his cruiser, guided my head below the roof and into the back seat, and shut the door. I grimaced in pain as we zoomed off into the night.

On the way, the cop checked his laptop, which lay on a stand next to him, and talked over his radio with tension and anger in his voice. My adrenaline rushed. Having never been to jail, I had no idea what to expect. After refusing to go with the tow truck driver, though, it seemed I had no choice. The cop had put me in an impossible predicament. I could only pray that no further harm would come to me.

15.

When we arrived at the jail, only a few square floodlights lit the side of the building and entrance. I saw next to nothing with my limited vision. The officer unlocked and opened a few heavy metal doors and walked me into the structure. He greeted the booking officers. "This guy refused to leave the freeway after his car accident," he said, explaining my arrest.

The area where I was booked was not as dirty as I envisioned it would be. The gray-painted floor was swept, the walls were lined with white cinder blocks, and a silence, besides the cop and the booking officers talking, caught my attention. The staleness of the air lay heavy; I avoided taking deep breaths.

A couple of other prisoners, both unkempt, with unshaven faces and haggard expressions, and both reeking of alcohol, were led away. They glared at me, and my legs trembled.

One booking officer was a short woman whose hair was tied back in a bun, while the other was a stocky man of medium height whose entire head was shaved. The overhead fluorescent lights of the jail reflected their light off its shiny dome. They both wore navy uniforms, contrasting sharply with my appearance. My blue jeans were bloodied down near my right shin and had a hole in them, and my sweater was pulled halfway up my torso from when the cop had searched me on the freeway.

"Put your thumb here," said the female officer, who then rolled it over on the electronic scanner. I winced from the pain in my wrist.

As the two guards processed me, I imagined what sort of individual or individuals would be in my cell. *A thief, a crazed man, a murderer? Will I be beaten and gasp my last breath in this jail?* So much was out of my control; I was in the hands of the guards now. I concentrated hard on not letting my fear show, but the guards must have noticed my body shaking and my voice quivering. They knew I was scared out of my wits. I wanted to plead mercy and not be thrown to prisoners like those I'd just seen. Somehow, I kept silent.

My exhaustion and shock at being in the horrific car accident grew. I began regretting not going to the hospital like the EMTs offered, but some horrible premonition that I'd have ended up in a mental hospital again had prevented me from climbing into that ambulance.

I remembered awakening to the car crash. *Did I hit my head? Could I be seriously injured?* There was no way to know.

A guard led me away to a cell. My legs continued to shake, and I limped noticeably. Other prisoners stared at me through their cell door windows. One, a young woman with long, bleach-blonde hair that was uncombed, had a crazed look on her face. Another, a black man with a beard and an Afro, laughed. Most of the others glanced at me but showed little interest.

To my surprise, the guards put me in a cell by myself. The cell walls were white with graffiti scattered on them. The door, which closed with a clank when the guard pulled it shut, had a square window. A metal toilet with a small seat jutted out from the wall across from the cement bench that served as my bed. I used my hands as a pillow behind my head and lay on my back on the green canvas padding with my face toward the door.

I remembered how the day had begun, safe and sound in my apartment. Never had I guessed I'd end up here! And Tracy and my family—what would they think of me when they found out I'd been arrested? I didn't dare imagine what my father would say or do.

The sounds of the jail were unfamiliar to me as I tried to rest, much like when one is first trying to sleep in any strange place. Other prisoners yelled out from their cells.

One threatened someone else, saying, "You better look out when I get outta here!"

Another yelled out, "Hey white boy! White boy!" I remained motionless for some time, taking shallow breaths so as not to breathe in the stale air.

I lay in a time warp. No day and night, just overhead fluorescent lights that always shone. No clocks, just the sounds of other prisoners and guards and my own beating heart and slow breathing.

I got up from the cement bench and started limping back and forth, still holding my left arm to my side. I looked out of the window of my cell door and called out, "Hey, soul sister!" to a female guard. Then I shouted and pounded on my cell door with my right hand and sang "America the Beautiful." Some of the other prisoners watched me from their square windows and cheered me on while another looked at me with fury.

I calmed down and managed to lie on the hard bed and canvas, trying to sleep. My right arm covered my face to block out the light.

Then a guard, a tall man, opened my door, called, "Galloway!" and said, "You're going to the infirmary. Let's go."

He cuffed me, walked behind me, and directed me to a cell where two members of the medical team tended to me. They wrapped my left forearm and wrist into a white bandage and put my arm in a sling. Then they patched up my right shin, dry with crusting blood.

The same guard put me in another cell with a cellmate, a medium-size man with long, wiry brown hair. I sensed him sizing me up as I slowly moved to the bed. I lay down and immediately rested.

My cellmate kept mostly to himself until I slowly sat up, propping myself up on the elbow of my good arm. The man, sitting just a few feet away, offered me a Bible.

"Thanks," I said. With my terrible vision, I held it close to my face, skipping around and reading various passages. One described the wrath of God, and I thought I was going to hell for sure now that I was in jail.

"You doing all right, man?" asked the disheveled cellmate. He fixed his eyes on me.

I didn't answer.

"You don't look so good right now," he continued.

"I'm OK. I'm just a little banged up." This man worried me. The way he studied me and talked made me ill at ease, though he hadn't done anything to merit such fear.

There was more silence. He came to a sitting position from lying on his bed and leaned forward slightly. "I don't know how you got here, bud, but don't worry too much. There're better days ahead." He grinned.

"Thanks." I let out a deep breath.

A guard gave us a meal, a plastic tray full of beans, rice, and a plain hamburger. I peeled back the container of juice and sipped on it. After making sure I didn't want my food, my cellmate helped himself to it.

"You should really try to eat while you're here," he said to me while he heartily gulped down my portion. "You've got to keep your strength up."

"How long have you been here?"

"Two years. I'm in here for killing someone."

I kept my cool, not believing him. My mind raced nonetheless. *This is it. This guy is going to attack me with his bare hands.*

Then all of a sudden my cellmate acted as if he did not care for me in the least. He burped, farted, snorted, and walked around the cell pretending that I wasn't even there.

I looked up from the Bible. "What's wrong?"

He didn't respond but rather kept up his vulgar behavior, farting again while he urinated in the toilet. I lay back and pulled the sheets and blanket close to my face.

I waited for something to happen. Then, a miracle.

The young guard outside the cell announced chapel time. My cellmate left, becoming jovial when he saw another prisoner. I got up to follow them but then hesitated. Without my glasses, I squinted to scan the hallway heading toward the chapel for trouble.

I stopped walking behind the other prisoners and turned around, starting back. Then, on a spur of the moment, I said, "I am not caring much for my cellmate," to the clean-cut guard.

"You mean your buddy?" he replied sarcastically.

"I was wondering if I could move to another cell," I said softly. "He's bothering me."

"How long have you been here for?" asked the guard.

"You mean in California?"

"No. In jail! You wait right there," he ordered me as I stood outside the open cell.

He began a search, tearing up the beds, turning over the mattresses, and spilling items onto the floor. "Do you have to tear up his bed, too?" I asked. There was no reply as he continued to dismantle the cell. I stood by helplessly and scanned the hallway.

If my cellmate returns to find the cell a wreck, he'll surely beat me.

The guard finished his search. He removed my sling, cuffed me, and directed me to another smaller cell. I heard him say something about solitary confinement over his handheld radio.

I entered the cell to try to rest. My eyelids were heavy, but I still didn't sleep. Another bright, buzzing fluorescent light shone into my eyes. *That bastard cellmate of mine probably had a hand in this—acting like my friend so that the guard became suspicious of me!*

Time stood still. My dream of becoming an engineer was surely dashed. I'd be a janitor for the rest of my life, cleaning toilets and picking up trash. I had no future now that I'd been arrested and thrown into jail. *What good is life?*

I made haphazard attempts to suffocate myself with the pillow. But after a short time, my body reflexed into a big gasp of air, which kept me conscious. I gave up and lay quietly on my bed, hopeless, trying to block out the light with my arm over my eyes and to ignore the buzzing. Sleep was impossible.

I began praying fervently, reciting a few prayers in a whisper. *Regain some composure!*

Then, longing to be free of my cell and mustering my remaining energy, I approached the cell door, banging on it with my good arm and shouting, "Let me out! Let me out!" I continued to pound on the door and scream.

A group of guards opened the door and stormed in. One covered me with pepper spray while another used a Taser. In a state of utter shock, I didn't feel a thing as they surrounded me.

Two of them took hold of me and walked me down a corridor and into a room. Three guards strapped me tightly in a restraining chair, the only thing in the room. "You're not gonna have any fun, now," said one of them who was helping the others strap me in. "You just handled fifty thousand volts from a Taser, but now you aren't going to do nothing but sit."

They left me there alone in my suffering and fatigue. Soon I was sore. My buttocks and back ached.

Time dragged. Finally a bevy of guards came and unstrapped me from the chair. They led me to another dimly lit section of the jail and put me into a cell by myself. The walls were painted dark gray, and my cell was one of about five in a row.

"Take that off and put this on," said one of them, who held out a one-piece smock that hooked together over one shoulder with Velcro and went down to my thighs. They left me alone. I heard some words spoken between the guards, including "suicide watch."

That's what the smock is for—so I don't hurt myself.

I sat on yet another cement bed, although this one had no padding. I stared at the adjacent wall, with my shoulders slouched and my hands clasped together in my lap.

This cell had a musty dank smell, as if it were underground from the rest of the jail like a cave. *How long has it been since my car accident—two, maybe ten hours?* I had no idea. Zach and my parents would be worried sick by now, not to mention Chrissy. She would worry the most. Tracy would wonder where I was, too.

Looking through my cell window, I saw multiple guards keeping watch. They sat and chatted behind plexiglass, which separated them from the space outside the cells.

My stomach growled, and my mouth was parched. My back still ached from being strapped in the chair from my previous cell, so I didn't even lie down on the hard flat surface. My bare feet touched the cold floor. I continued to sit, staring at the wall, spent.

I turned and noticed a razor blade on the floor near the cell door. *How did that get there?* I was positive it hadn't been there before. At any rate, there it lay, with the dismal light from above reflecting off it, contrasting with the dark cement floor. *Am I seeing things?* I picked it up and pushed it under the door and outside my cell.

I sat on my bed again. After some time, I looked back and the razor blade had reappeared! I was dumbfounded. *Some sick joke. They want me to hurt myself.* This time, I left the blade alone.

My cell door opened, and a nurse, accompanied by a guard, gave me a small plastic cup of water and a tablet in another plastic cup.

"Here, take this," she said.

I looked at the tablet doubtfully but took it and gulped down the water. After she left, I squinted toward the floor by the door and no longer saw the blade. At some point, someone had taken it away.

More waiting. I had experienced solitary confinement, pepper spray, a Taser, the restraining chair, and a suicide watch. What else?

Then, a visitor. She was a young woman wearing professional attire—a navy button-down dress shirt, gray slacks, and black shoes. After the guard let her in, she remained inside my cell with the door closed.

"Hello, I'm Cindy from Sun County Social Services. I'm here to do an evaluation. May I ask you some questions?" she asked, now in a crouched position opposite me. I sat.

"All right," I said despondently.

"Are you currently taking illegal drugs?" she asked.

"No," I said.

"Are you currently taking any prescription drugs?"

"Yes. Boost."

"Do you know the dose?"

I told her.

"Are you currently having any suicidal thoughts or thoughts of wanting to hurt others?"

"No." She wrote down my responses on a form as the interview went along.

"Have you been to a psychiatric hospital before?"

"Yes." *Is that where I'm headed—another mental hospital?*

She finished up, thanked me, and left the cell. I let out a few deep breaths, and my body stopped trembling. Since I'd arrived at the jail, Cindy was the first person to treat me like a real human, and I felt the effect.

16.

I came to, and an older male attendant leaned over my bedside. "You're at Holy Redeemer Hospital in San Vicente, Hank. You've been unconscious. We're glad that you're awake now," he said.

Still groggy, I propped myself up with my elbows and took in my surroundings. Like the windows at Bellevue in San Francisco, these were sealed with a fine grated metal covering, though the sun shone through them. An empty bed covered with white sheets sat to my right. The floor was linoleum, and the walls were white. Across from the foot of my bed was the doorway to a bathroom.

I had no idea how long I'd been unconscious, though I remembered the old woman who admitted me into the psychiatric hospital and the pain in my shoulder after slamming into a glass doorway to try to escape. The car accident, the jail, the ride in the police cruiser to the hospital—they were all fresh in my memory.

I asked the attendant, "Does my family know where I am?"

"Yes, Hank. They know you're here."

After sensing the soreness in my right shoulder, I took a minute to get out of bed. The attendant oriented me to the ward, showing me the medication window at the nurses' station. I looked over the daily schedule for the patients posted in the hallway and peered at the exit doors.

"Why was I unconscious?" I asked him after the tour was over and we were back in the room.

He hesitated before answering. "We had to sedate you the night they brought you here."

Patients walked around slowly and eyed me suspiciously, since I was still in my orange jail clothes, I supposed. They were of all colors, heights, genders, and builds. I didn't make eye contact. A young woman sitting in the hallway at one end with no expression on her face stared out the window. A tall, slim man walked the hallway, staring straight ahead as I passed him. An older man was unshaven and wrinkled. A teenage girl squinted at me and smirked. Some were dressed in hospital gowns, others in street clothes. Like the patients in the mental hospital in San Francisco, the ones here seemed silent and unpredictable. I couldn't trust them.

The long carpeted hallway and white-painted walls stretched straight, with entrances to patient rooms on either side. Patients lay in their beds, stood in the hallway, and sat in the common room across from the nurses' station.

After a shower and a bland breakfast, I went to a group session. The group leader, a middle-aged man with a bulging belly, asked my name. I told him my first name only.

He began the session. "We're covering some methods of caring for your mental well-being today."

I sat in my chair and stared straight ahead, as if I were in a trance, while I tried to get my bearings and make sense of what had happened since I left Halifax. The handouts that explained mental wellness didn't register. I let the other patients do the talking.

Before lunch I stood in line at the medication window. The nurse checked my identification band, gave me my tablets and a small cup of water, and asked me, "Can you take your medicine, please?"

My heart beat wildly, and my hand trembled. *Will my throat swell and choke off my breath? Or will I die slowly and painfully?* I swallowed the tablets. Then I left the nurses' station and walked back to my room. I waited, almost holding my breath, for a reaction. Nothing happened. Five minutes passed and then ten. Still nothing. I lay in my bed, feeling groggy but nothing more.

In the evening, I ate my dinner by myself in an empty group room as instructed while the rest of the patients went to the cafeteria. Afterward, I sat among them, slightly more at ease. Though I didn't speak to anyone, several of the others spoke to one another.

"Are you feeling better?"

"What's the name of the medicine you're taking?"

All of a sudden, I broke down sobbing. I covered my eyes with my hand to avoid anyone else's gaze. I was relieved, scared, and still in shock all simultaneously. As tears fell through my hand, I wondered what the other patients and staff were thinking. *Do they pity me, scorn me, or think of me as an outcast—even among their group?* Wiping my tears, I rose abruptly from my cushioned chair and walked briskly to my room.

That first night, I slept in fits and starts. I woke once to hear the staff member situated outside my room sighing and shifting in his chair, but otherwise all was quiet. The empty bed that stood next to mine still wasn't occupied.

The next day, the same cheerful attendant woke me again. "Hank, it's time for your medicine." He stretched out his arms, waiting for me to take the pills and water. I sat up and reluctantly washed down the tablets.

I didn't want to be in the hospital. I examined the exit doors, wishing them open. The pills, the other patients, the staff—they all bothered me. But I was an involuntary patient, meaning I couldn't leave without the doctor's permission. I hadn't even met the doctor.

After finishing breakfast, a nurse came to me and said, "Hank, the doctor wants to see you now."

This psychiatrist, Dr. Patel, was a young-looking man, dark skinned with thick hair and bushy eyebrows. He wore a suit and tie. I sat in a chair opposite him in a small office.

"How are you doing so far here in the hospital?" He spoke with an Indian accent.

"OK." I feared his authority. *He can put me away in a long-term facility, a state hospital, can't he?* I wasn't sure, but my intuition told me to be careful what I said.

"Are you feeling any better?" asked Dr. Patel.

"Yes, somewhat."

"If you don't mind, we're going to talk about your symptoms."

Adrenaline coursed through me. "Sure."

"Were your thoughts racing before you came to the hospital?"

I paused. My fear of my medication, my distrust of my family during my trip to LA, and my reaction to being in jail. I supposed my thoughts had been racing. "Yes."

"Can you tell me more about those thoughts?"

"I thought my medicine was poisoned and my father was responsible." My level of discomfort and embarrassment rose when I admitted such a thing. I wanted to be as honest as possible with him, though. I figured this doctor could tell if I was lying to him.

He paused for a few seconds to type something on a laptop computer.

"Are you afraid of being hurt by other people while you're having racing thoughts?"

Being hurt by others? That was another strange question that caught me off guard. The more I thought about it, though, the more I knew it to be true. "Sometimes."

"Do you see things that aren't actually there?"

Whoa! That's off the wall. "No," I said politely.

"Are you hearing any voices?" he asked.

Another strange one! "No."

"Any current thoughts of suicide or wanting to hurt others?"

"No." I didn't tell him about my attempt in the jail, nor did he ask about it.

He paused, typed again, and then met my eyes.

"This is your second time in a psychiatric hospital?"

"Yes."

"What led you to the hospital the first time?"

"I thought my neighbor was going to shoot me, so I left my apartment in the middle of the night."

"Was there anything that your neighbors did that caused you to have this thought?"

"The father was angry with me but otherwise…no."

He typed away. "What medicines have you taken since your first hospitalization?"

"Connect and Boost."

"Have you taken them as prescribed by your outpatient psychiatrist?"

"Yes." I was relieved to say this, though I didn't know exactly why. I always took my medicine, even when I didn't want to. I had been faithful to the regimen Dr. Allen in Sonoma County put me on—always.

"Did he ever give you a diagnosis?"

"He thought I might be suffering from depression." Then, "Do you know what my diagnosis is?" I was curious as to his thoughts.

"It's too early to give one on the first evaluation. I may have one by the time you leave here."

I wondered when my discharge would be but wasn't bold enough to ask right then. Dr. Patel ended the interview, and I walked out of the office, feeling uneasy, my heart still racing. Some of his questions were spot on. Dr. Allen had never asked me them.

It was Monday. That much I could see on the dry-erase board that served as the announcement bulletin for the patients and staff, though I still didn't have my glasses, which I assumed were lost.

New patients appeared later in the morning, while others disappeared. One of the new ones, a plump teenage girl, was crying while talking on the public phone, saying, "Mom, please come and pick me up. Why did you send me here? I want to go home." I steered clear of her negativity from that point onward.

As I walked about, a staff member approached me, saying, "Hank, it's time for group. Can you join us in room one?" I walked into the group room and sat with seven other patients.

"Today's group is about depression," said the same group leader, his belly pressed up against the table. His name was Wilson. "It's a common form of mental illness which affects a large amount of the population. Can anyone tell me a symptom of someone who might be suffering from depression?"

Silence ensued for a few seconds. A male patient with uncombed hair said, "You feel tired."

"Good. Fatigue is very common," said Wilson. "Anyone else have an idea?"

"Sleeping too much," said a female patient softly.

"Yes. Lack of energy causes one to stay in bed. What else?"

"You don't eat," said the same male patient, whose name was Al.

"Right, Al. A lack of appetite." He paused. "Anyone else?"

No one spoke. Two of the patients had fallen asleep while another stared straight ahead at the wall opposite him. One of those that slept snored softly.

"Hank?" asked Wilson.

I shrugged.

"Another symptom of depression is lack of interest in activities that you normally do," continued the fat man. "Can anyone tell the group if they've had any of these symptoms?"

There was a pause. Finally the patient with the uncombed hair said, "Yeah, I just sit around and start drinking when I get depressed."

"OK, thank you for sharing. What Al said is a good point because often when someone suffers from depression they begin taking drugs and alcohol. The individual thinks he can overcome his depression by abusing these substances. There is a term for this kind of behavior in mental illness. Does anyone know what it is?"

"Yeah, self-medication," said the woman from before, a little more boldly this time.

"Good, Susan. Self-medication. What happens when you self-medicate? Does it help or hurt your mental illness?"

"It hurts it," said Susan.

"Yes. It's important to stay away from drugs and alcohol."

"Because you end up in the hospital," said Al.

"Right, Al. Now what can you do to alleviate depression?"

"Spend time with friends and family," said a middle-aged woman.

"You can avoid isolation by being around those that care about you. Socializing is very important when we talk about staying mentally healthy. What else?"

There was a pause. Then Al said, "Take your medicine."

"Yes, Al. Sometimes side effects or just the idea of taking it make you feel ashamed or embarrassed, but taking your medication is also a very important step in staying mentally healthy. Is there anything else?"

No one replied this time. Another patient had fallen asleep with his head down on the table. The snores of the other sleeping one grew louder. The patient staring ahead continued to do so. Everyone else declined to make eye contact with the leader.

"How about exercise?" he asked. "Knowing that you are stressed out is important. You have to find healthy ways to relieve it. What are some other ways to cope with stress?"

"Read a book," said Susan.

"Reading a book—that's good," said the leader.

"Eat some ice cream," said the middle-aged woman.

"Right, Michelle. Treat yourself."

"Have a cigarette," said a patient who had previously been looking down at the floor the entire time.

"You want to try to stay away from cigarettes. I know that they relieve stress for you, but smoking is not a healthy way to relieve stress," said Wilson.

"But I like cigarettes," said the patient.

"I know you do, but what we are discussing are healthy methods, not unhealthy ones."

The patient turned his gaze back to the floor.

On went the group. I gave one or two answers but mainly sat and listened. It seemed most of the patients had been in the hospital before by their familiarity with the topic of discussion and the staff member. I was the new guy.

17.

The next morning, after a night of deep sleep, I called Tracy. She sounded upset that I was stuck in another mental hospital; I tried to reassure her. But given the circumstances, I didn't accomplish calming her down. We ended the conversation with her very concerned and worried; I heard it in her voice. My longing to leave the hospital and return home grew.

After the phone call, I strolled down the hallway, passing time. The nurse in charge of me, a short man named Larry, said, "Hank, can you follow me please?"

I obliged, walking with him out of the ward, down two flights of stairs, and down another hallway. Finally we came to a conference room that had a long white-topped table stretching the length of it. Larry asked me to sit at one end. A middle-aged woman dressed in a business suit sat at the other. Two other men in suits and ties were in chairs on either side of the woman and fixed their stares on me.

One of the men stated some kind of information, and I heard my name among all of the legal jargon. The woman's eyes focused only on me when I looked up from the floor briefly. After a minute or two of more legal talk, meaningless to me, Larry asked me to stand and walk out of the room with him.

When I returned to the ward, one of the patients approached me.

"Where did you go, Hank?" she asked.

"I had a meeting," I said. The patient pursued the subject no further and walked away. No one said anything else to me, though several patients looked at me intently. I made eye contact with no one and sat on a couch. Sweat ran down my sides, and I gulped.

I wondered about the meeting. *It must have been something to do with my arrest and stay in jail. The middle-aged woman seemed like a judge or some other important figure, in charge of the whole proceeding.*

Next to me on the couch was the patient with the age-wrinkled face. His name was Charles. "How're you doing there, young man?" he asked me.

"Better, thanks."

"You look like you're feeling better," he said. "Do you have the routine here figured out by now?"

"I'm getting the hang of it."

"Keep on eating your food. That'll help you get your strength back. And another thing," he continued, leaning toward me now and speaking in a lower voice. "When you get before the judge, tell her it was dark."

I stiffened. Everyone else in the area kept quiet. I watched the local news on the box television hanging in the corner of the common area and paid no one any mind. The patient went to his room, and a couple of patients began playing UNO on a small table next to me. *Does Charles know about my car accident? It seems there aren't any secrets in the psych ward.*

. . . . .

That evening, I called my parents' house from a public phone in one of the group rooms. My mother answered.

"Hi, Mom," I said.

"Hi, Hank! How are you?"

"I'm better."

"We were worried when you didn't show up at Zach's. And then we got the call from the police that you'd been in an accident…" Her voice trailed off, like she was fighting back the urge to cry. "How is the hospital treating you?" she finally asked.

"Good." I fought back the urge to plead with her to get me out of the hospital.

"Are you getting enough to eat?"

"Yes."

"We thought about visiting, but the doctor feels that it's best right now for you to not have any visitors. Did you speak with Tracy?"

"Yes."

"Zach was especially worried when we couldn't reach you on your cell anymore."

"Yeah, tell him I'm sorry." Guilt for what I'd put my family through rose in me. What pain my mother must be feeling! And Zach must have thought the worst when I didn't show at his house.

"I will. Your father and I are awfully sorry you had to go to that jail. The officer was very apologetic when we told him you were having an episode. Are you sure you're doing OK? Your voice is shaky."

"I'm OK. I'm just trying to get used to this hospital." My accident, the jail, and the hospital still had me in a state of shock, but I didn't relate all of this to my mother for fear that she'd be even more upset.

"Zach sent you a book to read. Maybe that'll help make you more comfortable."

"Mmm."

"OK. Our prayers are with you, Hank, and we love you."

"I love you, too."

I hung up, lost in thought. I still didn't know where I'd go after discharge. Holy Redeemer was only for short stays, not long ones. I'd have to go somewhere. My conversation with my mother gave me hope that my family still accepted me, but what about my father?

Two days later, the staff found me street clothes to wear—a white T-shirt and a pair of gray sweatpants. The rest of the patients glanced up at me when I joined them in the common room. Then, for lunch, I was allowed to eat with the rest of the patients in the cafeteria. The following day, Larry gave me my eyeglasses, which had been found in the car wreckage. Gradually, life in the ward improved for me.

When, on day eleven, the staff finally told me my discharge date was in three days and Chrissy would pick me up, my mind churned. I strode up and down the hallways, thinking of what life on the outside would be like. *What will my father do? Berate me for going to the hospital? I can't fathom living with my parents again, but that's exactly what's about to happen according to my nurse.*

Meanwhile, time dragged. I attended and participated in groups, but soon they began to overlap. My strength was almost full except for my broken left wrist, which remained wrapped in a cast. I saw Dr. Patel every weekday and another psychiatrist over the weekend. Though I asked numerous times, nobody gave me a definite diagnosis.

I continued to walk the hallway as well as read the book, a biography of

George Bush Sr., that Zach sent me.

My discharge day arrived, and Chrissy showed up and gave me a hug with tears in her eyes. When she composed herself, she requested a copy of my medical record.

We stood in my room, letting my nurse attend to his discharge duties. I was uncomfortable because, for a change, Chrissy was in charge of *my* well-being, at least for a few days until we returned to Atlanta together. The traditional roles had been reversed.

I knew I'd miss some of my fellow patients who remained behind after my two-week stay. Charles approached me. "See you," he said, embracing me. His eyes looked at me hard like they always did but with a hint of sadness.

Chrissy and I walked out of the hospital and climbed into a rental car on a dreary January afternoon.

. . . . .

The lawyer we met straight after leaving the hospital in San Vicente was a fast talker. He wore a beige suit even though it was wintertime. His office floors were all wooden except for the throw rug on the floor beneath his desk. The floors creaked as the three of us entered and sat.

I was confused about why we had to meet him. I had been arrested because I had no other way to leave the freeway after my accident, not because I had done anything egregious. *Or maybe I did some horrible crime and don't even remember? No, I remember everything. How can I not?*

As Chrissy and the lawyer exchanged formalities, I sat quietly, hunched forward, still in a stupor from the medicine in the hospital. Neither Chrissy nor the lawyer explained to me what exactly this meeting was about. She was pensive on the ride to the lawyer's office, not giving me much information. She normally was so cheerful. I passed it off as jet lag or the fact that she had to pick me up in the psych ward.

"We'll get this cleared up," said the lawyer. "Hank will get some good home cooking for a while." He smiled at us.

"Is there any chance we can expunge Hank's arrest from his record?" asked Chrissy. I perked my ears, since this was an important issue concerning my career ambitions.

"Since this is his first arrest, we can clear the record in about six months' time," said the lawyer. Relief flooded through me, sending life into my otherwise lifeless body.

I couldn't stay silent any longer. "What's this all about anyway? The officer gave me an ultimatum on the freeway—either leave the scene or go to jail."

The lawyer's smile disappeared. He and Chrissy exchanged glances, and then Chrissy turned to me. "I'll tell you later."

"And then in jail they put me in solitary. Can you believe that?" I searched their faces for some compassion, some understanding, but neither was present. "They stormed into my cell, pepper sprayed me, and used a Taser. Four guards against me. Does that seem fair?"

Again Chrissy and the lawyer's eyes met. Chrissy glanced at me. "Hank, let him finish, will you?"

The lawyer chatted away like a friendly car salesman. Finally, without him asking me a single question besides how I was doing in general, we all stood, and my sister and I shook the lawyer's limp hand.

. . . . .

Later on, in the rental car on the highway going to Los Angeles, where Chrissy and I were to fly to Atlanta, I asked Chrissy for more information.

"You hit the officer that arrested you in the chest before he handcuffed you," she said.

"No, I didn't!"

"And then in the jail, you fought with another inmate."

"Those are all lies!"

"That's what's in the report."

"Why would I be stupid enough to do those things, even if I was having a nervous breakdown?"

She shrugged with both hands on the steering wheel.

"You don't believe me?" I asked.

"I believe you, but everyone else isn't going to take your word over what's in a report, especially since you were acting crazy."

Chrissy had a point, which I hadn't thought about. Neither a judge nor anybody else would believe my side of the story, even if I were telling the truth.

The more I thought about it, the more serious the situation became. I was up against the law now, and I couldn't do much about it.

I contemplated bringing up the razor blade in my cell but figured now wasn't the time. Worry flooded my mind. On top of a mandatory stay with my parents, I had to contend with false accusations.

"How did you afford to travel out here? You don't have that kind of money," I finally said.

"Dad paid for it all, including the lawyer's fees."

"Are you serious?"

Chrissy nodded.

Stunned, I didn't say another word for the rest of the ride to Los Angeles.

18.

I was a sight to see when I arrived in Atlanta's airport with Chrissy. My entire left forearm and wrist were in a hard cast, and my forehead was still slightly bruised from ramming the glass door trying to escape the hospital. Soon after takeoff, the guy sitting next to me on my flight had asked if I was returning from combat. I told him I was in a bad car accident, shied away from any further details, and put on my headphones and feigned sleep for the remainder of the flight.

My parents, instead of letting Chrissy and me ride the train to the other side of town from the airport, came and picked us up straight from the baggage claim during rush hour. It must have taken them an hour to get from the mansion to the airport. My mother offered me the front passenger seat. My father got out to help with the bags and even closed the door behind me after I sat in his Lexus.

On the way from the airport, my father asked how I was doing. I answered that I was OK. I really wasn't, though. My state of shock was much greater than when I was first in the hospital the year before, and it, along with the antipsychotic medicine I was taking, held me in a kind of trance. Plus, I was in Atlanta, a place I'd never thought I'd live in again.

I braced myself for staying with my parents for the first time since high school. I really wasn't sure I'd survive being essentially unemployed with my only outside contact being another shrink. During the weekends Chrissy would visit from her college town, Athens, but during the week, my isolation from the real world would be greatest. I'd have to deal with my father's country club cronies if I joined him there or placate my mother's bridge companions when they all met at the mansion periodically. But the individuals my parents associated with weren't the real world, in my opinion. I wanted to be on my own again and not in my childhood surroundings.

Jocelyn greeted us when we entered the kitchen. She was baking cookies, one of my favorite foods of hers. "Hi, Chrissy! Hi, Hank! It's so good to see both of you. How are you feeling, Hank?"

"OK." In my shock, I'd forgotten to ask what Jocelyn knew about my accident and hospitalization—whether she knew about my "psychosis," as the doctors all called it again. But Jocelyn knew all the secrets in the house, perhaps more than she let on. I wouldn't have been surprised if she knew I'd acted strangely two times in California. Nevertheless, I assumed she referred to my physical injuries not my mental ones when she asked how I was.

"I'm so glad to see you. Really. You'll be staying with us a while then?"

"Yeah."

"We'll get you all fixed up. Does your arm hurt? How about your head?"

"They're all fine. Thanks."

"Very good. I got your bedroom all ready for you. Your bed's made, a fresh set of towels in the bathroom. You just let me know if you need anything. OK?"

"OK."

"I'm making stuffed shells, with the marinara sauce that you like. It'll be ready before I go this evening."

"Thanks, Jocelyn." I managed a smile despite all that had happened in the last three weeks.

"Jocelyn, did you clean that bathroom downstairs by the exercise room?" boomed my father, who had set down a suitcase on the oak floor. My father was all business with our maid, all the time. He didn't waste time on small talk with her, either.

Jocelyn straightened up from a slightly bowed position from talking with me. She was much like a soldier preparing to salute a superior. "Yes, Mr. Galloway. It's all clean."

"Good. It's been a while since it was done." He panted once or twice from the exertion of carrying my suitcase. "You can go as soon as the food is ready."

"Thank you, Jocelyn," chimed my mother. "Remember I'm having the ladies over for bridge next week. I have a list of appetizers for you to prepare for them."

"Yes, Mrs. Galloway."

"Good to see you, Jocelyn," said Chrissy, who also smiled.

"Why, Chrissy! It's so good that you're here. I don't see you as often anymore."

"I'm busy studying in Athens, but I'll be making the trip to see Hank on the weekends while he's back." Chrissy's entrance exam for medical school was in the spring.

"Oh, good!" exclaimed our maid. "I think you'll make a fine surgeon. Yes, indeed. Find yourself a nice gentleman and settle down, too."

Chrissy flushed red. "No one yet in that department. I'll let you know when I find him, though."

"Sure you will. Just like Zach has done. And Hank, too."

Later that night, I called Tracy to update her more on my situation.

"The cop arrested you for disobeying an impossible order?" she said when I told her about my car accident and jailing. "Can't you file a complaint against him?"

"I don't know," I said. "Since I went to another psych ward, I don't know if anyone would take it seriously or even believe me."

"That's crap. That cop took advantage of the situation when the two of you were alone on the highway."

"I know. Even my family doesn't believe my side of the story. Nor my lawyer."

"I believe you, Hank."

"Thanks." Though it didn't help my situation in a legal sense, having Tracy's support made me feel much better.

"So when are you returning to California?" she asked.

"It's going to be a while. I have to live with my parents until I get a psychiatrist's permission to live on my own again."

"Oh…" The disappointment in her voice was evident. Then, "I'll wait for you."

Relief flooded through me. I was afraid she'd break it off with me again.

．．．．．

Two weeks later, as I sat at the kitchen table eating cookies and reading the newspaper, Jocelyn entered with a basket of laundry, which she proceeded to fold on the counter. "How are you, Hank?" she asked.

"I'm better, thanks."

My mother had gone out to shop for food. My father was at his country club. Only Jocelyn and I were in the mansion.

"You going back to California?"

"As soon as I can, yes."

"I can understand why you want to be so far away," continued our maid. "You had it rough growing up here. With your father and all, you know?"

I stopped my reading and glanced up at Jocelyn. Then I continued perusing the travel section. "Yeah, he was pretty strict."

"Not only strict. His temper affected you in ways you and I don't even understand."

I looked up at Jocelyn, who continued to fold clothes. She had my full attention now. She wasn't one to mince words—when she said something, she meant it.

Although she didn't look up from her work, she knew I was listening. She'd known me since I was a baby and perhaps knew me better than I knew myself.

"Maybe it's for the best that you live there, after you get well again. Just be careful that you don't go to the hospital no more. You don't want to live in one of those state hospitals."

State hospitals? What does she mean by that? She must definitely know the real reason behind my two hospitalizations in California. I felt an impulse to defend myself, to say the two incidents were a mistake, but it was futile to argue. Jocelyn was usually right.

I decided to be humble. "Thanks, Jocelyn."

"And another thing," she continued, matching two dark socks with each other. "Don't be wasting your time with women who can't accept who you are. I see it all the time—women trying to change the man they is with. Men trying to change the women they is with. It don't work that way. You have to accept each other's faults."

"I understand." I didn't know if she was referring to Tracy. I convinced myself that she wasn't.

"I'm just giving some advice, Hank. Not trying to run your life. You hear me?"

That was Jocelyn's way of ending her talks. I said, "Yes."

19.

I sat on my couch in my apartment in California, back after a six-month stay with my parents. I had missed the entire semester at Dewey State, so I decided to take a year off and start again in January of the following year. I withdrew my applications to engineering schools.

Staying at the mansion in Atlanta had bored me to no end. I had no job, no classes to attend, and no close friends in the area. My only social interactions were with Jocelyn, my parents at dinnertime, and with my new shrink. Chrissy's visits broke the monotony and lifted my spirits, and occasionally I joined my father at his country club to play golf or have lunch. But mostly I left him to his leisure activities and counted the days until my return to California. Out of my bedroom window, I saw the seasons change from winter to spring to summer.

My second psychiatrist was another detached and boring personality with whom I didn't click. His long pauses between questions and his peering at me as if I were a freak of nature made me uneasy. He never brought up my arrest and jailing, nor did I. I was ashamed to do so and didn't think any good would come of it. So I let the past lie dormant.

One thing he did accomplish was a switch to a new medicine, called Elixir. It wasn't as sedating as Connect, the medicine I was on yet again after my discharge from Holy Redeemer. Now I slept eight hours a night and had my normal energy.

Over the phone, Tracy fretted about my accident, reiterating the fact that I could have died. I told her not to worry, but deep down I worried myself about the whole incident. My car accident could've been fatal. The guards in the jail had broken me, ending with me being spit out to a mental hospital. I was a year behind schedule in my career track. My life was on hold for the time being.

My father was largely subdued during my whole stay, though he didn't say why. *Is he ashamed to have me as a son?* I thanked him for letting me stay at the mansion when I arrived with Chrissy. He grunted, "You're welcome." After a few weeks his attentiveness wore off, and he was back to his old self, barking orders to Jocelyn and hounding my mother. My mother was relieved to have me safe at home, and I was not sure she wanted me to leave again.

As my time in Atlanta wound down my parents urged me to go on disability and stay with them, but despite their pleading, I left for Halifax as soon as my psychiatrist gave me the approval I needed. Six months with them had been way too long, and I longed to be independent again. I was determined to make something of myself and fulfill my dream.

Now, in my hands, I had the discharge papers from Holy Redeemer. Out of curiosity, I'd brought them along from Atlanta. I read the discharge summary for the first time in my apartment.

Holy Redeemer Hospital Admission Report for Hank Galloway

Patient, a twenty-seven-year-old male, was admitted to Holy Redeemer Hospital from the county jail. Before going to the jail, the patient's car crashed into an eighteen-wheel truck parked on the shoulder of the I-5 interstate. After the crash, the patient refused medical care and refused a ride to a hotel. Instead, the patient sat in the middle of the highway, ignoring the police officer on the scene that ordered him to move. The patient was subsequently arrested and taken to the county jail, where he was involved in a violent altercation with another inmate. Pepper spray and a Taser shock failed to subdue him.

After release from the jail, police transported the patient to a local hospital, where he received treatment for a left wrist fracture and a wound in the right lower extremity. CT scan of the head was negative. Patient was also noted to have a red left eye and bruised forehead, stemming from his fight in the jail.

Upon arrival at Holy Redeemer Hospital, the patient ran through a glass exit door, bringing another staff member through it and injuring himself as well as the staff. Patient was uncooperative when the staff tried to calm him down. He was then tranquilized.

My initial interview with the patient produced little information, as the patient was mumbling incoherently and could only give his name.

The information provided by the police and overnight staff was the principal source for this evaluation.

Unable to read further, I threw the pile of papers across my living room in disgust. I stood, seething, with my hands on my hips. The doctor's report was full of lies. I didn't sit in the middle of the interstate after my accident, nor was I involved in a fight at the jail. Even the part about injuring another staff member once I was admitted to the hospital was wrong. I had run to the glass door, but I didn't take a staff member with me. His initial interview with me was fabricated, too. *Why does the inpatient psychiatrist want to paint me as a monster? Why is the report so inaccurate?*

I was helpless to do anything to correct it. Too much time had passed, and, apparently I wasn't in a state to corroborate what exactly happened, according to the hospital. I had been labeled as psychotic again. No one would believe my side of the story, even though I remembered what had happened.

My phone rang. It was Tom. He knew about my second hospitalization and subsequent stay in Atlanta.

"Are you back in Cali?" he asked.

"Just got back last week," I answered.

"How are you feeling?"

"I'm my old self again. Looking forward to starting classes."

"What about a diagnosis?"

"Still don't have one. They gave me some possibilities."

"Like?"

"Psychotic depression, schizo something."

"Schizophrenia?"

"No." I would've remembered such a serious diagnosis. "I'd have to look at the discharge papers again."

"The psychiatrist in Atlanta didn't give you one?"

"No. He wasn't very personable, so I didn't pursue his thoughts about a diagnosis. His strongest reaction to anything I said was when I suggested going off my medicine during one of our last sessions. He said that it wasn't possible."

"So who are you set up with here?"

"I'm seeing a therapist once a week and another new psychiatrist monthly. My first appointment with the therapist is tomorrow. I've already seen the psychiatrist."

"What's he like?"

"About as good as expected, I suppose...I don't know. I'm fed up with shrinks in general."

"Mmm. Don't lose hope. What about your applications for engineering school?"

"I'm looking into applying for next year. I'll tell them I had to take a year off for personal reasons."

"Gotcha." Tom sounded somewhat resigned, but I didn't ask him why.

We set up a surf session for that weekend, which gave me some sense of normalcy after my long absence.

I wondered why Tom sounded disappointed. He was usually more upbeat. *Is it because I don't have a diagnosis yet? Because I ended up in a hospital again? Because I can't find a psychiatrist I like?* I couldn't put my finger on it. He was usually so straightforward.

I wondered at this point if my hopes for entering into an engineering school were still realistic. Having had two nervous breakdowns within a year was a real cause for concern, especially since I had to take a year off. I seriously questioned if I was really cut out to be an engineer. My first hospitalization was a blip on the radar, but this latest one, which had kept me for two weeks, was a serious matter, even if I wasn't mentally ill.

I gathered up the discharge report strewn on the floor and put it away in a drawer. My healing wrist kept me even from working my deli job; my removable cast kept it immobilized. My only routine for a while would be going to my therapy and psychiatry appointments and spending time with Tracy. The only bright spot was that the lawyer in San Vicente had expunged my record of my arrest. In a legal sense at least, my dream to work at NASA was still intact.

20.

I sat across from my new therapist, Paula Jacobs, and tried not to let my nerves get the best of me.

The week before, I'd met my third psychiatrist, not counting the ones I saw in the hospital. I visited him just for medication matters—prescriptions, refills, and side effects monitoring. The bulk of my time would be with Paula. She could send me to the hospital, just like a psychiatrist could.

She wore elegant black slacks, a cream-colored silk shirt, a black dress jacket, and a fair amount of makeup, which sharpened her beauty, although she was middle-aged. I could tell that she had once been even more attractive.

The office offered some elegance as well. It was brightly lit from two large windows and had a beige carpet and a white-and-red-striped sofa. The sofa was short and had full cushions and small pillows for the comfort of sitting, instead of reclining.

"So you were at Holy Redeemer Hospital in San Vicente?" she began.

"Yes. I was discharged almost seven months ago." I shifted nervously on the couch.

She eyed me. I wondered if she could tell that I was nervous. After a few seconds, she asked, "Is this the first time that you've ever worked with a therapist?"

"Yes," I said, almost under my breath. I broke eye contact with her.

"I read in the summary of your care in Atlanta that you were living with your parents after your discharge. How long have you been back in California since living with them?"

"About two weeks."

"I see." She paused and glanced at my cast. "How is your injury coming along?"

"OK. I'm waiting for the orthopedist to clear me so I can work again."

"Aren't you taking classes?" She sifted through the file on her lap.

"No. I don't start school again until January. I have only one semester left…hopefully. I'm finishing my prerequisites for engineering schools and waiting for acceptance."

"What brought you to California originally?"

"I prefer to live a distance away from my father." I had never told any shrink this. I trusted Paula right away, it seemed.

"Ah. But you just spent six months with him. How was that?"

"It was terrible. I appreciated the hospitality but basically just counted the days until my return. Chrissy, my sister, was the only bright spot. But she was preparing for medical school and wasn't around that much. My parents' house is big enough that I avoided my father most of the time."

"And your mother?"

"She's OK. Not someone I can have a deep conversation with, though. I'm closer with my sister than with anyone else in my family. Though I can't talk about…"

"Talk about what?"

"My hospitalizations. It's a taboo subject for some reason."

"Would you like to speak with them about your illness?"

I disagreed that I had an illness but let it go this time. "Yes. I mean…it would help my family understand me better."

"I agree." Another pause. "What about your girlfriend? What's her name?"

"Tracy," I offered.

"Yes. Tracy. What's she like?"

"She's been good to me, especially with understanding my long absence. Though I haven't told her what happened when I was in jail."

"Oh."

"I wasn't treated humanely while I was there, and nobody seems to believe my side of the story—not even my family. I'm embarrassed to bring it up to Tracy."

"Don't you think it would bring some closure to the whole matter if you did?"

"I'm too ashamed."

"I see."

"Maybe I'm afraid she'll break up with me if I do tell her about it. I don't know…" I imagined the worst. If we broke up, Tracy would be bitter and angry. She'd tell everyone I was psycho. Maybe word would reach Stanford, or even NASA, that I wasn't mentally fit for their program. Who knew? My life could be ruined!

"It seems trust is a big issue with you."

I had never thought of it before, but now that my therapist brought it up, it occurred to me that it was true.

There was a silence. I didn't know what to say, so I kept quiet. I'd had minimal social interaction—except with Tracy—so I was out of breath because of all the talking already. I relaxed. My palms didn't sweat anymore, and I sat farther back in the couch.

My therapist looked down at the file again. "And you have one more sibling, Zach, right?"

"He followed in my father's footsteps, into banking. He doesn't stir the pot like I do."

"Is that what you feel like you're doing—stirring the pot?"

"With my career choice especially. If I could only make him understand."

"Some parents never understand, Hank."

My anxiety rose. *Will I ever gain my father's acceptance?*

My therapist continued. "But your sister chose medicine. What does your father think of that choice, since it's not banking?"

"He's more of the breadwinner personality, so he's more concerned with what Zach and I do for a living. He expects that Chrissy will marry one day, so he's not worried about her."

"Does he think engineering doesn't garner a big enough salary?"

"Maybe…I've never asked him directly."

"Communication is lacking in your family. You aren't sure why your father is against your career change; no one talks about your hospitalizations. That's something that needs attention."

Another pause. I burned with curiosity and, sensing an opportunity, asked my own question. "Did my psychiatrist in Atlanta give a diagnosis?" I asked.

Paula searched her papers for a moment. "I don't see one here."

"Is that normal? Not to have a diagnosis after being in the hospital two times?"

"In psychiatry the diagnosis can take a long time."

"I read a couple of possibilities in my discharge papers from Holy Redeemer—psychotic depression and schizoaffective disorder."

"Well, Hank. After working together for a while, hopefully we'll have one for you." She met my eyes. "Tell me what *you* think has caused you to go to the hospital those two times."

I leaned forward slightly. "Both times I had lost a lot of sleep. And I think that growing up I developed some sort of depression or something. So with the lost sleep and depression, I suffered some sort of nervous breakdown. Episode. Whatever. I'm doing a lot better than I was six months ago, though."

"So you're leaning toward some sort of depression?"

"Right."

"It's quite possible. I think with time we'll figure it out."

The appointment continued. Paula mixed in some small talk with more questions about my family and my interest in working for NASA. Before long, the time was up, and we made plans to meet the following week.

I walked out of Paula's office building with a feeling of having taken an exam. My brain was on overload after so much talk about my family, something I hadn't done with my previous psychiatrists. I had to concentrate to unlock my car door, open it, and slide into the driver's seat. Slowly I pulled out of my parking spot and away from Paula's building in Santa Rosa, headed for the main road, and tried to regain my senses.

. . . . .

I studied the financial aid form for Dewey State at my desk in my new, smaller apartment on the outskirts of town. For the first time in my life, I needed help, via loans, to get through my last semester. My bank account was quickly depleting, despite my working at the deli for the past few months, and I couldn't afford tuition on my own anymore.

My private health insurance that I'd taken out during my absence from school cost a bundle. I cut down on my surfing trips to save on gas. I didn't eat at restaurants so often and shopped for clothing at less expensive stores.

With some resignation, I signed the form and stuffed it in an envelope.

. . . . .

"Hank, where are we going from here?" Tracy asked while she sipped her beverage at a sandwich shop in the middle of wine country. We both sat on a wooden bench outside on the front porch of the shop and finished our sandwiches. It was the last day of vacation before we both started our last semester.

"I thought we'd go back to my place and watch a movie. I know it's cozy, but—"

"No. I mean our relationship. This is our last semester at Dewey. Are we staying together or not?"

I met her worried eyes. "Of course we're staying together! You know I love you." I put my arm around her and drew her close. "Don't you want to be with me?"

"Yeah. It's just that, even if you get accepted to Stanford, we'll both have to move away from Sonoma County. I've never lived out of the same county as my parents. And MIT, Georgia Tech, Premier University…well…those are all the way on the East Coast."

"And I know you don't like snow."

"I hate it."

"But half the programs I'm applying to are in snowy climates. Are you sure you can't tolerate it? It's just until I finish the program, and then we move back to California for good."

"I'll think about it." She looked away and surveyed the vineyards across the street.

We finished our meal and headed back to my place in my used Subaru, which I'd bought after my accident with the Audi. Despite it being the middle of January, the sun was out and the temperature mild.

"How are things going with your therapist?" asked Tracy, breaking the silence once again.

We didn't talk a lot about my therapy. Just like my family didn't. The question caught me off guard. "Good. We're working on some things."

"Anything you can tell me about?"

"You know, family stuff."

"Like what, your father?"

All the joy of the date disappeared. My father was still a sore subject.

"Yeah...look can we talk about something else besides my therapy?"

"I was just curious, that's all. We don't have to talk about it anymore. If you want to shut down on me, that's fine."

"I'm not shutting down. It's just that my father's my least favorite subject."

"Why do you have such ill-will toward him? He did get a lawyer for you and send Chrissy to get you from the hospital. Not to mention house you for six months after the hospital."

I exhaled a deep breath.

Tracy continued. "He is harsh, I'll give you that. But he loves you."

"I'm not so sure."

"He wants you to have a good life. Maybe he thinks you're taking a big risk shooting for NASA."

"That's my dream, though! If he can't handle that, then we're gonna continue to have friction."

"I'm just telling you what I see. You don't have to get upset."

"I'm not upset." But I was. My breaths were deep and quick, my voice loud. *Why does the mention of my father always ruin things?*

Silence ensued. I realized I had soured the afternoon. "I'm sorry."

"You don't have to apologize."

"Yes, I do. I got upset." I felt guilty now.

"I just thought you'd want to talk about your illness, since your family is so hush-hush about it."

There was that word again. *Illness!* How I hated it! It was up there with "disease" and "condition," two other words I'd heard that described mental disorders. I let it go, though, because I didn't want to get into an argument with Tracy. Enough damage had been done for one day.

"There's nothing to talk about. We work on my issues so I don't have to go to the hospital again. That's it."

"Did you get a diagnosis yet?"

Yet another sore subject! "No."

"That's bullshit. You should have one by now. All these doctors that you've had are giving you the run around. That's what I think."

In the back of my mind, I knew Tracy was right, but I still didn't admit it. I said nothing.

"You've been to the hospital twice, seen three psychiatrists and a therapist.

They should have it figured out by now," she continued. "I'd be pissed if I were you. Demand some straight answers for once!"

I sensed Tracy's frustration. My nervous breakdowns had already caused enough problems, along with my six-month absence from California. Tracy had had to fabricate a story about my father having heart surgery to explain my absence to her conservative family and her friends at the university. All had gone well with the alternate explanation, though, as far as I knew.

Does her family question her about me when I'm not around? How about her friends? These thoughts bothered me but I didn't pursue them with Tracy. I considered them minor problems that would work themselves out eventually.

21.

I sat in Paula's office for my weekly session in February. I'd been seeing her for six months now. We discussed a recent phone call with my parents.

"My father keeps hounding me to move back to Atlanta," I said.

"Haven't you told him that you're doing well in your classes and that you're waiting for interviews for the programs you applied to?"

"He won't listen to any of it. He says it'll be a miracle if I get into one."

"Just don't let your thought process be destructive. I know you're frustrated and angry with your father, but don't let these emotions get the best of you like they have in the past. You don't want to end up in the hospital again," she said.

"You think my hospitalizations have to do with my relationship with my father?"

"I do. You harbor strong emotions toward him. The dysfunctional father-son relationship is a common problem. If you can learn to recognize and deal with these emotions when they arise, you'd be in a much better spot in life. What about the rest of your family? Are they supportive?"

"Zach and Chrissy are enthusiastic about interviews. They want me to call as soon as I get one. My mom wants me to attend Georgia Tech's program and live at home. I really do hope I get into one outside Atlanta. Ideally, I want to attend Stanford's so Tracy and I can stay in California."

"I agree that it wouldn't be healthy for you to live with your parents if you decide to attend Georgia Tech. It may make them happy, but in the long run, it isn't healthy for you."

I let out a deep breath.

My therapist, in her usual slacks and a blouse, crossed her legs. "Your father's harsh ways don't translate into a healthy relationship with your mother or you, for that matter. I think you respond better to encouragement and nurturing rather than threats and belittling."

"I agree." I met her eyes.

"Growing up you had very little nurturing. You, Zach, and Chrissy listened to arguments and criticism instead. In some respects, you were traumatized."

"Not Chrissy! I protected her from my father. She came to my room when my parents fought, and I put her back to bed and stayed with her until she fell asleep."

"You were a surrogate parent to her," answered my therapist.

I cocked my head to one side. "No one ever put it that way."

"None of you ever dared to speak about it outside the family. Perhaps the only one outside the family who understood what you went through was your maid, Jocelyn."

"Jocelyn was nice to us. I distinctly remember that. She took care of us while my parents were on vacation."

"She might've been the only strong parent figure in your life. Your father busied himself with making money, and your mother was the victim when your father got home from work. Neither of them acted as a strong parent figure." My therapist paused. "Do you understand?"

I nodded. "Yes, I do."

A silence followed, while I digested her analysis. Then a question came to me, born from this talk about my family. I hesitated at first. Then I asked, "So do I have some sort of mental illness, or am I messed up from my family?" I waited for a response, holding my breath.

She uncrossed her legs and looked at her lap, then back at me, something I'd never seen her do. "I don't know exactly, Hank. It could be like you said during our first appointment—that you suffer from some sort of depression because of your childhood. The medicine you take is used off-label for that. Your doctor hasn't given me a definite diagnosis otherwise."

"What about schizoaffective disorder?" I had read up on this diagnosis. It was in the family of schizophrenia but milder.

"I haven't seen any symptoms of that. Holy Redeemer gave that possibility based on your admission data, but based on our work, I don't think you're schizoaffective."

My eyes widened. "Really? You really think so?"

She smiled. "I do."

I rested both arms on the sofa, completely relaxed now. The prospect of having a serious mental illness had grown in my mind ever since my last hospitalization. Now those fears disappeared. Almost everyone suffered from depression. I'd let it get the best of me two times, but now I was working on my issues and taking a different medicine. I was taking good care of myself.

A long pause ensued. Paula switched the subject. "How's it going with Tracy?"

My smile faded. "She's still deciding whether to stay with me when I get into a program."

"It's a big commitment for her. Following her boyfriend away from her family."

"Yeah. I know. She's torn. I'm staying positive, though. It'll work out." I forced a smile.

"That's all you can do. It seems she understands your condition—the medicine and your visits to me. That's good."

"Yeah. She's not freaked out about it. That gives me some relief."

"Have you received any invitations to interview yet?"

"No. I'm still waiting for my first one."

"Stay positive. You'll get one."

. . . . .

On a crisp, sunny late February morning, I arrived at the lobby of Lightning Incorporated in downtown San Francisco for my interview with Premier University. My interview with Stanford in Menlo Park, south of San Francisco, had taken place a week prior, and I hadn't heard anything from them since.

I gathered myself together mentally for Premier's interview. The university was in Philadelphia, which I knew hardly anything about. Even so, it wasn't in Atlanta. MIT hadn't offered me an interview yet, and Georgia Tech's came the following week.

A mechanical engineer who worked for the company appeared from a hallway to greet me. My throat was dry from nerves as I extended my hand. He showed me into his spacious office, where his diploma from Premier hung on the wall behind his desk.

"So, Hank," he began after we'd settled in our seats. "Your grades are quite impressive for the most part. I see you had some trouble with your calculus class but managed to do well in multivariable calculus the following semester. Any reason for the slip up?"

"I was sick the week before an exam. That caused a poor performance and a drop in my grade." I wanted to tell as much of the truth as possible without revealing that I'd been in a mental hospital. That revelation would doom me for sure!

He gave a quick smile, seemingly satisfied with my answer, and turned his eyes to my curriculum vitae again. "You have a degree in finance and worked in a bank for several years. Why the switch to mechanical engineering?"

"Engineering is my true passion. I didn't know this at the time of my undergraduate studies, but three years ago, I decided that a career change was in order."

"I see. Career changes are common these days." He studied me. "Any awards or promotions while you worked in banking?"

"I worked my way to assistant manager before resigning."

"Tell me about that position. I'm unfamiliar with the industry."

"An assistant manager opens accounts, approves loans, grants mortgages—pretty much does all the services that a bank provides. I worked closely with the branch manager and other assistant managers, so a lot of teamwork was involved."

"You'll be working in conjunction with other engineers both in engineering school and beyond. That's a good skill to have," he continued. "Why Premier? You used to live in the South. Now, you're out here in California. Nice weather, friendly people. Philadelphia would be quite a culture shock for you."

From the little I'd heard about Philadelphia, it was a small New York City—lots of rudeness and impatience, not to mention cold, blustery winters, which I'd never experienced. "I'm ready for the change. I moved from North Carolina to California when I decided to pursue engineering. I believe I can make another transition. As far as Premier's program, its reputation is solid. It would prepare me well for a career in NASA."

"Ah, yes. The Ames Center in San Jose. They're always in need of a good mechanical engineer. Any program that interests you?"

"I'm interested in rockets."

"You're ambitious. I'll give that to you. As you can see, I've done quite well with my degree." He gestured with his hands to take in his office. "Here at

Lightning, we design aircraft, mostly military. You may have even seen one of our products. The Speed Demon, for example."

I shook my head to indicate that I hadn't seen that one.

My interviewer smiled. "It's only a few years into production. For use in the navy on aircraft carriers." He changed the subject back to Premier University. "As far as the winters in Philadelphia, they can be severe. I would invest in a heavy coat."

My thoughts turned to Tracy for an instant, but I smiled. "I'll keep that in mind."

He turned more serious again and continued, resting his hands on his desk all the while. "Any family in the Mid-Atlantic area?"

"No."

"Your closest relatives are in Georgia?"

"Yes. My parents live there, my brother lives in Los Angeles, and my sister lives in Georgia as well."

"Hmm. It would be nice to have some family close by, but students in the program come from all over the country—even internationally. You'll be in the same boat as many others."

"I understand."

"You took a year off at Dewey State for personal reasons."

My heart rate doubled. "Yes."

He waited for more.

"My father was sick for a while, so I went back to Georgia to be with him."

"Oh…How is he now?"

"Much better, thanks."

"Certainly a break from your studies would be in order in a situation such as that."

"Right." I didn't break eye contact and kept calm.

I relaxed. I told him of my hobbies and how much I enjoyed Northern California. In typical California style, he was easy going and friendly enough. Explaining my year off was over now, which put me at ease.

"Any questions for me?" he asked.

"What advice do you have for doing well at Premier?"

"Keep up with your reading and assignments. Don't let much time go by without getting something done. You can't afford to take much time off to party or whatever, even when you're getting excellent grades.

"The curriculum is quite challenging. If you graduate, you'll be a top candidate for an organization like NASA. I recommend you opt for something related to NASA for your internship."

He paused, rubbing his goatee.

Stay strong! The interview is going well!

"Any other questions for me?" he continued.

"Not at the moment."

"Any reason for concern about your capabilities, Hank?"

For a split second, I pictured my skeptical father, and then my last hospitalization came to mind. "Absolutely not," I replied.

22.

Two months later, I pulled out the letter from Premier from my mailbox. From past experience with colleges, I knew the fat, eight-by-eleven-inch envelope was probably an acceptance package. Rejection letters were short and came in smaller, standard envelopes. I raced inside to my apartment to open and read the contents.

Sure enough, the letter stated that I was invited to start with the freshman engineering class in September provided I finished my present semester at Dewey State with a good performance, especially in my prerequisite physics class.

It was April. Only a month of school remained; I had As and Bs in all of my classes. It would take a total collapse for me not to start at Premier in the fall. I yelped with joy in my kitchenette and called Tom.

"Just don't get complacent with your health," he said. "You don't want a relapse at this point."

"I know." I'd heard all this before—from my family, from my psychiatrist, from my therapist. The last person I thought would lecture me was Tom.

"Look. You don't have a diagnosis yet, but be careful, is all I'm saying. I have an uncle with bipolar, and he kept relapsing until he became faithful to taking his medicine and seeing his psychiatrist regularly. I'm not saying that you have that illness, but you've worked too hard and accomplished too much to throw it all away now."

He paused. "I'm not going to say anything more. Don't take what I said the wrong way. You're doing great now. You deserve to be in an engineering program. Remember, though, I'm not close by if you begin to have problems again. You'll have to manage things on your own."

I knew now why Tom had been miffed when I'd told him that I didn't yet have a diagnosis. He'd been comparing me to his uncle, which was a mistake. I wasn't *that* sick. Maybe some depression mixed in with a couple of nervous breakdowns, but nothing as serious as bipolar.

"Don't worry," I said. "I'll be fine."

I called my parents to tell them the news and spoke to my mother first. She responded by asking, "Does this mean you'll never come back to Atlanta?"

"I can't say for sure, Mom." I knew I wouldn't live in my hometown again.

"What about Georgia Tech's program, Hank?" she pursued. "Don't you want to study in Atlanta, even if you don't live with us?"

I had been accepted to that program as well, but I wasn't going there! "I've made my mind up. I'm going to Philadelphia."

"It's your choice. Hold on. I'll put your father on now."

There was a pause. "Hank? Are you there?" It was my father's booming voice.

"I'm here." My voice sounded flat despite the circumstances.

"Hank, I'm happy for you. I really am. Just remember what your mother just told you, all right? I know you and I disagree on whether you have an illness or not, but don't come to me if you end up in the hospital again. It's your responsibility to get through this program and take care of yourself. Do you have a doctor lined up in Philadelphia yet?"

"Not yet."

"You better get started. You can't let a lapse in your care happen. Are you taking your medicine?"

"Yes."

"Has your present psychiatrist given you a diagnosis, by any chance?"

"No."

There was a pause. "All right. Just because he doesn't have a diagnosis doesn't mean you can stop your medicine. Remember that."

After I hung up, I sat on my cot and read the acceptance letter once again. It ended saying, *Congratulations, Hank!* A smile crept back to my face.

I signed and dated in the appropriate spaces and put it in the return envelope, along with a deposit to secure my spot in the freshman class.

I texted Tracy to give her the news because I knew she was in class. The only response was "Congratulations!" Nothing about whether she was staying in California or going with me. My nerves grew, and I paced back and forth in my garage apartment before leaving for campus to meet her.

Will I move to the East Coast alone or with the love of my life?

My hands slickened the steering wheel of my Subaru with sweat. I tried to take deep breaths to relax. I thought of our differences, especially of how we viewed my father. I had been angry again the last time we talked about him. Did she think I was an ass for feeling this way? Would she stay in California based on this friction that now spilled into our relationship?

Tracy's parents were devout Catholics, so when she told them she was considering moving with me, they objected to our cohabitation. Tracy wouldn't have paid any mind except that she was broke and had loans to pay. If she moved with me, we'd have to at least set up separate apartments. Only then would Tracy's parents help her with expenses.

Then there was my so-called illness. I assured her it was under control. Some mild depression. Dysthymia was what my therapist called it. I was taking my medicine and had assured her I would tell her if things weren't right. No cause for concern, yet it entered my mind as I made the drive to campus.

I made it to the main quad after speed walking from the parking lot. A bright spring sun bathed the students sitting on the stone steps from the adjacent classroom buildings. I didn't see Tracy at first. Then she appeared from the exit of a building with a huge smile, something I hadn't seen on her face for months, it seemed.

"We're Philly bound!" She ran to me and hugged and kissed me.

My relief was instant. I held her tight, not wanting to let go. A tear rolled down my cheek. I almost choked on my breath, which came in little gasps.

Tracy pulled back with a look of surprise. "Are you OK?"

All I could do was smile. There weren't any words to describe my feelings.

She took my hand, and we walked to her dorm. She sat me down on her bed and closed her bedroom door. She took off her clothes and helped me off with mine. I still didn't know what to say, but words weren't necessary as we lay down on the bed and made love. We hadn't had such passion in months.

23.

Five months later, I was alone in the waiting room of my fourth psychiatrist's high-rise office in Philadelphia. I fidgeted in my seat and looked out of the window, not reading any magazines that lay on the small square table next to me. The doctor appeared.

"Hank?"

I nodded.

"I'm Dr. Sloane." He smiled. Short and stout, he wore a suit and tie. His nose was pudgy, and his black hair thick and wavy, neatly combed.

"Hi." I managed a smile and shook his hand after rising from my chair.

"Let's go back to the office." He led the way and motioned toward a long leather sofa as we entered. "Would you prefer to lie on the couch?"

"No, thanks." I sat in a brown lounge chair opposite the psychiatrist, who sat in a green leather one. The smell of leather pervaded the office, which provided the atmosphere of one wanting to have a cigar. Plush wall-to-wall carpeting, a full bookcase stretching almost to the ceiling, and partially drawn blinds all contributed to this thought.

"What part of town do you live in?" asked the doctor.

"University City. I live near Premier."

"That's close. Did you walk here?"

"Yes."

He got out a pad of standard-size paper and clicked a pen into writing position. "Well, let's get started. As an initial evaluation, I'm going to ask you some questions about you and your family. All right?"

"OK."

"Any mental illness in your family?"

I told him with some reluctance. Dr. Sloane began writing down my responses.

"Any suicides?"

"Not that I know of," I answered, taken aback.

"Any complications while your mother carried you or at birth?"

"No." Already, I had a difficult time following his line of questions.

"How did you do in school as a child?"

"I got all As and Bs."

"Friends?"

"I had friends."

"Any suspensions or chronic problems with teachers or classmates?"

"No."

"Did you experience any abuse?"

"No." I lied, not wanting to send my father to jail.

"Any history of drug abuse?"

"I tried marijuana a few times, but that's it."

"When's the last time you used it?"

"Ten years ago."

"Are you or have you ever been a smoker?"

"No."

"Any legal history?"

"No."

"How are your finances?"

"I get student loans."

"And you're at Premier, right? That's what I read from the report that your psychiatrist in California gave me," he said.

"Yes. I'm studying mechanical engineering."

"Great." I couldn't tell whether he was sincere with this answer. He kept on writing with hardly any eye contact.

He continued. "Are you single, married, or divorced?"

"Single."

"Heterosexual or homosexual?"

"Heterosexual." *This is exasperating!*

More writing. "What are your hobbies?"

"I like to surf."

The doctor looked up. "On the Internet?"

"No. Surf real waves with a board."

"Interesting."

"Yeah, thanks."

"Can you interpret the saying one shouldn't throw stones at glass walls?" He returned his focus to his notepad.

"It means you shouldn't do things that you know will turn out badly."

Dr. Sloane changed gears. "Let's talk about symptoms, if you don't mind. Do you ever hear voices or see things that aren't there?"

"No," I said, annoyed.

"Do you have periods of time with high energy when you feel energetic enough to go without sleep and then periods of time with low energy when you can barely get out of bed?"

"No." I gave a questioning look, but Dr. Sloane ignored it and continued.

"Any loss of interest in activities or isolation from friends and family?"

"No."

"Any instances when you go on spending sprees with money?"

"No."

"How much sleep do you get daily?"

"Eight hours."

"How is your appetite?"

"Good."

"Eating three meals a day?"

"Yes."

"Are you making friends at Premier?"

"We've had only an orientation so far. Classes start next week."

"Any significant other in your life?"

"My girlfriend, Tracy, moved here with me from California."

"Excellent. Are you living together?"

"No. We have separate apartments. Her parents insisted she get her own place."

He stopped writing, smiled, and looked up at me. "How do you like Philadelphia?"

"It's different. Busy and dirty."

"I imagine it's quite a change coming from wine country in California. Are you ready for the biting temperatures?"

"I don't know." Dr. Sloane's direct manner put me on the defensive. I made my answers to his questions as short as possible, not wanting to give away any information that he might use against me, if he decided I needed to go to a psych ward.

"What medicines have you taken in the past?" he asked, looking back down at his pad of paper.

I told him.

"And right now you're taking ten milligrams of Elixir, right?"

"Right."

"How many hospitalizations?"

"Two."

He paused after each answer to write my response. I looked at his pen working away, which made me nervous. None of my other psychiatrists had bothered to write my responses word for word. They only jotted down some notes from time to time. My psychiatrist in Atlanta hadn't even bothered with any notes. I could predict with certainty his next question, but with Dr. Sloane, so far, I didn't know what to make of the information he was gathering.

"So you saw a therapist and a psychiatrist in California, right?"

"Yes."

"With me, you'll see me weekly. I do the psychoanalysis and psychotherapy myself. I don't work with any therapists—just so you get the best care possible."

"So how much will the weekly appointments cost?"

"Two hundred."

"Two hundred? That's not in my budget. I mean—you don't take any insurance."

"Let's see how much reimbursement you get after you make the claims. We can work something out to fit your budget."

I frowned.

"Have you been taking your medicine as prescribed?"

"Yes. Do I really need it?"

"You've been in the hospital twice."

"My therapist said I had only a mild depression."

"Working with me, that could change. In fact, one of our goals is to get you a proper diagnosis. Going to the hospital multiple times usually indicates something more serious."

"Do you have any thoughts right now as to what it is?"

"No, not yet."

I frowned again. *Same old shit.*

When the appointment was over and I was on my way back to my one-bedroom apartment, some of Dr. Sloane's probing still ran in my mind and made me uneasy. None of my other psychiatrists thus far had been so direct and thorough.

24.

My first day of school I rode an old twelve-speed bike I'd had for years along Market Street to Premier's campus, about a mile away. The street teemed with activity. Cars filled the lanes in both directions, street vendors sold food on the sidewalks inside their portable metal kitchens, and delivery trucks double-parked momentarily along my path. The morning was bright, and the humid September air stuck to my skin as I dodged vehicles and pedestrians. I made it to the bike rack near the vast engineering building and entered.

The chatter of my classmates filled the air as I settled into my seat for our first lecture. I gulped at being in the presence of them again, slid out my laptop, and tapped my fingers on the slide out writing surface in anticipation of the arrival of our professor.

"Hey," said a student who had curly red hair and sat a couple of seats to my left. "Are you ready for this?"

"I hope so," I replied. "I busted my ass to get in."

"Yeah, me too," he said. "Some others are bragging about their future As, but I'm with you. Getting through and graduating is my priority." He surveyed the rest of the mostly male students, who were joking and carrying on lightheartedly. I wondered if he was in awe as well. "We're in a hard program," he continued. "I heard that last year six people either dropped out or switched majors. That's a lot."

"Sounds like we have to be dedicated."

"Once we're through and have that degree, though, we're set. An engineering degree from Premier is like gold in the working world. As long as I pass, I'll be satisfied. The others can have their straight As."

"I'm with you," I said.

"You sound like you're from the South."

"From Atlanta. What about you?"

"Phoenix."

There was a pause in the conversation as we watched the professor enter the lecture hall. He approached the podium, asked for quiet, and began a speech about the importance of chemistry in engineering. He showed his first slide, which gave an overview of the course, and then began his lecture on the atom. Classes such as these—chemistry, calculus, and physics—would be repeats from the courses required to enter into the program, but the material was more in-depth and the exams more difficult, from what I'd heard. I paid close attention and typed notes on my laptop.

After the lecture was over, we took a break.

The student sitting next to me joined me in the lobby adjacent to the lecture hall. "What did you think?"

"The pace is definitely quicker than my prerequisite chemistry," I said. "We covered a week's worth of material in just one hour!"

"Imagine. That's what it'll be like for us the next four years. Better get used to it. Those fluff courses we took before we started here are over." He had a look of resignation on his face, as if he realized the good times were over and it was time to get to work. "Well, at least we're in the program. That says a lot already."

"I just hope I can keep up."

"You and me both."

. . . . .

Two weeks later, in October, I picked up Tracy outside her apartment. She wore a short denim skirt and a pink sweater that showed her curves once again. Her hair flowed, and I heard the click of her heels as she walked to the Subaru and climbed in. She was gorgeous in the fading autumn evening light.

Luckily, I got a parking spot near Pat's, the famous cheesesteak venue in South Philly. That was the plan for the date—go to Pat's for my first submarine cheesesteak sandwich and go for an ice cream afterward.

Litter lined the streets and sidewalks in this part of the city, which put me off. Sonoma County was so pristine comparatively. Tracy didn't seem to mind, though. She liked the famous Philadelphia cheesesteaks, so when I told her that I'd never had one, she suggested Pat's.

As we walked to get in line to order our sandwiches, other men noticed Tracy in obvious ways. Some even whistled as we walked past them, which made me uncomfortable. I didn't say anything to them, though. My southern gentleman roots kept my jealousy in check.

But I already surmised the different environment that we'd been thrust into after our first six weeks in our new city. Downtown was east of Premier, just a couple of miles away, and West Philadelphia, an area of generally lower income, lay even closer. Fortunately Tracy had brought a car from California, so she could avoid the aged and crowded public transit system. Dr. Sloane was right. Wine country differed a lot from Philadelphia.

We stood in an endless line, which wrapped around the side of the restaurant on the sidewalk. The sound of metal spatulas chopping the beef on the giant metal stoves and the scent of the beef, the main ingredient, filled the air. A touch of autumn chill came, as day turned to night.

"So when is your first exam?" asked Tracy. She seemed to ignore the glances of other men sizing her up.

It cooled my enthusiasm for the date to talk about school because I was still intimidated by all of the fast-talking, type-A students, but I answered. "Tuesday. In chemistry."

"Are you ready?"

"Almost."

"Chemistry, wow! That sounds hard."

"I'm nervous," I admitted.

"I'd be, too."

"What about you? Any job leads yet?"

Tracy's attempts to get a job at one of the many museums in Philadelphia weren't successful thus far. Her goal was to work at the Philadelphia Museum of Art on Benjamin Franklin Parkway, the one with the famous Rocky statue outside it. Fortunately her parents were helping her out financially until she got a job.

"It looks like I'll be doing temp work until something opens up at a museum. I applied at an agency. They're supposed to call next week with an assignment."

"Any idea of what type of work?"

"Probably data entry."

I felt sorry that Tracy was about to do such mindless work just to be with me. And the cooler weather was moving in. Snow wasn't far off. I prayed the winter wouldn't be awful in that regard, since Tracy hated the snow. She even abstained from vacationing with her parents at Lake Tahoe in the winter in California because she disliked it so much.

We stood close to each other. Tracy's eyes were dreamy and attentive. I smiled.

After we finished our hefty sandwiches, we walked slowly along a busy one-way street looking for an ice cream shop.

"How is it going with your new doctor?" asked Tracy.

My joyful mood turned uneasy. Just the mention of Dr. Sloane made my stomach churn. His random questions went through my mind over and over, though I wished they would stop. I had managed to put them in the back of my mind until now.

"All right, I guess. He seems competent, unlike some of my other doctors in the past." I couldn't tell Tracy about my uneasiness! She'd probably question whether Dr. Sloane was a good fit for me. And I didn't want my mental health causing even more friction between us. Tracy had been asking regularly if I'd been taking my medicine. I'd even yelled at her once, saying she had become like my parents. She'd cried when I said that, and I'd apologized right away.

"How did you find him anyway?"

"My last doctor referred me to him, which was lucky. Otherwise, I would have had to start from scratch looking for one here."

When we found an ice cream stand, we ordered and sat on a bench. We watched passers by and vendors of nearby small shops go about their evenings and took in the scene while gobbling down our cones. A breeze rustled trash in the gutter of the street, and cars passed slowly, occasionally honking at one another. Tracy's sweet-smelling perfume was evident. After we finished gathering in the scene, we rose and strolled back to the Subaru.

As we rode back to University City, I asked Tracy, "Do you want to come over to my place for a little bit?" She'd been spending time at her apartment a lot so far, setting it up and looking for work, and I'd been busy with school. Although we saw each other often, this was our first official date out of

University City. Time had flown by. Again, I wondered if the magic between us had waned.

"Of course! Don't think that I haven't missed spending the night with you." She covered my hand with hers.

Relief! She still loved me. And I loved her. "I hope it'll happen more often."

25.

I was in Dr. Sloane's office yet again. Five months had passed since our first appointment, and Philadelphia was in the dead of winter. The top layer of the Schuylkill River, which separated University City from downtown, called Center City, had frozen over, leaving a white surface from freshly fallen snow. The cold wind had whipped through my coat and frozen my face as I walked toward the office, and now I sat in the brown lounge chair and rubbed my hands, trying to warm them.

Though at first I had met weekly with the doctor, the past few months I'd visited him every other week. It was too much, with my studies and seeing Tracy, to visit him weekly. Even though he gave me a break with his fee because the reimbursement I received from my insurance company was low, my appointments every other week fell more within my budget, too.

I plugged my nose, which had started to run, with Kleenex. "So have you thought about lowering my dose like I suggested?"

"Not right now. I don't think it would be wise in your case."

"I don't understand."

"If you were to relapse, you run the risk of hurting yourself and others."

I furrowed my forehead and squinted, not fully comprehending.

"You get combative when you're having an episode, Hank," he said, with his stomach protruding from underneath his suit jacket.

I had a feeling about where this line of questioning was going but played it cool. "What do you mean?"

"I read the report from your last psychiatrist about your last hospitalization. You got into an altercation while you were in jail, and once you were in the hospital, you brought another staff member into the glass door that you rammed."

"That's not true."

"You also endangered yourself by sitting in the middle of the highway after your car accident, which led to your arrest in the first place."

"All of that is lies." My blood boiled. "I read the report from Holy Redeemer. It's full of them."

"Why would the report be wrong?"

"I don't know, but I remember what happened. I was standing on the shoulder of the highway when the officer arrested me, not sitting *in* the highway. In jail, the guards pepper sprayed and used a Taser on me. I didn't get into a fight with an inmate. And at the hospital, I tried to escape, but I hit the door by myself. No other staff was around me."

The doctor nodded.

Despite this indication that he understood, I sensed the doctor's doubt by his frown. "You don't believe me, do you?"

Dr. Sloane sighed. "Hank, you were psychotic during all of this. It's highly unlikely that you remember anything that really happened. You may think you remember, but your version of the events differs from what is in the report. Why would a professional, such as a police officer, guard, or even a health-care worker, fabricate such events?"

"To justify his own actions, even though he was wrong."

"I still don't follow you."

"The guards who used excessive force with the pepper spray and Taser. All I was doing was banging on my cell door and yelling to be let out. And then the razor blade they placed in my cell—"

Dr. Sloane glanced up from his writing. "A razor blade in your cell?"

"I saw it. Even when I pushed it out underneath the door, someone put it back."

"Hank, your imagination was running wild at the time. Why on Earth would a guard put a razor blade in your jail cell?"

"To see if I'd hurt myself."

"To see if you'd hurt yourself. Right."

I knew from the months I had worked with him already that Dr. Sloane still doubted me. "Look. I know what happened. Obviously, you don't believe me. Let's just talk about something else."

There was a long pause. I took deep, audible breaths to relieve my anger and focused on the plush carpet.

"I understand that you're frustrated with the report. Not everyone is skilled enough to deal with cases such as yours. Mistakes do happen."

"But placing a razor blade in my cell?"

Dr. Sloane's expression remained unchanged. Stoic as usual. Now he did change the subject. "Can we talk about your childhood some more?"

I continued to study the carpet. "That's a sore subject, too."

"I know it is. But if we're to make any headway in here, we have to tackle some sensitive issues. The way you survived your childhood, by clamming up your feelings while your father went on his tirades, doesn't translate into how to survive adulthood. Recognizing your emotions and taking appropriate measures to express them, rather than bottling them up, will help you cope better with life."

I leaned my head on my fist. "My childhood was shitty. I'd give my right arm to have had a decent father. When I spent time at other friends' houses, their fathers weren't as cold and explosive. That's when I knew my family was messed up."

"You're twenty-nine. Don't you think it's time to put the past behind you?"

I remained silent.

"Dealing with your family issues would help you to live a much healthier life. I can't force you to work with me, though. You have to choose to do that. As for the medicine. We discussed it last month—you can't go off it entirely. You need it to manage your illness."

"No one's sure of the long-term side effects. Besides, you haven't given me a diagnosis. I don't even know why I'm taking it."

"You've had two psychotic episodes. Something is amiss, I assure you. As far as the medicine goes, it's a very safe one."

Again, I stayed silent. My frustration rose.

"Besides, I wouldn't want to see you go to the hospital again and risk everything you've worked for in school. Not to mention throwing away what we've worked on to keep you healthy in here. It's not worth it," continued the doctor.

"I'm doing great. I got a good grade point average my first quarter. Things are fine with Tracy…"

"Things could change quickly. I'm not trying to scare you, but that's the nature of mental illness. I hope you understand that."

"Nothing will happen, Dr. Sloane. I promise."

"You promise to call me if you begin to have strange thoughts like in the past?"

"Of course."

"No matter what time of day."

"*Yes.*"

"All right," said Dr. Sloane. "When can you come in again?"

"In two weeks," I said.

"You know you really should be seeing me every week. We should be meeting twice a week, but you've been reluctant to come in even once a week."

"Why twice a week? I thought a weekly appointment was enough."

"We have a lot to work on."

"Like?"

"For instance. Your relationship with your father. It's not a healthy one. It affects your day-to-day life adversely. Meeting me every other week doesn't give enough time for us to explore what needs fixing. Right now, with our meetings every other week, we're barely maintaining your mental well-being."

"I just can't meet more often right now. I have too much schoolwork."

Dr. Sloane sat back in his chair, flipped through his appointment book, and wrote down something. "I'll see you in two weeks." He sounded deflated.

I walked back to my apartment through the frigid cold, annoyed. It was obvious that Dr. Sloane didn't trust my ability to stay healthy. I was determined to prove him wrong.

26.

I ran. No, not a jog. But an all out sprint across the open lawn in front of the mansion. My feet were shoeless, bare. The Bermuda grass tickled their soles and wet them. A thought crossed my mind—it must have just showered, maybe a thunderstorm. Or had the sprinklers just been used? I couldn't figure it out. I continued to sprint, so fast that my heels didn't touch the grass.

Where am I going?

And the darkness! No light from the sky. No stars, no moon. Only the gas light, set on a lamppost and encased in glass along the walkway to the front door, showed the way. The mansion was dark, save for a light upstairs, Chrissy's room. *That's where I'm going!*

From outside I heard the shouting from my father. For a second, I wondered if the neighbors could hear. The thought flashed into and out of my mind.

"Damn it, Evelyn! You're no good, just like your father! And I have to support you, along with the kids!"

Slowly I clicked the front door open and shut it quietly behind me. I had to go undetected. My parents were in the kitchen. I could go through the spacious foyer and up the stairs without being seen, if I were silent enough.

Now that I was inside, I heard my mother weeping. *Oh, the pain I feel swelling in me!* I wanted to save her, but I couldn't. I was just a kid. Too young.

As I climbed the stairs, the tirade continued. "I pay for a maid to do the cooking and cleaning! Can't you even do the one errand I asked you to do?" my father screamed. Each word cut into me, stabbing me with grief and shock.

Ignore him! But it was impossible.

Concentrate, Hank! Get to Chrissy! Then a squeak from the spiral staircase as I tread on a step. The yelling stopped. I heard a roar. "Hank! Hank, is that you?" But before he entered the foyer, I was gone! Up the stairs to the hallway.

Then I heard my father return to the kitchen.

On to Chrissy's room. From the hallway, I saw the light from behind the closed door. I waited for the shouting to continue before I turned the handle and opened it, so as not to be heard.

Chrissy sat up in bed. She was wide awake. "Hank, what's going on? Why is Daddy yelling?" She was five years younger than me. Too young to understand.

"Don't worry, Chrissy. It's OK." I tucked her in and sat on her bed. Then I read a Dr. Seuss story to her. Finally, she closed her eyes. I turned the light out and sat with her until she was asleep.

I woke. But I wasn't in my parents' house. I was in my apartment in Philadelphia, with Tracy at my side. It was morning. Tracy was awake, staring at me.

"You mumbled in your sleep. Something about green eggs and ham. Isn't that a Dr. Seuss story?"

"Yeah. I was dreaming."

"Do you want to talk about it?"

I brushed through her straight black hair with my hand and looked into her green eyes. "No."

. . . . .

Five months later, Tracy and I visited the Philadelphia Museum of Art. It was July, and I had completed my first year at Premier. This summer would be my only free one, as the following two summers I had to do my internship.

The winter had passed with plenty of wind, snow, and cold. It was nothing like Tracy and I had ever experienced. The ice and snow caked on sidewalks and on the outdoor stairs, making it difficult to walk without slipping. Tracy did slip on the sidewalk leading to her small parking lot one morning on the way to work, which caused a bruise on her buttocks. She was particularly cranky that night.

Then there was driving in the white stuff. I crashed my Subaru during a blizzard, when I slid into the car in front, and Tracy had two separate accidents in her Toyota due directly to poor road conditions. Luckily hers were fender benders, and she escaped without injury. I was unhurt as well.

But spring finally arrived and then summer. Tracy had been to the museum alone a few times, so this was our first time to it together. I wore khaki shorts and a red button-down short-sleeved dress shirt. Tracy wore a navy summer skirt and white blouse with sandals.

She had still yet to secure a job in a museum like she'd planned, and she tired of doing temp work in offices around the city. So since I had the summer off, it lifted her spirits that I could spend more time with her than when school was in session. We'd driven up to the Pocono Mountains one weekend and down to Washington, DC, another. This Saturday we stayed local.

An aura of magnificence filled the air as we entered the museum. Another grand stairway, apart from the one outside, led the way to the various galleries from the main entrance. Attendants roamed from room to room to keep an eye on patrons.

Tracy and I met with a group of patrons to take a tour with a guide. The guide was a clean-shaven young man of medium height with long black hair down the back of his neck. He touched on many of the famous paintings by Renoir, Van Gogh, and Monet, among others. He seemed gracious enough and knowledgeable. Tracy knew him by name from her previous visits.

After chatting with the tour guide when the tour was over, Tracy and I drifted with the other patrons from room to room on the first floor. Silence dominated as everybody took in the beauty of the paintings and of the museum.

We found ourselves in a small alcove studying Monet's "Marine View with a Sunset." It was Tracy's favorite painting. An attendant followed us into the small room and then left. We were alone.

This was the moment I'd been waiting for. I fumbled in my pocket to find the ring I'd bought, dropped to one knee, and took Tracy's hand in mine. Her face turned from a dreamy state to one of pure joy when I asked, "Will you marry me?"

"Oh, Hank. I can't believe it!"

"Will you?" I asked again.

"Yes!"

I rose to my feet, and Tracy kissed me and wrapped her arms around me. I was on cloud nine. Everything had worked out perfectly. Tracy had stuck it out in Philadelphia with me so far. Now she wanted to be my wife. What more could I have asked for?

The same attendant as before showed up again since Tracy had yelped for joy after hugging me. He asked for quiet. Tracy and I laughed and hand-in-hand, we headed for the exit.

After leaving the museum, we headed to her favorite restaurant in Center City to celebrate with champagne and Italian food.

Tracy chatted away like a bird in springtime. "We can invite our friends from Dewey to the wedding. Wouldn't that be great?"

"We can invite as many as you like."

"And then we'll settle down after you've finished your program and have babies."

"Sure."

"I can even work from home with my watercolors while you're at NASA during the day."

"That's what I was thinking!"

On and on we went about a wedding and starting a family. Both of us were overjoyed at the prospects the future held. All I had to do was get through my program, and then I'd be golden.

Tracy admired the ring on her finger and how it sparkled. She spread out her fingers so she saw its beauty. I'd chosen a small but elegant diamond and was relieved that she liked it so much.

I'm getting married! The thought itself gave me such happiness. The journey to proposing had been bumpy, but that was in the past. That and going to the hospital again. I trusted Dr. Sloane's care would help me achieve my goal of staying healthy mentally. I had even visited him weekly during the summer at his request, since I had no classes.

Tracy was the one I wanted to be with for the rest of my life. I had thought of my decision to propose very carefully and even brought it up to Dr. Sloane. She made me happy and understood me. We would make each other happy for the rest of our lives.

27.

My classmates and I were back in class for our sophomore year. Though the days were warm and the quarter was young, the professors, as I anticipated, had no mercy. Assignments and exams piled up, and I spent most of my time either in class or in the library, though I managed to see Tracy every few days and Dr. Sloane every other week.

Then, during the same quarter, in November, it happened.

I lay on my couch and watched ESPN on a cold Saturday night after going out to dinner with Tracy. She had complained of a headache and returned to her apartment to rest.

During a commercial break from the football highlights, I looked up at the vent right above me. For some reason, with its balls of dust behind the vent grates, it caught my eye. I moved a chair from the kitchen table into the living room and stood on top of it, trying to get a closer look.

Yes, there is definitely something curious there. Behind the grate was a dark ball of dust. I had never noticed it before.

I wondered what the ball could be and if someone had maybe put it there. *There could be a listening device of some sort in it!* I continued peering into the grate and tried to pry the ball out with my fingers, but it was too big to pass through. I imagined who could be listening to me, if there were a device in it—the apartment management, the local police, or even the federal government!

I tried to convince myself that the government would have no interest in what I did but found myself instead walking quickly to the kitchen. Its vent encased another ball of dust! I raced to my bedroom—same thing.

I began hyperventilating, and my adrenaline rushed. I searched through a kitchen drawer and found a screwdriver. Then, I stood on my kitchen chair in my living room and began unscrewing the screws holding the grate in place. With some difficulty at first, I pried the grate back from the vent and took a closer look. There was nothing much to it—just a ball of dust that had collected. I picked at it and carefully examined it for any electronic chips.

How small are listening devices used to spy these days? I didn't know.

Then I noticed something else. The sprinkler heads. They could house some minute camera. *Someone could be videotaping me as well as listening!* I examined the sprinkler head in my living room ceiling. There were some tiny nooks and crannies that could house a device with today's technology, I guessed.

I sat back down on my couch and ran my hand through my hair. I moved to dial 911 on my phone but stopped short. Instead, I took the screwdriver in my hands and climbed onto the chair once more to look at a sprinkler head in the living room, clinking it lightly.

Convinced that someone was monitoring me in some fashion, I gathered my coat and cell phone and slipped out of the apartment quietly. After lightly closing my apartment door, I barged out of the building lobby and marched on the sidewalk toward Tracy's apartment, a ten-minute walk away. I looked behind me—the coast was clear. Then I dialed Tracy.

"What's wrong?" she asked. "It's midnight."

"Yeah, I know. Look, is it all right if I stay at your place tonight?" I asked.

"What? Why do you want to stay here?"

"I think someone's spying on me in my apartment."

"Someone's spying on you? What are you talking about?" she asked, her voice concerned.

"I think that someone's monitoring me from the vents and sprinkler heads," I said, trying to sound casual, but even I noticed the tension of fear in my voice. "So I thought to stay with you."

There was a slight pause. "Hank, I don't think you're acting yourself."

I stopped walking and froze. "What?"

"You don't sound like yourself. Have you been taking your medicine?"

"Taking my medicine?"

"You're not making sense with this talk of being monitored inside your apartment," she said. "I've never heard you talk like this before. You're worrying me."

"But I—" I was shocked she didn't believe me.

"I'm sorry. If you want me to go to the hospital with you I can, but I can't have you spend the night if you're not acting your usual self."

I hung up the phone without saying goodbye and stood on the sidewalk leading to Tracy's apartment in utter disappointment. My predicament seemed so real. How could she question me when my life was in danger? I wondered briefly if she could be right, that I was imagining everything.

No, I'm certain my fears are justified. It's fortunate I escaped when I did— before the authorities came to get me!

I continued to her apartment. *Maybe there are cameras and microphones in her apartment, too! I have to see for myself. Warn her of any danger she's in. Save both of us from this mess.*

I broke into a jog and made it to the lobby of her building. Up the elevator and to her door. I was just about to rap on her door when I heard it. A moan coming from inside, then a yelp of ecstasy from Tracy.

Is that actually her? I paused and heard a man's voice, then laughter from Tracy. She was with another man!

Someone came down the hallway, and I casually slipped away from the door and headed back to the lobby. But not all the way to the exit. I needed confirmation of my suspicions first. I sat on a beat-up sofa in the lobby, waiting for the secret lover to emerge.

Then he did. At first I didn't recognize him. Then his long black hair and tall, wiry frame registered. The tour guide at the art museum! The guide Tracy had introduced me to right before I proposed. He didn't recognize me as he strolled out of the building and to the rear parking lot.

My jaw dropped in astonishment. All these years of building a relationship were lost. Oh, the heartache! The pain! Never had I thought Tracy would be unfaithful. I couldn't forgive her for this. It was over, just like that!

I had a mind to bang on her door and yell a few choice words, but I stopped short of going up the elevator. She'd call the cops on me. Maybe she already had! Her lover had seen me in the lobby. Had he recognized me after all and warned her? I had to get out of there fast!

The night chilled my core, and the wind blew both leaves and litter. Most hotels were in Center City across the Schuylkill River. *Maybe I can find a hotel for the night and plan my next move in the morning.* I began walking toward Market Street, which led downtown.

All of a sudden I heard some quick footsteps coming from behind, and I felt a blow to the back of my head and fell, groaning. A voice said, "Hurry, man!

Check his pockets!" Someone took my cell phone and wallet while I lay on the ground, trying to get my bearings. The footsteps hurried away, and I lay on the sidewalk in the fetal position with my hands holding the back of my throbbing head.

I lay there for a few minutes when a group of young men, talking to one another in loud voices as if they'd been drinking, came upon me. They quieted down. Then one said, "Look at that guy."

I heard approaching footsteps and a voice. "Call 911. He's bleeding. Are you OK?"

I moved to make eye contact with the one who'd just spoken and groaned again.

Another one said, "I think he's been jumped." Then to me, "Hang on, man. We called for help."

Moments later, the siren of an ambulance approached. Two EMTs hovered over me and loaded me up into the ambulance on a stretcher. The EMT in the back applied pressure to my head and asked questions on the way—my name, my medical history.

"What medicines do you take?"

"Elixir."

"What do you take that for?" asked the man, writing down my answers while he spoke.

"Depression."

We arrived in the frenetic emergency room of Philadelphia Hospital. I got into a gown and got another scan of my head. A nurse cleaned and sewed up the head wound. The bays were full of patients, and the staff scurried to and fro. The police came by and got an account of the mugging and then left. I waited alone in the bay, trying to stay calm.

Finally, an older man who looked like a doctor arrived. He wore a dress shirt with a stethoscope hanging around his neck and a long white lab coat. He was dark-skinned and heavy-set and moved and spoke at a slow pace.

"Can you tell me what happened, Hank?" he asked me.

"I was on the sidewalk, and these guys hit me on the back of the head with something and took my phone and wallet. Then they ran off," I said.

"I see," said the doctor. "And what were you doing out at such a late hour by yourself?" he asked.

I paused and let the reality of the situation sink in. Then it all came back to me. My apartment, the vents, the sprinkler heads, the phone call to Tracy.

The doctor asked me again, "Hank, do you remember why you were out on the street?"

I paused. "I was on my way back from my fiancée's place…"

"You do realize that your neighborhood isn't safe at such a late hour, right?"

"I had to leave my apartment. I…"

"You had to leave your apartment?" The doctor's eyebrows rose.

I hesitated answering, knowing full well what the truth would bring. *Can I trust this doctor, the emergency room staff, and the staff of the psychiatric unit? Will these strangers take care of me or do something awful?* I took my chances. "I thought there were listening devices and cameras in my apartment," I said.

"Listening devices and cameras? Can you tell me more?"

I looked away from the doctor's eyes, down at the shiny linoleum floor, and then at the curtains of the adjacent bays and said softly, almost mumbling, "I thought they were monitoring me."

A short silence. Then the doctor said, "You thought you were being monitored inside of your apartment, so you left?"

"Yes," I said.

The doctor examined me, looking at my head wound again, listening to my lungs, checking my heart, and moving his finger in front of my eyes. He asked me, "Have you ever been admitted to a psychiatry unit before?"

"Yes."

"Would you be opposed to being admitted into one tonight?" His face was set, his eyes fixed on me.

I looked away and paused for a few seconds. "No."

That was it. I would be stuck in a psych ward again. I waited for some time until an orderly wheeled me back to the psychiatry unit in a wheelchair with my head wrapped a large bandage.

28.

This psychiatry ward had a similar setup to the previous ones. The nurses' station stood adjacent to the common area. A long hallway jutted from the nurses' station to the exit with patient rooms along both sides. Lighting was minimal, as it was late at night.

My arrival disturbed some of the other sleeping patients, who began to emerge from their rooms and carry on.

"Man, I can't sleep with all the noise!"

"Who's the new guy?"

A staff member greeted me and began her questions, but soon the disturbance was too great for her to continue. She stopped the interview. "Please return to your rooms! Please!"

Another female staff member, who had been sitting idly by, stirred to action. She corralled patients that had strayed and lightly directed them back to their rooms. Some patients returned faster than others. Order was ultimately restored, and the staff member resumed her questions. I remained uneasy about the disruption.

"What brings you to the hospital?" she asked.

I hesitated at first. "The doctor in the emergency room sent me here because I thought there were cameras and listening devices in my apartment."

She interviewed me for about ten minutes, asking all sorts of questions. My head still throbbed even though the emergency room staff had given me a painkiller. My adrenaline rush from the night faded and fatigue set in. I longed to go to bed.

My small, empty room had two neatly made beds. I laid my head on my pillow and tried once again to get accustomed to my surroundings. Within minutes I was up again, looking for signs of trouble outside. I put on my glasses, studied the ceiling, and searched for places where a camera or sound recording device might be. The light was round and fixed into the ceiling, and the only sprinkler in the room hadn't been tampered with, as far as I could tell. The vents were clean. I lay back down.

I managed to sleep deeply for a couple of hours until wakeup time. My head still throbbed. Other patients noticed my stitched-up wound and my overall disheveled state. They gave me curious looks, similar to the ones I'd gotten when I was in jail clothes and a cast during my last hospitalization. During breakfast, I sat next to a heavy-set man, who seemed to be minding his own business at one of the circular tables in the common area. I didn't make eye contact with anyone.

For the first time since my arrival at the hospital, I thought over my situation. Not only was my academic career in jeopardy, my health was a major concern again. I remembered Dr. Sloane's warnings about seeing him every other week.

He was right after all.

The footsteps of my assailants kept playing over and over in my mind. What happened wasn't the worst, but I imagined what could've been—a repeat attack by some other ruffians or even death! I'd thought I was in control of my mental health, but by now it was obvious that I wasn't.

I decided to call my parents, so I approached the public phone in the common room. One of the other patients, a tall, slim black man with a graying beard called to me from his seat. "You trying to call local or long distance?" he asked.

"Long distance," I replied.

"You have to speak with the staff then," said the patient. "You can use the phone here only for local calls."

"Thanks." I moved to the nurses' station.

Soon I was on the phone with my mother. She sounded distraught yet again and asked me what I would do about letting my university know about my situation. I told her I'd have to tell them I was in the hospital. I didn't speak to my father. I remembered his warning, that if I went to the hospital again I was on my own. My stomach churned at the thought of being kicked out of my program for having a mental illness.

Could that happen?

I went back to my room, lost in thought. In the common room, most of the other patients watched a professional football game, hollering whenever there was a good play for the local team, the Eagles. Since it was Sunday, most group activities were not scheduled, and only the medical doctor and the weekend psychiatrist came to see me.

I spent most of the day in bed and worried about what was to come in the hospital and at school. I found myself checking for cameras and listening devices as I stared at the ceiling.

The second day my headache almost disappeared. Outside the day was dreary and windy. My suspicions about my hospital room being bugged and wired to videotape me weren't as strong. I continued to take my medicine, double the dose from what I'd started with when I saw Dr. Sloane.

I had a roommate. The man who had helped me with the phone the day before moved into the bed next to mine after the staff rearranged some patients' room assignments. We didn't say much to each other at first. I rested with my eyes closed until it was time for the first activity of the day—drawing in the common room. I rose and ventured out of the room.

Most of the other patients drew with markers, although a few still lay in their beds. The staff member in charge strode from table to table, checking on the progress of everyone and making comments. "Oh, that's nice. Good job!"

All of a sudden, one of the female patients, a young woman who wore a hospital gown as well, stood up abruptly, shoved her markers and drawing on the floor. "I ain't fucking doing this shit anymore! This is bullshit!"

One of the nurses immediately spoke up. "Tina, what are you doing? Please calm down!"

But the patient continued her tantrum. "I'm not calming down. I'm sick of this place! I want to go home!"

The staff member continued to try to gain back control of the patient. "Tina, please. Sit down. You know this behavior is unacceptable."

I sat down at one of the tables and tried to ignore the drama, but the patient persisted. "Stop telling me what to do, bitch! I want to go home!" She began walking toward the exit. Several staff members followed and slowly surrounded her.

One of them, a male nurse, said, "Tina, you're being disruptive. Do you want something to calm you down?"

"No!" she said. "I don't need another damn shot! Get away from me!"

She struggled after they grabbed her. A staff member who had prepared an injection moved toward the fracas. "Let go of me!" said the patient. Two other staff members eventually got her into the quiet room, a room with padding and no furniture, and shut the door. In a few minutes, they all emerged, and the patient was quiet. The staff member with the needle went to the nurses' station to dispose of it. The rest of us resumed our drawing.

After the activity ended, I went back to bed. While several staff members talked among themselves about the sedated patient at the nurses' station, my roommate said in a low voice, "Be careful here. The staff doesn't have control over the patients."

I turned my head and looked at him and then looked back at the ceiling. "Thanks."

He wore a clean white T-shirt and tan pants that were torn and frayed in the knees but clean.

After a moment, he said, "You've got to be careful in the hospital when you're sick."

I looked at his worn-out face and then back at the ceiling, sensing that he was warning me again of possible danger.

He continued. "Some patients make life hard on the rest of us, carrying on and starting fights. You've got to stay clear of that trouble so you can leave here and go home."

He paused. "And whatever you do, don't hit any staff, no matter what they say to you." He rose from his reclined position and sat on his bed so that he was closer to me. He spoke almost in a whisper. "I did that back when I was sick in the emergency room. I hit the orderly—I knew it. I was 'delusional,' as the doctor said, thinking that he was going to start a nuclear war. Anyway, right after I was discharged from the hospital, the police came and took me to jail. They gave me the police report for what I did. I couldn't believe my eyes when I read it. It said I was biting a nurse, hitting the security guards and other staff who came near, and destroying hospital property. None of that happened. They lied, making everything sound worse than it was, and no one believed my side of the story because I was 'delusional.' When I got in front of the judge, there was nothing that I could say. No one would believe my side of the story."

"Aren't you pissed off at the ER staff?" I said.

"I sure am. They were supposed to help me." He stared straight ahead at nothing in particular, as if his thoughts were way back in the past instead of in his present situation. I waited for more.

"You just be careful, is all I'm saying," he said. "If you get physical with the staff, they'll retaliate with lies and get you in more trouble than you're already in."

We lay in silence for a few more minutes. Then my roommate got up and left the room. I lay thinking about what he'd said and remembered the ER staff during my first hospitalization—the orderlies pinning me down and later claiming that I'd bitten one of them. My roommate was in a similar situation but much worse. I wondered again why psychiatric patients were treated in such a manner.

29.

Later that morning, I called Chrissy but didn't get an answer. I wondered why she didn't pick up, especially after what had happened with my hospital admission. My worries added to one another with each passing minute. Tracy must've found out from my parents that I was in the hospital because she kept calling the psych ward, but I didn't take her calls.

A young man with straight brown hair, a medical student, came to my room.

"Can you come with me, Hank?" he asked, smiling.

We walked briskly down the hall, through the double doors marking the exit of the ward, and into a small conference room, where an older, broad man in a suit and tie sat at a desk with a laptop computer. As I entered the room, he gave me a piercing glance and then stood to extend his hand. "Hi, Hank. I'm Dr. Hargrove." He gave a firm handshake and showed me a chair. His full black beard contrasted with his receding hairline; his deep, resonating voice carried substantial weight and authority.

"How are you feeling today?" he asked me after the medical student had closed the door and the three of us sat down.

"Better," I said. His booming voice forced me to tell the truth. I feared he'd know if I was lying.

"Good. The staff notes indicate that you've been taking your medicine and sleeping through the night thus far. Any problems with the higher dose of Elixir?"

"No." My heart pounded. His blunt style of speaking put me on edge.

"And what about your fears that someone is monitoring you through hidden cameras and recording devices? Do you think they're still real?"

"Not as much as before I came to the hospital." It was a different feeling speaking to this psychiatrist, as if I both respected and feared him. I knew he wanted to help me.

"That's good to hear," Dr. Hargrove said. "Just remember that no one is recording your voice here or filming you. When you're in your room, you have your privacy. Do you get along with the staff and trust that they'll take care of you?"

"At first it was hard to trust them, but now it's better." I shifted in my chair.

"Great. Just remember that they're here for your care," he said. "They're not going to hurt you in any way."

I eased back a little more in my plastic seat. The medical student, who was sitting directly across from me, smiled again.

"Now," said Dr. Hargrove, typing on his laptop as he spoke. "This is the third time that you've been hospitalized?"

"Yes." Shame filled me. I answered his questions about my previous times in the hospital.

He looked at my chart. "You've never taken a dose as high as twenty milligrams of Elixir before, right?"

"No," I said, fidgeting with my hands.

"That's what you're taking now, just so you know," the doctor continued. "What about sleeping patterns? Do you go for periods without sleeping or sleeping too much?"

"I always go without good sleep for about a week before I go to the hospital," I said. "But I never stay in bed all day."

"And racing thoughts?"

"Again, right before the hospital I have them."

"And this time your thoughts led you to believe that someone was monitoring you in your apartment?"

"Yes, that's right."

"Now, from reading your intake from Saturday night, it looks like you don't have a diagnosis. Am I right?"

"I thought I suffered from some sort of depression. But I don't know…"

"By the time you leave here, I might have one for you. I'll have more by tomorrow." Dr. Hargrove stopped typing and turned to me. "Very good. That'll be all for today. Do you have any questions for us?"

"When do you think I'll be discharged?" I asked. "I have to let my school know when I'll be back in class."

"I don't expect you to be discharged for at least a week," he said. "This is my first evaluation. I'll have a better idea in the next couple of days when you can go home. I'm working with the medical doctor, who wants to make sure your head is healing."

More bad news.

After the doctor dismissed me, I rose from my chair, wondering what he thought of my answers and of me in general.

The medical student walked with me back to the common area, where patients chatted with one another. I went to my room and lay down to relax. My mind was a whirlwind, and my heart still pounded, though. I concluded that my discomfort was due to the stress and fatigue that came with being in the hospital.

In the afternoon, the uncomfortable feeling persisted, and I concluded it was Dr. Hargrove that worried me. His direct manner and his no-nonsense personality made me wonder what sort of diagnosis he might give me. I forced myself to consider other problems that needed attention.

I had to call my university, so I went to the public phone and dialed the main number of Premier and then asked for my advisor's extension. My advisor, Edith, answered.

She sounded concerned when I told her I'd been mugged and was hospitalized with a head injury. I left out that I had suffered a psychotic episode and was confined to a psychiatric ward. She bought my story that the hospital was keeping me for the rest of the week to monitor me.

The next morning, after wakeup, showers, and breakfast, the medical student came for me as I played Scrabble with two other patients. I walked down the corridor leading to the conference room with the same uncomfortable feeling. The medical student's smile was absent today. Outside light rain fell from a dark-gray sky. With each step, I tensed and braced myself for the unknown.

The medical student's pace picked up as we neared the conference room. I tried to keep calm, but fear of this meeting overtook me. I concentrated on breathing—in, out, in, out. The medical student opened the door, and I entered and greeted Dr. Hargrove.

"Hello, Hank. How are you doing today?" His booming voice seemed to bounce off the walls. His dress was exquisite again. There was utter silence while he and the student waited for my response.

"Better. Thanks."

"How did you sleep last night?" Dr. Hargrove turned and looked me square in the eyes.

"I slept well."

"How about your thoughts? Any about others monitoring you?"

"Hardly any."

"Good," continued Dr. Hargrove. "The medicine is taking effect."

I stayed quiet, waiting for more. The doctor seemed to collect his thoughts and prepare himself to say something.

"Hank, have you ever been told that you have schizophrenia?" he asked, again meeting my eyes.

The word "schizophrenia" sent a chill throughout my body. It was a serious diagnosis, the one that patients feared the most, though bipolar disorder was a close second. I was frozen but managed to get out a no a few seconds later, though my voice faltered. Suddenly, the tension in the room increased. The student dropped his gaze to his palms. The doctor's hard stare continued.

"I'm afraid this is your diagnosis. You have schizophrenia, subtype paranoid," he continued.

I stared at the wall across from me in a trance, utterly at a loss for words. It was as if someone had punched me in the gut. I knew the doctor and the student waited for a response, but I continued in silence and shock.

Dr. Hargrove began to type. "There's a brochure about schizophrenia that I want you to look at while you're here. The nurse handling your case will give it to you. It will help you learn about your disorder."

"All right." The words were deep in my throat, and I had to will them out of my mouth.

"Good. Now what questions do you have for us?"

I was speechless. It was as if my whole world had caved in, and I suffocated under all of the debris. I struggled to process my diagnosis. My mind was stuck.

"Hank," said the psychiatrist. "Are you still with us?"

"Yes…" I stared blankly at the carpeted floor now. Nothing else came from my mouth.

He stopped typing. "Well, you've got a lot to digest, so I think we'll end the meeting for today. We'll see you again tomorrow. Make sure to keep taking your medicine, attend group sessions, and try to read about schizophrenia."

The student rose from his seat, and I blindly followed him down the shiny white corridor to the entrance of the ward. Walking was like a new experience for me; I managed to make it down the hallway only because someone led me. Just before arriving at the common area, I braced myself for the stares from the other patients. The student left me and searched for the next patient. I tried not to let my emotions show, but I knew from the looks on *their* faces something was wrong with mine.

I went on to my empty room and closed the door behind me. *Deep breaths!* The will to move was gone. I sat alone, still wearing a hospital gown and in a trance.

I felt like a different person, though when I finally moved to the bathroom to look into the mirror, the basic essence of my body was still present. My eyes were the same baby blue, though they showed obvious fatigue behind my glasses. The stubble of a beard; my long, thick brown hair combed back after my morning shower; and the bald spot where the stitches were—all the same. But my mind wasn't right. Something was wrong with it, though no one, not even I, could see it.

Schizophrenia! Never in my wildest dreams did I think I had it. Some patients I'd seen in psych wards with it were completely incapacitated. They seemed like they would always be in the hospital. I could handle depression and even bipolar disorder, another common diagnosis, but schizophrenia! I didn't know if I could handle that.

In the afternoon, when most of the patients attended a group session and the common room was clear of all but one patient snoring in his chair, I called my parents.

"How are you feeling, Hank?" asked my mother, her voice full of worry.

I stood at the semicircular counter with my elbows resting on it. One hand held the phone to my ear while the other propped my head up, holding my forehead. "OK...The doctor says I have schizophrenia," I stammered. The nurses within earshot glanced at me and then continued on with their chatting and paperwork.

"I'm sorry. Your father and I were afraid of that. Do you want us to come up and visit you?"

"No, I'll be fine. I called Chrissy. She won't pick up."

A foreboding pause ensued. "We weren't going to tell you."

"What? Tell me what happened!"

"She was stuck with an infected needle during her surgical rotation."

"Infected? With what?"

Now my mother began to cry. "With—with HIV."

"HIV?" My mind whirled into action. *I have to get out of the hospital and go see her!* I hung up with my mother and slapped my hand on the countertop of the nurses' station to get their attention. "I need to leave here! My sister's sick in Georgia!"

"Hank, you can't leave now. Your discharge date isn't for another week. And then you have to attend the day hospital for a week. Those are the doctor's orders." The nurse returned to her work.

I paced back and forth in front of the station. I longed to be free, only to see my sister. But I remained in the psych ward, trapped at the mercy of the doctors. If I'd only had this diagnosis sooner, this admission could've been prevented. Unable to hold back, I pounded the wall with my fist in anger.

30.

I called Chrissy.

When she answered, her voice wasn't her own. It was broken and forlorn, like a lost child's.

"Chrissy? It's me, Hank. How are you?"

All of a sudden, the voice became slightly stronger. "Hank? Are you still in the hospital? I don't recognize this number."

"I'm calling from a hospital phone. How are you?" I repeated.

Chrissy began to cry, something she hadn't done over the phone since she broke up with her high school boyfriend when I was in college. "Oh, it was such bad luck! I volunteered to help with the surgery. The nurse next to me was giving an injection of some sort, and the needle from the syringe punctured my glove…I'm so scared. If—if I contract HIV I don't know what I'll do!" She tried to stifle her emotions but didn't have much luck.

"What are they doing for you?"

"I have to take antivirals for twenty-eight days. They're already making me nauseous. They already got a baseline HIV test that was negative. Then they test me again at one, three, and six months to make sure I'm not infected."

"So it's six months before you know for sure?"

"Yes."

"What about your studies? Can you continue?"

"I'm going on in the program. I need to pass my boards, though. I'm not a hundred percent obviously."

"Do you think you *can* continue?"

"I don't know…I'm going to try."

"How are Mom and Dad reacting to it?" I could predict with certainty my father's reaction, but I had to know for sure. They had been the first to hear the news and were the only relatives nearby to support her.

"Dad is irate that they let a student scrub in on an HIV-infected patient."

"And Mom?"

"She's really worried. The toll it would be on my personal life. My quality of life going forward if I do become infected. Oh, Hank! I'm so sorry to put everyone through this!"

"It's not your fault! It was just…an accident."

"Are you coming to Georgia anytime soon? To visit?"

Those questions cut through me like a knife. I knew I was a better comfort than my parents, but I was stuck in the hospital!

"I—I can't right now. They're holding me for another week, and then after that I have to attend a day hospital for another week."

"But what are you going to do about school?"

"I don't know. I have to meet with my advisor after discharge to see."

"I'd come to visit you, but I'm in the middle of my semester. I have finals to study for—" She cried audibly, which broke my heart. I'd have rather seen my fiancée in bed with another man than hear my sister cry over the phone and not be able to see her in person to console her.

She gathered herself and continued. "I tried to persuade Mom and Dad to visit you. But Dad said to let you be—that you had to work out your problems by yourself."

"Mmm." I didn't know how else to respond. My father's analysis of the situation actually sounded right.

I ended the call amid more sniffles from Chrissy, went to my room, and slammed the door shut, done with the hospital. I promised myself I'd never return to one for my mental illness, now that I knew that I had one. I had been too complacent about my care, and from now on, I would be on top of things.

I felt helpless as I lay in the room alone. "Fuck!" I yelled.

A few minutes later, a nurse knocked and opened the door. "Hank, you have a phone call."

I wondered who it was. I'd already talked to my parents that day, as well as Chrissy. Was it my school? Had they found out I was in the psych ward? My hands shook with nerves as I took the receiver and answered.

"Hank?"

I knew that southern drawl anywhere. Tom!

"Tom! How are you? How did you know I was in the hospital?"

"I kept calling your cell, but it wasn't turned on. Then I called your parents to see what was going on. How are you feeling?"

"Not good. I relapsed, they diagnosed me with schizophrenia, Tracy cheated on me, Chrissy had a crisis in medical school—"

"Why didn't you call me sooner?"

"I didn't think to." Relief flooded through me as I spoke. It'd been months since I'd heard from my best friend.

"I'm worried about you. You sure you don't want to move back to Atlanta with your parents? I know you and your dad have issues, but you might want to think it over. My uncle had to live with my grandparents until he was forty."

"Doesn't sound inviting to me. But I'll think about it. I want to finish my program. That's my top priority now."

"All right." Tom sounded resigned. "Just take care of yourself. You don't want to wind up in a state hospital like my uncle did."

"How long was he there?"

"Almost a year. He punched a cop while he was psychotic. The law didn't look too kindly on what he did."

"Mmm." *That could have been me after my car accident in California!* I really had to be careful going forward. Even if I didn't break the law, someone could claim I did if I got sick again. Any judge would believe a sane person over an insane one, even if the insane one remembered exactly what happened and hadn't done anything against the law. It was just as my roommate said.

I promised to call Tom when I returned to my apartment. Then we ended the conversation. I returned to my room with some measure of hope and calm after speaking with him.

. . . . .

The next afternoon, during visiting hours, a nurse approached me. "Hank, you have a visitor." In the common room sat Tracy. When I walked up to the table where she fidgeted, she stood and hugged me. I didn't return the gesture.

I collected myself and sat in a plastic chair opposite her. "You've got two minutes to explain yourself."

She gave a questioning look. She still didn't know I knew about her lover. "How are you? I had to call your parents to find out you were in the hospital.

And then you wouldn't take any of my calls. What's going on?"

"I know about you and the tour guide from the museum."

That stopped the conversation in its tracks. Now I moved in for the decisive blow.

"The night I was mugged I was at your door and heard you and the tour guide making love."

Tracy's mouth hung open, and she remained silent. She tried to recover. "I don't know what you're talking about."

"Oh yes, you do. I even waited in the lobby for him to leave. I recognized him. It's over between us. The engagement is off." My voice quivered with anger, but I stayed calm.

Suddenly, Tracy broke into an angry tirade. "You're breaking it off! After the three hospitalizations that I had to deal with? I should break up with you! You crazy fool. And you think you're going to work for NASA? Your career is finished! I'm glad you know about the tour guide! At least he isn't crazy." She stood with her hands on her hips.

"You can go now," I said calmly.

But she wasn't finished. Not yet. "I came to tell you—I'm moving back to California. I'm sick of this city. I should've never moved here in the first place! I'm glad it's over! I'm sick of dealing with you and your issues with your father. And don't call me when you relapse again!"

"Go!" I shouted. By now we were the center of attention in the ward.

Tracy threw her engagement ring at me and stomped to the exit. I calmly returned to my room, though my hands shook with fury.

31.

It had been almost three weeks since I had attended a class.

I met with my advisor, Edith, after my discharge, as she instructed. Entering her office, I saw books and stacks of papers piled everywhere. A small circular fishbowl with a goldfish in it sat on a little table over by her window.

"So you finally recovered from your injury?" she asked. Edith was soft spoken but always to the point. She wore black slacks and a crimson sweater. Her facial features were condensed. Her eyes, mouth, and nose all seemed set in close vicinity to one another like a mouse's face.

"Yes," I said, fidgeting with my hands.

"And you missed almost three weeks of school," she continued.

"Yes." My hands were still now, and I broke eye contact. After discharge from inpatient care, I'd had to attend a day hospital for further education about my disorder and prevention of relapse. I was way behind in my classwork.

"This is a very serious situation."

I said nothing and sensed more bad news.

"If you want to continue in the program, you would have to file for incompletes in the courses that you are taking now and take off a year to begin again with this quarter next fall."

"I was wondering if my hospitalization could be considered a special circumstance and an exception could be made. I can catch up quickly and take the exams I missed."

"I've looked into it already, and Dean Bryant said that there are no exceptions right now."

"No exceptions?" My heart sank.

"None." Now Edith was leaning forward with her hands clasped together on her desk, forcing me to make eye contact again.

"I'm afraid that you must file those incompletes immediately," she said in her usual quiet voice. "You can register to begin the program again next year, at the appointed time."

I glanced at the floor again and tried to comprehend the situation. "How am I going to pay my bills if I take a leave of absence? My loans will stop coming while I'm away from the university. I can't get a loan from a bank to support myself."

"That is completely up to you," said Edith without any expression. "I hope to see you back here next year."

I collected myself, forced out a "thank-you" to Edith, and grabbed the door handle.

On the elevator ride, I felt like screaming in frustration but held my emotions in check. I ambled on a sidewalk back to my apartment. The brisk December wind kicked up between the buildings lining the streets of University City but didn't coerce me into walking faster. The sun made its way to the western horizon, and darkness began to pervade the alleys and small streets. My nose and toes began to go numb, and the closed wound on my head stung from the cold.

In my apartment, I turned on a lamp and the heat to counter the dreary light and cold. The silence of the place added to my despair. I tossed my book bag on my brown, frayed sofa.

I was frozen with shock and grief. I merely stared at the ceiling of my apartment, which had discolored brown rings from a leak and faint cracking in some places.

I spotted a bottle of rum that I seldom used. Though I wasn't supposed to drink alcohol, I took a small glass, poured myself a shot's worth in it, and gulped it down. Then another and another, until I lost count and woke in the middle of the night on my sofa.

. . . . .

My phone ringing the next morning woke me. It was my father.

"What's going on?" he asked.

"I had a meeting with my advisor yesterday. It didn't go well," I said, propping myself up with my elbows.

"What happened?"

"I missed too much school, and I'm forced to take a leave of absence until next fall."

"What? Did you explain to her that you were in the hospital with a head injury?"

"Yeah, but she said there were no exceptions."

"I can't believe this. What are you going to do now? You've taken out loans on a lot of money."

"I don't know," I said morosely. Shortly afterward, the conversation ended with my father demanding I move back to Atlanta.

I put the phone down, leaned over, and put both hands over my face and pressed with my hands. I sat on the bed and listened to traffic pick up slightly. It was a Saturday, and the street noise was calm. Outside a bark from a tenant's dog sounded. The heat clicked on. Slowly the familiarity of life in my apartment motivated me to stand up and open the drapes.

My health, my personal life, my professional life. They were all in shambles. I was at the bottom of the barrel—*no place to go but up from here.*

. . . . .

I went to Dr. Sloane's office the next day. As usual, he met me in the waiting room.

In his office, his legs were crossed and his usual standard-size notepad was on his lap. A few seconds passed before he spoke. "So I see from the hospital report that you were diagnosed with schizophrenia."

"Yes," I said, resigned.

"Mmm…I'm sorry, Hank. I know it must be tough to hear that news."

I remained silent, staring ahead of me.

"And your university? What's the situation there?"

"I had to take a leave of absence. I missed too many classes." Now I met his eyes. "And Tracy and I are finished."

Dr. Sloane peered at me. Then he began writing on his notepad. "Yes, that's unfortunate. You've had quite a month since I last saw you." He finished his writing. "And how are you holding up with all that has happened?"

"OK, I guess."

"You know, if you continue to avoid seeing me, you're going to end up in the hospital again. I'm not threatening you—I'm just telling you like it is. You're lucky to be as high functioning as you are with your disorder, but if you don't make some changes, you're going to continue to spiral downward."

He continued. "How about your finances?"

"Not too good. My financial aid will stop in the next couple of weeks."

"So you're going to need some income pretty quickly." The doctor scribbled some more.

"Yeah."

"Have you thought about moving to Atlanta to be near your family and cut down on your living expenses?"

"I've thought about it."

"Of course, if you decide to stay in Philadelphia, I would be happy to continue on with you." He paused. "You're in a tough situation. No one would think less of you for moving back in with your parents and going on disability."

"That's out of the question."

"Considering your diagnosis, it may be your only choice. Many patients with your disorder deteriorate mentally and lose their ability to work. On the other hand, there are individuals with schizophrenia who work demanding jobs. It's a wait and see situation."

"I don't see any future on disability. I'm going to continue to pursue engineering."

"It's your life. No one is stopping you. You're very ambitious. I'll hand that to you."

"But how is it that I have schizophrenia? I don't have any relatives with it."

"Good question. I'm sure in the brochure that you read and in most textbooks it talks about the genetic component of passing it down from generation to generation, but a more plausible theory for you would be that of experiencing childhood emotional trauma. This is a newer theory."

"You mean listening to my parents fight and fearing for my mother and sister might've given me an illness?"

He looked me in the eye. "Yes. I do."

"And is there any chance of it going into remission, or am I going to be in and out of hospitals?"

"Remission is impossible, unfortunately. You'll always have to take your medicine. If you do that, and if you can recognize that some of your thought process isn't real, you should be able to stay out of hospitals. Improvement from your present state comes only with some effort on your part. Some patients improve, and some deteriorate. I can't give you a definite prognosis."

I sat silent for a moment, pensive, and remembered the countless nights when I lay in bed frozen with fear as a kid, praying that my father wouldn't hurt my mother during an argument. I never imagined this past would lead me to have a mental illness.

I sank in my seat. "Are there people who suffer from schizophrenia who are able to function at a high level for the rest of their life?"

"There are few, unfortunately. The majority of patients have a decline in function eventually."

"Oh…" *Didn't want to hear that right now!* Would all my effort to become an engineer be for naught? Even if I made it through the program at Premier, would I be fired from NASA from a lapse in performance because of my disorder?

Dr. Sloane continued. "But don't give up hope. With the newer medicine that you're taking and the fact that you're doing so well now, you could be one of the exceptions." He paused again. "How is your sister? You told me over the phone that she'd been stuck with an infected needle."

"She's shaken. I've never heard her so distraught from our phone calls. She isn't herself."

"Can you go visit her?"

"I can't afford to, and she's busy studying for her boards. She can't come here, either."

"It must be very difficult for you." Dr. Sloane pulled out his appointment book. "I would like to meet with you twice next week."

I let out a sigh. "All right."

I walked back home, hoping I would be one of the lucky ones that lived without any more hospitals and worked at the profession I loved. I remembered some of the patients from my hospital stays, incapacitated and silent.

Will I end up like them? The future was so uncertain, especially now that my world had been smashed to pieces.

32.

I arose with a hint of energy for the first time in two months. I shook off the dreariness of my apartment and of the January weather, dressed myself in a collared shirt and slacks, and gathered a business notebook full of resumés. I mapped out a course that took me to as many restaurants as possible and then rode the regional rail from Thirtieth Street Station to Suburban Station near city hall in Center City.

I stood outside the classy restaurant, Pots and Pans. I looked over the huge windows showing the tables, chairs, and a bar inside. With some exertion, I opened the heavy wooden door.

The restaurant gleamed. Fresh white tablecloths, silverware, and glasses covered every table. The bar top was immaculate—no dirty glasses or plates, not even a crumb or wet ring. Liquor bottles reflected the overhead lights and sparkled. A young woman approached me from the kitchen. Through the doorway behind her came the sounds of cooks, who carried on with one another and clanged cooking utensils.

I asked the hostess about speaking with a manager. Then I waited.

Soon a robust man with a tie came from a swing door in the back. "Kevin McClure. I'm assistant manager. What can I do for you?"

I shook his hand. "I'm Hank Galloway. I was wondering if you have any server positions available?" I tried to sound as energetic as he did.

"Do you have any experience as a server?"

My voice dropped. "No."

"We require at least a year of experience," he said, smiling.

"OK." Disappointed all of a sudden, I turned to leave but then caught myself. I had an idea. "Excuse me, Mr. McClure?"

"Yes?" He did a turn from walking back toward the kitchen.

"What about bussers? Do they need prior experience?"

Now the manager looked at me with some interest. "No, our server assistants do not. Is *that* a position that would interest you?"

"Yes, sir. I have experience in customer service, and I've worked in food management before."

"Is that right? Do you have a resumé?"

I took one out of my business folder.

He glanced it over. "Supermarket, eh?" There was another pause, as if he were considering something. "How about you fill out an application for me?"

Kevin motioned me toward a booth. I kept calm while I wrote down my information.

I finished the application, and Kevin returned from the back to look it over. He raised his eyebrows and said, "Premier University. Did you graduate?"

"No. I decided to take a break from my studies."

"And you can begin right away full-time?" He studied me with steely eyes.

"Yes. What is the pay for the position?"

"Seven fifty an hour plus tip share."

It's a start at least. "I can begin right away."

He returned his eyes back toward the application. "I'll give you a call in a couple of days at this number and let you know what we've decided." Then he rose, shook my hand, and walked quickly back to the kitchen area and out of sight. My glimmer of hope continued to flicker as I walked out to the street.

I went on my quest that morning and afternoon. I dropped off resumés and filled out applications for server positions at various other restaurants, but since I had no prior experience, none other indicated they might hire me. Pots and Pans was my best bet.

·   ·   ·   ·   ·

The next two days, I applied at more restaurants but got no offers. I began to lose hope that I would be able to stay in Philadelphia. Waiting tables was the only job I was qualified for that could pay my bills while I was away from my program. The frigid weather and my dreary apartment grew on my nerves, as did my current state of unemployment.

Then, while I was searching for jobs on the Internet at home in a desperate attempt to possibly do temp work, Kevin called.

"Come back on Monday in uniform—black pants and shoes, a white shirt, and tie—and we'll begin your training."

After hanging up, I breathed a sigh of relief and tried to imagine what it would be like to work in the restaurant. I really had no idea what I was getting into.

. . . . .

On Monday, I arrived at the restaurant at the appointed time, a half hour before opening for lunch. Servers zipped through the service area, preparing clear glass jugs of ice water, slicing lemons, carrying clean, empty salad bowls to the cooler by the salad station and dinner plates and platters to the cooking line. The kitchen was full of food prep workers who washed lettuce, chopped carrots and onions, and mixed ingredients for the soups in giant metal pots on gas burners. Deli-style food slicers chopped lettuce and tomatoes on automatic—going back and forth, back and forth.

My senses were overloaded, though no one paid any attention to me.

"Hank," Kevin shouted above all of the commotion. As I turned to face him, I slipped on the wet plastic floor and awkwardly regained my balance without falling.

"Be careful in the kitchen. These floors are slippery," bellowed Kevin. "Let's go to the front, and I'll show you around."

He showed me the various appliances—the ice machine, the coffee maker, and the soda fountain. I struggled to take in everything and stay out of the way of the servers, who were busy preparing the dining area.

"Mario, make sure we have water pitchers at every station," Kevin barked at one of the bussers.

"Sure," said a short, dark-haired and tan-skinned man, who walked quickly to the dining area and disappeared around the corner.

"Let's get the entrées out hot and the salads out cold, everyone," said Kevin. "Yesterday we lost two dishes because they sat too long." He showed me a diagram of the layout of the tables. "Take this home and study it. I'll be giving you a written test at the end of the week. Today, you'll be training alongside Mario. Mario! Come over here! I want you to meet your new trainee. This is Hank Galloway."

Mario and I shook hands. Mario said, "Aww, Kevin I have to train again? Let Vinny take a turn."

Kevin turned on Mario and stared him down. "Vinny trained last time, Mario. It's your turn." He walked away.

Mario looked me over for a split second. "C'mon, man. I'll show you our station."

In the dining area, Mario pointed and said, "These four tops are our tables, as well as the two tops in either corner. This your first time bussing?"

"Yes."

His shoulders slouched all of a sudden. Mario looked like he was letdown even more. "Oh, boy. Well, let me tell you how it's gonna be, Hank. Lunchtime is fast paced. Guests want to come in for their meal and get back to work, quick. We've gotta move fast, or everyone will be on our ass—the guests *and* the management. Just keep water glasses filled and clear dishes when the meal is finished. That's your job today. And keep your cool if any guest hassles you. The fastest way to lose your job is to get angry at a guest."

"OK." I tried not to sound intimidated.

"And try to lose that accent. It won't get you any tips here."

I didn't respond.

The restaurant opened, and the first guests arrived. My heart beat fast as they were seated in our section. Mario passed me a pitcher of water and said, "Let's go, man."

I followed him and filled up a water glass in front of an elderly woman while he filled glasses on the other side of the big round table. All the while, Mario wore a smile on his face and moved quickly from glass to glass. I awkwardly reached around the next guest, a stout man, and barely reached his glass and maintained my position as I filled it. He sensed that I was straining and moved so I could better reach around his portly torso, but he seemed bothered by my presence. I continued on.

The shift progressed. I could tell the physical expense of my new job right away. My back and legs strained from bending over the table and around guests to fill their glasses. My feet ached from walking from one end of our station to the next and then back to the kitchen.

"Hank, you need to speed up some, bud," Mario said after the third table of our section had been seated.

I worked as fast as possible, walking around guests and filling up glasses. One glass I overfilled in my haste, but the elderly female patron said, "Don't worry about it, son."

The restaurant shifted into high gear. "I need a food runner," yelled Kevin from the food line.

"Give me a ram of Italian!" said one of the servers to the salad man.

"Back up platters," yelled one of the cooks.

All was commotion coming from the kitchen and food line. Glass after glass I filled and refilled. I began to clear empty dishes from the tables full of guests. I tried to stay on Mario's heels and out of the way of the hostess, the servers, and other bussers, but my stamina was spent after a short time.

All the while, Kevin barked at the cooks and servers along with another manager, who was in the dining room, or "on the floor," as the employees coined it, mingling with guests and overseeing the work of the staff. I felt this floor manager's and Kevin's eyes on me.

"Hank, refill that guest's water on table 18," said the floor manager.

I tried to figure out which table he meant but couldn't remember the diagram.

"Over there in the corner." He pointed impatiently.

"Right." I tried to sound upbeat, walking away toward the table as fast as possible.

After a couple of hours, the number of guests dwindled. I recovered from the frenetic pace. Mario slowed down, too.

"Let's get these tables cleared before you go," he said.

The work never stopped. Noticing the efficient way that Mario bussed the tables, I learned from him. He was fast and put my work to shame, though.

"Do I get a tip share?" I asked him after he told me to go home.

"No. No tip share until after your training is finished."

I walked to Suburban station, worn out and deflated. My training would last for another week at least. So far, my earnings wouldn't be enough to pay my bills.

I arrived at my apartment and settled on my couch. My first day had been a blur. I had speed walked, tended to guests, negotiated the slippery kitchen floor, and kept up with Mario. I couldn't fathom doing this for another eight months, but that was how long I would have to support myself until my loans kicked back in when I started my program again.

33.

After two months of work as a server assistant, I began to press Kevin regularly to become a server. A month later, I started my training at this position. I had been scraping by paying my bills, even putting my rent on my credit card for a couple months. I needed the added income of a server to get out of debt.

I sensed the increased intensity and workload immediately as I learned to put orders in to the kitchen and interact more with guests. I did side work with my trainer, Vinny, a tall and slim man who always smiled in front of guests but had a short fuse with bussers and cooks. He quickly showed me how to prepare my receipts at the end of the shift.

I took home the menu and studied it for an oral exam that I had to pass on my last day of training. I made a chart of the seasoning and side dishes for some of the entrées, such as the salmon and filet mignon, and yet another for the ingredients of the salads.

I fidgeted in my seat the morning of the exam. Kevin rattled off some salads and entrées, and I recited the ingredients. The Cobb salad tripped me up, but at the end, Kevin congratulated me with a handshake and told me to order food on the house. I had passed and was now a server!

My mental capacities were stretched to the limit. The managers put more pressure on servers to perform. Mistakes cost the restaurant money, as entrées had to be prepared again and the restaurant picked up the check for more egregious errors. Everyone was angry with me if I put in orders wrong, and my tips, the most important part of my job, suffered directly.

Like the work of a busser, the physical aspect still took its toll. I delivered or "ran" food for my tables and did side work, such as rolling silverware into napkins or wiping down countertops, at the end of the shift. Sometimes I worked lunch and dinner, a double shift lasting twelve hours, in the same day.

One lunch shift, six individuals were seated in my section at one of the big round tables. I worked diligently in anticipation of a large tip. Opportunities such as these didn't come everyday for me. I quickened my pace and attended to their requests. All was going well until I saw the floor manager speaking with the guests at length. Soon after the discussion, he approached me in the kitchen and took me aside.

"Table 8 is complaining that you didn't serve the women their food first."

"I thought we don't follow that policy—that we serve the food as it's ready."

"I explained that to them, but they're not happy. The restaurant's going to pick up the tab."

"What?" I tried to control my anger. "They aren't going to leave a single dime."

"I'm sorry." He walked away.

I stood in the kitchen, trying to compose myself. That complaint, over which I had no control, cost me at least fifteen dollars, a large portion of my tips for the shift. On top of that, I had worked so hard to give good service, and the guests didn't pay anything for their meal.

The rest of my shift, I tried hard but couldn't keep a smile on my face. Some other guests noticed and complained about my attitude to the manager. My tips suffered, and I was tempted to keep a large share of my tip out to my busser and the hostess like most of the other servers did, but I refrained. Instead, I sulked as I handed over my bag of cash and receipts to Kevin when I was about to clock out for my break between lunch and dinner.

"Go home, Hank. I'll see you tomorrow," he said.

"But I'm scheduled for dinner as well."

"Don't worry. We'll manage."

I walked back to my apartment on that May afternoon from Thirtieth Street Station, still angry. I needed the money from the more lucrative dinner shift in addition to the tip from lunch I missed out on. Most guests were fairly cheap, so missing a big one was a crushing blow.

At my apartment, I sat on my couch, fumed, and tried to get over it. Waiting tables was a cruel line of work.

· · · · ·

It wasn't long after that day that I met Claudia Barbosa. She had been a server at a restaurant that closed. We looked at each other with interest when Kevin introduced us on her first day of training with Vinny. Her pearly smile made her look even more beautiful and accentuated her brown skin and black eyes. She had an athletic build and a youthful exuberance, as well as a Brazilian accent. When she began to work for her own tips after training, she dazzled everybody with her beauty and charm and put guests at ease with her efficiency and warmth. Customers even asked for her when they returned.

One day, while rolling silverware into bundles in the kitchen, I asked her, "Why don't you give some of your guests to me? You have too many."

She smiled. "Hank, you have to get your own guests. I need my guests to pay my bills."

"I need a vacation. Can you give me just a table or two of yours, just to cover a good meal?"

She laughed. "No. I'll get in trouble with the managers."

"No one will know. Just say that it was a mix up."

She laughed again. "No!"

Claudia continued to wow the rest of us. To my surprise, she gave me some pointers on how to work more efficiently and garner better tips.

"You have to be firm with the cooks, especially the ones who are lazy," she told me off to the side one day. "They'll take all day to prepare dishes, especially when a manager isn't around. And always take care of your own guests before helping a manager with what they ask you. The manager may be annoyed with you, but he doesn't pay your tips. The guests do."

After a few weeks my income improved. Kevin was irritated that I wasn't as much of a team player and the cooks complained at me for being such a stickler all of a sudden. I even built up a clientele who asked for me every time they visited the restaurant—like Claudia. With my higher income, I was able to cut down my hours to five days a week with no double shifts.

One day Claudia came to work for the lunch shift almost in tears. I didn't ask what was wrong. Later she almost lost it in front of a table of guests and hurried to the kitchen. I made my way to the kitchen as soon as I could.

"Is everything OK?" I asked.

"This morning, I found out that Bruno cheated on me." Tears rolled down her cheeks. She rarely talked about her Brazilian boyfriend. "I'm not going to see him anymore."

I was at a loss for words. We were alone in the kitchen. I put my hand on her shoulder as she sobbed. "You can't go back onto the floor like this. Let me help you with your guests. You stay back here and do side work."

"Kevin will be upset that I let you have my tables," she said in between sobs.

I reassured her. "Don't worry about it. I owe you one anyway."

I went back to the floor. It was a busy shift, and almost all of my tables as well as Claudia's were full of patrons. I braced myself mentally for a race to cover them all and set to it, writing up orders and running food from the kitchen.

Kevin noticed I was working two stations and that Claudia had disappeared. Soon he approached me by the fountain machine. "What are you doing, Hank? Where's Claudia?"

"She asked me to cover her tables for her. She had to take care of something." I didn't make eye contact with him and continued to fill glasses with Dr. Pepper.

"Where is she?" continued Kevin with his jaw muscles clenched and brow furrowed.

"I don't know."

Kevin went back toward the kitchen as I finished putting drinks on my tray and headed back out onto the floor, where I remained as long as possible to let Kevin cool down and avoid any more conversation with him.

When I came back to check on some food being prepared, Kevin said to me, "Vinny will help you out on tables 18 and 19. I can't find Claudia."

The rest of the shift was hectic. Claudia emerged from the employee bathroom in the back as I was bringing some dirty dishes to the Hobart, the huge dishwasher.

"Kevin's looking for you," I warned her.

The whites of her eyes were clear, and she looked composed. "I know. I'll handle it. Thanks, Hank."

I said no more about the breakup or what had happened during the shift. I did my side work and handed my bag of receipts and cash to Kevin before heading home. Kevin still looked annoyed but didn't say anything to me about the shift—a huge relief.

34.

Registration for the fall quarter came in May, so I signed up for classes and arranged my financial aid to begin again in September.

With renewed hope in August, I reviewed old material every day on top of working at the restaurant. I covered the concepts of diffraction, static equilibrium, and corrosion of solids in my various textbooks and notes.

As September arrived, I was more focused on the beginning of school than the dressing that the guest wanted on his salad. Even though I needed the income from my job almost until school began, I couldn't help but think grander things lay ahead.

I stood at a table waiting for the patrons to give me an order, but my mind wandered to a concept I had studied the previous night.

"Waiter. Excuse me, waiter, did you hear me?" said an elderly man.

"Uh…I'm sorry, sir. Could you repeat that?" I said.

"I said I would like the salmon special." The man gave me an impatient look—his lips pursed, his eyes unforgiving.

"Yes, sir. Right away." I took his menu and started back toward the kitchen in a hurry.

The next day I stood at my station trying to remember external and internal forces in structures when Kevin approached me. "Hank, table 16 needs to be greeted. Come on, man. You're losing focus."

His words spurred me. While I moved to the table, another patron stopped me. "Where is my salad? I ordered it fifteen minutes ago."

Claudia was within earshot and heard him. "I'll go get it," she said. I continued on to the new guests and got their drink order.

"Hank, you really need to come out of the clouds. The guests are getting impatient with you," said Kevin as I checked out at the end of the night.

"Sure."

"I mean really. Forgetting about salads and asking guests twice about their order—that's been happening a lot lately."

"I understand. By the way, I'm going back to school—I'm putting in my two weeks."

Kevin's jaw dropped. He said nothing as I walked out of the small office adjacent to the kitchen. I hadn't intended to quit in that manner, but knowing that Kevin had given Claudia a hard time the day she broke up with Bruno, I suddenly felt the impulse to put in my notice that way. So I did.

By now, I was an embattled veteran of restaurant work. I had switched to a crew cut, dispensing with my longer hair, and had lost ten pounds. My right index finger had a scar on it from when I nicked the automated slicer in the kitchen. My left thumb had a mark from a hot plate that I picked up without a glove. My legs were weary.

Claudia came to me with obvious sorrow in her eyes the next day, as word that I was leaving had already spread. I rolled silverware into napkins in the kitchen; she joined me, doing the same task. We worked in silence, and from the months of getting to know her, I could tell she wasn't herself. Her head bowed slightly, and her shoulders slouched. She moved deliberately, not as quickly as she usually did.

I continued on. Finally, when one other server finished rolling her silverware and left the kitchen, leaving us alone, I said, "Don't worry, Claudia. I'll be by to see you."

She looked at me with her eyes glowing and gave me a quick smile. Then her pace of work picked up, and she left to return to the floor.

My last two weeks flew by. Mario and Vinny bid me farewell and good luck. It was the usual routine working with Claudia. During my last shift, a sense of calm and pride filled me. I joked with the guests and slowly gathered my receipts after it was over. The journey back to the classroom had been rough. Doing blue-collar work for a living entailed grit and endurance, and I admired those who did it their whole lives. I was lucky to be a student again.

After turning in my receipts, I strode out of the restaurant with a sense of victory. I felt as if I'd overcome a huge obstacle in my quest to work for NASA. With knowledge about my mental illness, which I'd learned in numerous meetings with Dr. Sloane, I was in a better spot to manage any symptoms that might occur in the future and fend off the necessity of going to a hospital. I was prepared as never before to complete my program.

The weekend before my classes resumed, I flew Chrissy up from Georgia for a visit since she couldn't afford the ticket. I hadn't seen her since her needle stick, but luckily her tests had all come back negative. The doctors had said officially that she was healthy.

But she still wasn't her normal self. She expressed doubts about pursuing her goal of becoming a surgeon. The needle stick had been a reality check to the dangers. I told her it was natural to have those feelings but to give it some time.

"You'll put it in the past," I said.

Then she brought up my career aspirations. "Do you really expect to work for NASA, let alone complete your program? You've been in the hospital three times."

"I have a diagnosis now. And I'm on the right dose of my medicine. My psychiatrist and I are making progress."

"Like what?"

"We're identifying the triggers of my psychoses. Making sure to prevent a relapse. He suggests ways to deal with Dad. I'm improving."

"I've heard that before."

"I'm not going to the hospital again. I promise."

She stayed silent, then replied, "I hope not. You weren't there for me after the needle stick. That's the first time in my life I was on my own when the shit hit the fan. If we hadn't been able to talk on the phone during that time, I don't know if I would've made it."

"I'm sorry I wasn't there for you."

"It's OK. You were going through your own hell."

"I'm better. I'm ready to kick some ass."

. . . . .

The Saturday evening after I started classes, I went to Pots and Pans. After greeting the bartender, I settled in at the bar and ordered a Pepsi and an appetizer.

I scanned the expanse of the dining area and spotted Claudia zipping in between tables, heading for the kitchen. Her beauty radiated, even from a distance. In fact, she was even more beautiful than I remembered. Her curves were more accentuated, as if she had gained some weight, making her more voluptuous. Her hair was down; she usually wore it in a bun. I wondered if she had a new boyfriend. I hoped not.

Eventually she spotted me from a table where she was writing an order. Her dark eyes flickered briefly. I played it cool, tending to my Pepsi and continuing to catch up on the latest news from the bartender. Claudia disappeared behind a wall to the service area.

I ordered an entrée. Soon Claudia stood at my side, smiling. "Hi, Hank."

"Hi, Claudia!" I said, surprised that she made the effort to walk up to the bar to speak with me while at work. "How are you? Is Kevin still getting on your nerves?"

"Yes, always." She put her arm around the empty seat beside me.

"How many tables do you have right now?"

"Just two. It's slow tonight."

"Any good tips?"

"None." Her face, wearing a frown, showed dismay. I remembered from my time as a server that tips were everything. The hourly pay alone just didn't cut it.

"Maybe you should switch careers, you know?"

"I want to go into nursing, but I can't afford the tuition right now. I have my GED already."

"Nursing. That's a noble field. I'm impressed, Claudia."

She smiled, but then it faded away, as if she were sad all of a sudden. I could empathize with her about being stuck waiting tables while trying to get a career on track.

"You'd make a good nurse," I said.

"Thank you. How are your studies going?"

"Always challenging. I can't complain, though." I studied her frown. "You'll get into a nursing school sometime. Don't worry." This was something that she'd say to someone else, like me, back when we waited tables together. Now I was saying it to her.

She looked at me with those soft black eyes and broke into a smile again, as if she appreciated the encouragement.

We surveyed the restaurant together, watching two servers glide through the dining area and hearing Kevin bark at the cooks. Then I sensed an opportunity

I'd been waiting for. "I was wondering if I could get your number? Maybe we could catch a movie."

Her face brightened, and she wrote on her pad. She ripped out the paper and gave it to me.

After Claudia left to attend to some guests, I ate my entrée while watching the Phillies play the Mets in baseball. The bartender tossed drinking glasses in the air while he prepared orders. As far as I saw, he didn't notice me admiring Claudia.

My steps were light and quick from Thirtieth Street Station to my apartment, making the journey seem shorter than when I toiled night after night and made the trip with tired legs and a weary mind. As always, I looked for signs of danger, since it was dark and I'd already been mugged in the same neighborhood.

. . . . .

The following weekend, on a clear evening with a hint of chill in the air, I drove out to Claudia's apartment in East Falls, northwest of Center City. I did a double take when I first saw her walking to my car from the driveway of her basement apartment. Her hair was down again. She had on makeup, something that she didn't wear when working. She wore blue jeans and a sweater. She was stunning.

"So do you like living in East Falls?" I asked her as we sped along I-76 to King of Prussia, a suburb a half hour's ride west of the city.

"Yes. It's my favorite part of Philadelphia. But I want to leave and move somewhere where the people are happier."

"Like the people in Brazil, I imagine."

"Yes. Like the Brazilians." She turned her head to me and grinned.

"Yeah, I'd like to leave Philadelphia, too. I grew up in the South where the people are much more congenial than here."

"Congenial?"

"Uh…friendlier. Here they're too gruff and nasty. In California, where I lived before I came here, people are more tolerant of each other and relaxed. That's where I want to go after I graduate."

"I'd like to go to a California beach," Claudia said with a big smile that I saw from the corner of my eye.

We watched the movie, a comedy, which Claudia didn't fully understand because the actors spoke too fast for her. I had to explain some of the jokes both during the movie and on the way back to her basement apartment, which the owner of the house lived above.

When we arrived back at the driveway, our eyes met, and I leaned over and kissed her on the lips. We said good night, and I slowly pulled my hatchback away, as if I weren't yet ready to leave. When I got on the highway heading back to University City, my heart pounded with excitement. I never thought I would be so enthralled by a woman after my breakup with Tracy!

I put things in perspective. This was just the first date. But I couldn't help but be happy.

35.

Claudia and I sat in her basement apartment a month later. Signs of autumn had appeared, and the temperature began dropping. Leaves covered most of the backyard grass within view of the apartment window, and the lawn within view was dry. Two massive oaks that stood in the yard were beginning to look bare.

Claudia paid bills online on her laptop computer at a small desk. To her right was her checkbook, which she wrote in every few minutes. I sat leaning forward on her couch with an open textbook and my laptop illuminated with notes. I had an exam in two days—a difficult one.

We'd dated during this time, going to restaurants and spending time at each other's apartments. I'd cooked for her at my place the previous week. Now, it was her turn to host me for the afternoon.

"Are you coming to the restaurant tomorrow for dinner? I'm working a double shift," said Claudia.

Deep in thought, I turned my head toward her. "What?"

"Are you listening? I asked if you were coming to the restaurant tomorrow evening."

"Sorry. Uh…no, I can't. I'm studying with someone in my class for the exam on Wednesday."

"Who are you studying with?"

"The same person as last time—Nancy." I turned my attention back to my computer screen.

Claudia, who'd had her back to me, turned and faced me. "Do you like her?"

I studied my notes. "Do I like her? What do you mean?"

Claudia slammed down her pen on her desk. "I mean what I asked!"

I caught her glare. "Are you asking if I'm interested in her? Is that why you're so mad?"

"Do you like her more than me?"

"Of course, not! What's wrong?" I paused. "You're jealous. That's it!"

She turned her head back to her computer. "No, I'm not."

"Yes, you are." I thought for a second. "It's because your old boyfriend cheated on you, isn't it?"

Claudia was silent.

"You think I'm cheating on you because of what happened with Bruno." I stood with my hands on my hips. "Let's get something straight. I'm not Bruno, and I'm not unfaithful."

"I thought—"

"You thought wrong. You've got to put the past behind you, or our relationship won't work." I glanced at the door leading outside. "I have to get some fresh air." Without bothering to put on a jacket, I went out onto the back patio, which lay just outside the entrance. A sparrow flew onto one of the shrubs and sounded his call. The wind rustled the remaining leaves of the oaks.

I wondered if it could work out between Claudia and me. Everything had gone well until now; I'd never seen this side of her. I stood with my back to the door.

I felt the pressure of a hand on my shoulder.

"I'm sorry," said Claudia.

I turned around to see streaks of tears on her cheeks.

"I was wrong," she continued. "Come back inside. It's cold out. Please?"

We both went inside. Claudia shut the door, put her arms around me, and squeezed. Even though she wore a heavy sweatshirt and sweatpants, I felt her bosom on my chest, her forehead against my shoulder, and her hips against mine. She sniffled.

I put my arms around her. "I know it might be hard for you, but you have to trust me more."

She lifted her head off my shoulder. "I know. You're so patient with me. Thank you."

She kissed me, her tongue searching for mine immediately. I squeezed her tight in my arms. Our breaths became forced and hard.

I had the sudden desire to make love to her, though we hadn't done so yet. I gently kissed her neck. She continued to squeeze me in her arms. I pulled her sweatpants and panties down part way, feeling her buttocks. Her breaths were audible now.

I knelt and finished removing her bottom clothes. Then I kissed the hair above her privates, slowly, all the while massaging her buttocks and the back of her thighs. She ran her hands through my hair.

Still standing, she parted her legs a little, and I kissed the inside of her thighs, getting closer and closer to her privates. I kissed their outer lips.

"I want you inside me," said Claudia, between breaths.

I removed her sweatshirt and bra and let down her hair. I undressed myself, showing my erection. A glimmer of delight passed over Claudia's eyes.

I removed a condom from its packaging and put it on. "Lie down on the couch."

Claudia obliged and looked into my eyes with anticipation.

I moved slowly inside her, then deeper. Claudia wrapped her legs around me and arched her back. Finally, we reached a climax and moaned with pleasure. We peeled away from each other with our skin perspiring.

. . . . .

On a date the following week with Claudia at a sushi restaurant in Center City, there was a pause in the conversation. We watched plates of the fresh raw fish go by on a tiny conveyor belt. Claudia loved sushi—it was her favorite food. The conveyor belt made the experience all the more interesting to her. She looked on as each little entrée passed and commented as to whether it looked appetizing. Occasionally, she grabbed a dish, removed the transparent plastic lid, and ate the pieces, one by one.

After we'd had our fill and waited for the check, Claudia broke the silence. "Hank, I want you to come to Miami over Thanksgiving to meet my parents."

"Of course." I took her hand, kissed it, and smiled. "I'd love to."

"But I haven't met your parents yet. And you don't talk about them very much." Claudia's eyes showed confusion and worry.

She was right. I had avoided talking about them, especially my father. He was such an unpleasant subject that I didn't bring him up. *Am I afraid that Claudia might break up with me if I tell her about him?* I put my fears aside and leveled with my girlfriend.

"My parents and I have very different views about how I should live my life.

I don't talk about them too much because there's a rift between us. They think I should be living with them and collecting disability instead of pursuing engineering."

"Collecting disability? Why?"

I took a deep breath and exhaled. "I have schizophrenia. I haven't been to the hospital in almost a year, but I see a psychiatrist every week to make sure that I'm doing OK." I looked at her intently, expecting the worst. *Will she walk out of the restaurant on me? Slap me?* I had no idea.

She looked away, out of the window of the restaurant. All I heard was the music over the speakers, playing Elvis's "Wooden Heart."

Can't you see I love you?
Please don't break my heart in two.
That's not hard to do,
Cause I don't have a wooden heart.

I tried to corral her gaze back to my eyes by folding my hand around hers, but she continued her thousand-yard stare.

I had known this subject would come up but was still taken by surprise. The conversation had shifted toward it so suddenly that disclosing my illness was like one of those waves that broke overhead without warning, crushing anything below.

Finally, Claudia took my other hand in hers. "Don't worry. I'll still be your girlfriend. I wouldn't leave you just because you have schizophrenia."

"Seriously? You won't leave me?"

She squeezed my hands. "No. You're ambitious, handsome, hardworking, intelligent. I'm proud to be with you."

A huge weight lifted off my heavy heart. I was suddenly giddy with joy. "You have no idea what it means to hear that. I was worried about telling you." I hesitated. Claudia's thousand-yard stare had me second-guessing what she had said. "You really believe all those nice things you said about me?"

"It's all true." She leaned over and kissed me on the cheek. "But I don't know how it'll work out between us." She turned solemn. "My family isn't crazy about me dating an American."

"Really?" My heart sank.

"No. They wanted me to marry Bruno because he was Brazilian. Now that they know about you, they're furious." Tears began falling down her cheeks.

"Please don't cry. We'll work it out."

"Oh, Hank!" She leaned on my shoulder, and I put my arm around her. I paid the check, and we left.

After departing the train from downtown, we took our time. Silence dominated, though Claudia had stopped crying. I held her hand as we strolled. It was Halloween, and children scampered from house to house with their parents in tow.

Back at her apartment, I expected to drop Claudia off and leave, but she invited me in, led me into her bedroom and took off her dress. We made love.

Afterward, as we lay in bed, I felt as if in a pleasant dream. Claudia was asleep next to me with her hair splayed out on her pillow. *She is a true blessing in my life.* I decided at that point that she had to be with me.

I moved closer to her so that our bodies touched. For the first time in years, I was truly happy. My nose nestled in the pillow, full of her sweet scent. When she woke, she gazed at me with sleepy eyes and smiled.

"I love you." I stroked her hair.

"I love you, too," she answered.

．　．　．　．　．

I traveled to Miami with Claudia to meet her parents. Miami's tropical setting contrasted sharply with Philadelphia's late fall. I sensed the climate change right away as we walked out of the airport to the curb and searched for her parents' Mercedes amid the sun and humidity.

Once in the car and on our way to their apartment, Claudia and her parents chatted in Portuguese while I zoned out and looked at the Miami skyline. The open windows let in a breeze as we traveled to a section of town called Kendall.

When we arrived at their apartment, which was neatly arranged inside on a bare wooden floor, we drank traditional Brazilian tea.

"Claudia tells me that you are studying to become an engineer," said her father, who wore a pressed, starched white shirt and brown pants. He was of small stature and had straight jet-black hair.

"Yes." I brushed my hand through my hair, which I did when I was really nervous, and then clasped my hands together.

"That's a difficult field. How are your studies coming along?"

"I'm doing well…in my second year."

"Do you know where you'd like to work after you graduate?" He studied me with his soft black eyes, the same ones Claudia had.

"Near San Francisco."

"But that's so far away. If Claudia goes with you, we'll miss her being on the East Coast." A look of obvious concern crossed his face.

"Don't worry Mr. Barbosa. I'll take good care of her. I love your daughter."

He didn't answer but only looked at me with those soft eyes with a hint of sadness. The mother, whose skin was much darker, sat quietly, pensive while listening to the two of us.

The next day, Claudia and I ventured out to South Beach. We massaged our feet in the sand and lay in bathing suits on towels, soaking in the sun. The beach was almost full of sunbathers, and the water was a crystal light blue.

Once again, Claudia broke the silence. "Are you really sure about going to California?"

"Of course. What about you?"

"I don't know. I've never been so far from my parents before. And what if it doesn't work out between us?"

I stopped reading my book and turned to her. "I've thought about this. You can take classes, you know, the nursing ones that you always wanted to take, instead of waiting tables. That's after you've established residency. With your GED, you could enroll at a university. We'll get a place together so you won't have to pay rent."

Her eyes drifted into a vacant stare again, as if lost in thought. "I just don't know."

"Just think about it."

Despite her doubts, Claudia became my rock. She made my worries disappear, and I could tell by how happy she was with me that our love was strong. Her eyes lit up when she spotted me entering the restaurant. Others stared at us in admiration as we walked the streets of Philadelphia. Her laughter and accented chatter caught the ears of bystanders and made them turn when we were together.

I worried that something would go wrong—a failure in a course, a fading of the magic between us, another hospitalization. But Claudia dismissed my anxiety with her compassion and unwavering love, which made me stronger.

Nothing, not even my father, can prevent me from achieving my dreams now.

36.

In school, I amped up my efforts to do well on assignments and exams. I worked with a tutor, met with professors one on one, and spent extra time in the library.

The first quarter reviewed ideas that I'd studied the previous year, until final exams approached. Then new material I'd never been tested on before appeared because of my hospital stay. During finals, I calmed myself with deep breaths, waiting in my seat for the professor to hand out the exam, though my hands shook visibly. I cleared my head as I read questions and marked my answer sheet. *Stay calm!* After the exams, my heart pounded when I checked my scores online. B minus (not bad), C plus (could be better), B plus (Great!)

. . . . .

I made it through the following two quarters and my first summer internship. Then Claudia and I scrounged up some money for a flight to Los Angeles to take a vacation before my third year began in September. We planned to stay with Zach and Jenny in their three-bedroom house. Fortunately, they kept a guest room for visitors.

A warm breeze greeted us when we exited the airport and waited on the curb for Zach to pick us up. The sun shone, and the glitz of LA showed already, with fancy cars all around. It was Claudia's first visit to California. The locals' loud outfits and cars fascinated her.

I wondered about Zach's reaction to Claudia. No one in my family knew that she was mulatto, only that she was Brazilian and worked as a server at Pots and Pans. While Claudia took in the Southern California flavor, I stood bracing myself for Zach's reaction. I didn't tell my girlfriend of my worry, though.

For the most part, Claudia's skin color hadn't been an issue. Philadelphia was a melting pot of ethnicities. In the back of my mind, though, I knew it would be an issue with my father. He was a bigot through and through, ever since I could remember. Even though Jocelyn was black, my father didn't want anything to do with black people in general. No black neighbors, no black coworkers while he worked, and no black country club members.

My mother was kind to Jocelyn, but I didn't know how she'd feel about Claudia, either.

Zach's BMW pulled up. His eyes went wide when he saw Claudia standing next to me. His lips parted in astonishment, I supposed. I held my breath as he got out and shook Claudia's hand with no expression on his face, as if he were stunned. Claudia was gracious, not showing any disdain.

"How was your trip?" he asked me after he greeted Claudia.

"Everything went smooth," I replied.

We loaded our baggage, and Zach pulled the car away.

"Jenny's excited to finally meet you, Claudia," said Zach. "And Michaela's always up for company."

"It's been so long since I've seen Michaela," I said. "How old is she?"

"She's four."

"And how is Jenny?"

"She's good." Zach's continued stoic expression worried me. I couldn't tell for sure if he was still stunned at the color of Claudia's skin or if maybe he was just tired or preoccupied.

"What about work?" I asked, changing the subject in the hopes that the conversation would liven up.

"Work is good. Can't complain."

We drove on. I wasn't having much luck with conversation with Zach, so I turned my head halfway toward Claudia. "How you feeling, Claudia?"

"Fine. It's so different here! It reminds me of Miami."

"Claudia's parents live in Miami," I said to Zach.

"Mmm," said Zach.

Zach definitely wasn't his usual gregarious self. I just hoped Jenny wouldn't have the same cool reaction. It would be a long visit if she and Zach didn't warm up to Claudia.

We pulled up Zach's driveway, and Michaela came running out the front door. Finally, Zach's expression changed to one of happiness, and he picked up his daughter. "Hi, my little princess. How are you? Look who's here!"

Michaela glanced at Claudia and me. "Uncle Hank!"

"That's right, Uncle Hank!" said Zach. "And look who's with him. That's his girlfriend, Claudia."

"Hi, Claudia," squeaked Michaela.

Claudia broke into a smile and reached to touch Michaela on the arm. Zach's happy expression didn't change when Claudia did this, which relieved me.

Then Jenny came out the front door of the white stucco house with orange Mexican roof tiles. She and Claudia shook hands. Jenny stroked Michaela's light-brown hair. "We have visitors, Michaela. Did you say hello to them?"

"Yes, Mommy."

"Good girl."

Without so much as a glance at Zach, Jenny continued. "We have the guest room all set up for you two. Make yourselves at home. We've got plenty of food. Excuse the toys in the living room. Michaela's always making a mess."

Jenny's welcome was a relief. On top of the issue of getting along with Claudia, she never knew that I was in jail during my second episode of my battle with schizophrenia. I always wondered if she'd treat *me* differently if she knew I'd been arrested, but now wasn't the time to tell her, I decided. Even if Zach had told her, she wasn't showing any signs of being distant.

"Let's go inside," said Jenny, taking Michaela from Zach, who then took the suitcases inside. "Hank, when's the last time we saw you? Christmas a couple years ago?"

"It's been a while." She'd forgotten about, or didn't mention, that she saw me briefly after my hospital stay in San Vicente. I'd stayed a night at their house with Chrissy before flying back to Atlanta. Even though Claudia knew about my hospitalizations, I was glad Jenny didn't bring it up. It would have been a downer to the happy occasion.

In the evening, we settled around the back patio table to have hamburgers from the grill. Zach let out a sigh as he sat down after taking the last of the burgers off the fire and setting it with the rest on a plate. He helped himself to one and dressed it. The rest of us had a head start on our food.

Michaela, who'd already had her dinner, played in the backyard. Zach broke the silence. "So how did your internship go? You were telling me that you had to do one over the summer."

"It went well. I have to do it again next summer," I said as I piled more potato salad onto my plate. "I worked in a professor's lab. A professor who used to work for NASA."

"Wow!" exclaimed Jenny, her eyes wide.

"It was pass or fail, and I passed."

"What sort of work did you do?" asked Zach.

"I helped to run experiments and gather data on designs that the professor himself made. It was intense work."

"That's pretty cool, Hank," said Zach, who then turned his head to Claudia but didn't say anything. His expression went flat when he considered her for a split second. So far, I was the only one who'd noticed Zach's lack of interest in my girlfriend.

Jenny, who'd been eyeing Michaela and hadn't seen that Zach ignored Claudia, turned her attention to my girlfriend. "Do you have any siblings, Claudia?"

"I have an older brother, but he lives back in Rio de Janeiro. My parents live in Miami."

"How long have they lived in the United States?" Jenny asked.

"I moved here with them ten years ago."

"And what made you move to Philadelphia?" Jenny continued.

"A friend from Brazil who worked as a server already lived there. She invited me to work in the same restaurant. I wanted to live in a city where mostly English was spoken to improve my own, so I moved three years ago."

"Claudia's English is better than when I first met her. It's been, what, over two years that we've known each other?" I asked.

While we carried on about learning English, Zach left the table without having finished his meal to play with Michaela.

"Honey, don't you want to eat before your food gets cold?" asked Jenny.

"I'll be back in a minute," said Zach, who began pushing Michaela on the swing set.

Zach's behavior didn't change throughout the visit, but fortunately Jenny and Michaela got along well with Claudia. When Claudia and I were alone sightseeing or spending time on the beach, she didn't mention Zach's cool demeanor. But I was afraid she'd mention it sooner or later.

Is it my schizophrenia that causes these fears or my own rationale? I couldn't figure it out.

. . . . .

The morning after Claudia and I arrived back in Philadelphia, my phone woke me. Even though it was 9:30 a.m., I was on West Coast time still. It was my father.

"Hank, Zach tells me that Claudia is black. Are you serious about her?"

"Of course. Why wouldn't I be?" I said. Anger that Zach had given this information to my father grew inside me.

"You know I don't approve of this relationship, don't you?" asked my father, his voice rising.

"You haven't even met her."

"Son, there's never been anyone of color in our family, ever. I don't intend to let Claudia be the first to taint our bloodline. Do you understand me?"

"If you're going to be that narrow-minded about who I might marry, then I don't want to talk about it."

"Now listen. We *are* going to talk. I want you to break it off with her."

"No. I'm doing nothing of the sort." My voice was calm but firm.

"I don't know what's got into you. First, this engineering dream and now a black woman."

"Claudia and I get along very well. I'm not going to stop seeing her because you don't approve of her skin color."

"You don't realize what you're doing! Consider your mother and my feelings, as well as those of the rest of the family. Your grandfather would turn over in his grave if he knew of this!"

"This is the twenty-first century. Times are different from when Grandpa was alive."

"Shit," muttered my father. "She's not welcome in my house, so don't bother bringing her here. Your mother feels the same way. Goodbye."

I felt a knot in my stomach. Again, my father had caught me off guard with his severity. Claudia would eventually catch on, if she hadn't already, that my family didn't accept her. There wouldn't be any easy way to tell her, either.

37.

I trudged through my third year and completed my second summer internship. For my last year, I had to prepare a senior project to present in May.

At the beginning of my senior year, I waited in the office of my senior project advisor and tapped my fingers together. Dr. Hill, the calculus professor, was my advisor.

"What do you have for me today?" he asked. His desk was neatly arranged, with a desktop computer keyboard and screen to his left and a stack of papers to his right.

"A new proposal, Dr. Hill," I said.

"Ah, good. The deadline is tomorrow. I hope this one is satisfactory."

I had attempted one proposal already, which Dr. Hill had nixed because another student in the program had already proposed the same topic. I wanted to do my original project on the different aspects in the construction of rockets, an idea stemming from my strong interest in them. Another student, a hot-shot straight-A student, had beat me to it. I'd had to scramble to come up with something different.

I handed my advisor my proposal, and he began reading.

If this one wasn't acceptable, I'd really be in trouble. I took a deep breath to calm down. Dr. Hill put an index finger to his cheek and a thumb under his chin; his poker face didn't reveal any emotion. I couldn't stand the suspense!

Finally, he spoke. "So the former banker wants to investigate the construction of two bridges and compare and contrast them. Am I right?"

The faculty and students knew by now that I used to work in a bank. I was an anomaly since I switched careers. Almost everyone frowned on that fact. I didn't know why. *Because I'm older? Because I passed on a more lucrative career to pursue engineering?* Some students had even said I was crazy for giving up banking.

"Correct," I replied.

"Mmm…the Walt Whitman and the Chesapeake Bay Bridge." He paused. "Do you have any initial thoughts about them?"

"The Walt Whitman is a standard suspension bridge, much shorter than the Chesapeake Bay Bridge. The westward span of the Bay Bridge is also suspension, but the first span built, the eastern span, is a cantilever bridge, a much different type of construction. Comparing and contrasting the two would be feasible and interesting." I exhaled.

"I see you've done some initial research—good. For a project such as this, there are plenty of resources."

"I checked out several books from the library. I've looked up some information online."

"I'm not going to lie, Hank. This is a challenging project. Not for the weak of heart."

"I can do it, Dr. Hill," I said with a smile, though inside my stomach was doing flips.

"For a student, this project is ideal. The idea is original and fresh." Dr. Hill leaned forward and put his hands in a fist on his desk. "Go for it, Hank."

. . . . .

I did my research, studying the construction of the Bay Bridge in Maryland and then doing the same with the Walt Whitman, the bridge in Philadelphia named after the famous poet in United States history.

Living in Philadelphia gave the opportunity to travel across the Walt Whitman, but the Bay Bridge lay two to three hours away by car.

In January, after I'd done the bulk of my research, I made the drive to see the Bay Bridge myself. Claudia came along with me as the Subaru huffed across the behemoth. A wind howled across the Bay, made white caps, and pushed the hatchback toward the shoulder of the highway at times. As I made the crossing, I remembered the support system and appreciated that it had withstood over fifty years of use. I was impressed by the volume of traffic it handled, especially in the summertime when beachgoers from Washington, DC and Baltimore went to Ocean City, a popular tourist resort that was easily accessible because of the bridge.

The Walt Whitman also accommodated plenty of vehicles, letting commuters from New Jersey travel to and from Philadelphia over the Delaware River. The suburbs in New Jersey were heavily populated, and this bridge was one of the main thoroughfares into the city.

I prayed that I had reviewed the right resources. They needed to be effective in presenting enough information to give me a solid background in my understanding of the engineering involved in bridges. If they didn't give me this foundation, I was in trouble, especially for the question and answer portion of my presentation, which came at the end. I had been meeting with Dr. Hill regularly, though, and there wasn't any cause for concern, at least none that I could foresee.

· · · · ·

Dr. Sloane and I sat in our respective lounge chairs in his office in late January. As usual, he clicked a pen into writing position and prepared his notepad. I leaned back in my chair and breathed easy. This was our fifth year of working together; I had become accustomed to our weekly appointments.

"How is your schoolwork going?" he started.

"My main concern is my senior project. The rest of my courses are electives or easy requirements. I finished my research, so now I'm beginning to write up my findings."

"It seems the most difficult part is over then."

"I'm anxious about presenting in front of my class and faculty, though. I have a phobia when it comes to speaking in front of crowds."

"That's a matter of experience. The more you practice, the more comfortable you'll feel."

"I hope so."

"How are things with your parents—your father?"

"I haven't visited them in over a year. I speak with my mother once a week, but I seldom talk with my father. They're still upset about me dating Claudia."

"When's the last time you spoke with him?"

"Two months ago. It was a short conversation about how I was doing in school. Nothing of much substance."

"At least he's acknowledging your studies. Before he kept insisting that you go on disability."

"But now that Claudia and I are serious about each other, I want my mother and him to accept her. That's even more important to me."

"You can't have everything, but I understand how much it hurts you to not have their approval of Claudia. Even adult children want the acceptance of their parents."

"And her parents still don't approve of me because I'm not Brazilian. We're both upset about that, too."

"Mmm. Yes, it's hard for both of you." He paused. "You have to live your life, Hank. Even if it means going against your father's wishes. If you and Claudia are right for each other, your father has to accept that fact. If he doesn't, you aren't bound to him financially or in any other way. Don't feel obligated to bow down to his view of how he wants you to live. The same goes for Claudia's parents. You can't please everyone all the time."

"I've struggled with wanting to please my father and live my dreams at the same time, but I'm finding that it's not possible."

"Of course not," exclaimed Dr. Sloane. "He's wanted you to follow in his footsteps all these years, something that you're not willing to do."

"I still worry about my mother. I mean, Chrissy is fine now that the needle stick is behind her. She's working a general surgery residency in Atlanta and dating a guy that makes her happy. But my mother's a different situation. She can't escape like my siblings and I did."

"You do all that you can to maintain your relationship with her. Don't feel you have to be responsible for her happiness." He wrote on his notepad. "How does she feel about you dating Claudia?"

I frowned. "She sides with my father, always asking me when I'm going to date someone more conventional."

"You're not in an easy position, Hank. It's hard to break family tradition."

"I'm seeing that. And, of course, my future with Claudia and NASA hinge on whether I can complete my program. That's stressful, too."

Dr. Sloane raised his eyebrows. "Is there any cause for concern?"

"Nothing. It's just that relapse is always a possibility. It's something I fear. One more extended absence from my program and I'm out. Another hospitalization could cause that." I changed the subject, leaning forward slightly. "So how *am* I doing with my illness?"

"Very well, Hank. Very well. I don't see any symptoms of relapse. You've been taking your medicine as always and coming to see me every week. You're stable."

I leaned back. "Awesome!"

"Just keep taking care of yourself, especially at this critical point in your program."

"I have interviews coming up for work after graduation. I travel to California in two weeks to meet with a representative of NASA for my first of three interviews."

Dr. Sloane's eyebrows rose. "Really? That's great!" He scribbled something down. "They might ask some difficult questions, Hank. You'll have to be prepared."

"I'm working on that."

38.

I sat in a room outside the office of the human resources contact who was about to interview me at NASA. I'd had a phone interview and two in-person interviews with various personnel and had made it to the final in-person interview. Though the weather in California that February day was mild and sunny and the temperature in the lobby was comfortable, my hands perspired, and my mouth was dry. I hadn't expected to make it this far in the hiring process. The time had come to close the deal.

My year off at Premier came up in each of the two previous in-person interviews. I explained it just as before. I suffered a concussion during a robbery and missed too much school to continue with my original class. I figured I'd put that hurdle behind me.

The representative behind the closed door won't ask me about it again, will he?

The HR representative appeared, wearing a gray suit and burgundy tie. We went into his office. He motioned toward a plush leather chair in front of his expansive desk. "Please, have a seat."

"How was the trip out from Philadelphia?" he asked after we'd settled into our chairs.

"Everything went fine. A long flight but otherwise, the trip was good." I smiled, exuding a friendly persona. I fought to not let my nerves show, trying not to run my hand through my hair. I'd had a couple of other interviews with two smaller engineering firms—one in Texas and one in Florida—but they weren't located in the Bay Area and weren't as prestigious as NASA.

The HR representative examined what must have been my curriculum vitae. He scratched his cheek with an index finger. "Your CV is impressive. Your grades are solid. Your experience with the Premier professor served you well over the two summers of your internship. You discussed your career change from working in finance with my colleague already." He paused. "One thing I'd like to cover is that you took off almost a year from classes. What prompted you to do that?"

There was that question again! I kept a straight face to hide my surprise. "I was mugged and suffered a head wound and concussion. By the time of my discharge, I'd missed too much school to continue with my original class. So I worked in a restaurant until the following fall, when I joined the class a year behind."

"That sounds terrible!" he said. His eyes were wide. "Did they ever find the perpetrators?"

"Unfortunately not," I replied.

"Wow. That must've been some blow to the head." He studied me.

I looked him straight in the eye. "It was. It knocked me out for a couple of seconds."

"I'm sorry to hear that." He leaned back in his chair. "And tell me about your work experience in the restaurant." My temporary job had been a subject of previous interviews as well. Again, I answered the same as I had before.

"It was hard, both physically and mentally. I definitely appreciated being a student again when it was over. But I met my current girlfriend there, though. So I feel lucky, in that sense, that I took the time off."

"Of course. Tell me the most important lesson you learned from your break, aside from meeting your girlfriend."

I paused. The most important lesson was not to get complacent about my schizophrenia, after it had been properly diagnosed. But I didn't go there. "I learned to be grateful for the opportunity to study engineering and possibly work for an organization such as NASA. I believe God has blessed me."

He nodded. "And what made you look for employment with NASA, Hank?"

"The opportunity to work with so many brilliant minds. Ever since I was a boy and visited the Air and Space Museum in Washington, DC, I've been amazed at the technology involved in what man has accomplished aboveground since the twentieth century. And rockets. They've always fascinated me ever since I was old enough to watch fireworks on the Fourth of July." I'd prepared this answer long before I even applied to the organization.

"It certainly is a unique agency. Have you heard about any missions our mechanical engineers have worked on here?"

"The Kepler mission, the Hubble Telescope, the International Space Station—all incredible projects!"

My interviewer must've seen my face light up because he smiled broadly.

I was quiet, waiting for more.

"We're constantly improving our teams. Not only is the importance of your foundation from Premier key, but also your own personality and how you work with others on your team. We realize no one is perfect, but we strive for perfection in our missions. As an individual at NASA, you must constantly assess your own personality as well as your work performance. If there are any deficiencies, you must strive to correct them. Do I make myself clear?"

Again, I thought of my schizophrenia but put it aside. "Yes, sir."

"We work with the model set forth by Charles Pellerin, a past astrophysicist who worked here. He set the gold standard for assessing performance among team members—even wrote a book about it. I suggest you take a look at it." He raised his chin in a show of pride, I supposed. He continued, "What are your other interests besides engineering? Tell me what you do in your free time."

I told the representative about my experiences surfing in the Bay Area. Then, after answering some questions about my family, which I portrayed to be as normal as possible, I observed my interviewer putting both hands on the armrests of his chair as if about to stand.

"I'd like to introduce you to your potential immediate supervisor. Follow me please."

We stood and walked down a corridor and into another building, took an elevator to the fifth floor and after my interviewer scanned his access key, entered a lobby. He walked with his head high, as if he were a head honcho, even on the floor of another building.

My potential supervisor came out of his office to greet us. He had a crew cut and a goatee. He offered his hand. "How are you, Hank?"

We proceeded into his office and sat. "I'll tell you more about what you'd be doing if you are hired," he began. "The International Space Station project has been ongoing for decades now. We're sending more supplies and astronauts up to it as time goes by. That means more and more rockets are launched from various locations every year to transport these supplies and men and women. Not only must we maintain the safety of these individuals and cargo, but we also must ensure the efficiency of the rockets. We're even working on reusable ones at this time. The type that land safely back on Earth after their return from space. You'd crunch numbers, gather data, and so forth, working under senior engineers such as myself. I can't tell you more until you sign the contract and are on board officially."

"I understand," I said.

"This project is already underway, so you'd have to jump in and get your feet wet quickly. Do you think you're up for the challenge?"

It was as if my potential supervisor didn't waste time beating around the bush because he needed to return to his work. His intensity matched the importance of his job title.

For me, working on rockets bound for the International Space Station piqued my interest. It was something out of my wildest dreams!

"Of course," I replied without any hesitation, trying both to tone down my excitement and hide my intimidation of the whole interview process.

He continued. "Along with knowing the principles that you learned in school, you'd have to juggle a whole lot of personalities, some of which are more impatient and exacting than others. The key is to be as precise as possible with your work.

"We enjoy what we do, but with the limited funding we have and the deadlines that we face, there isn't much room for error. Working under pressure will be a daily occurrence for you as well as the rest of the team, but remember, you aren't by yourself. You'll have others to back you up and to lean on."

Again, I thought of my illness—whether I'd relapse under such working conditions. My hands became clammy, and I gulped. For a moment, I pictured a headline in the newspaper: "Glitch in Rocket Sends Astronauts to Their Death; Engineer with Schizophrenia to Blame." But I put it out of my mind and replied, "I can handle it."

He smiled broadly. "That's what I like to hear." He shook my hand and showed the HR representative and me out back to the elevator.

Back in HR, I stood ready to leave.

"One more thing, Hank," said my original interviewer, standing in front of me.

My heart beat wildly, wondering what he was about to say. I had made it through the gauntlet so far, but I couldn't help feeling that the interview could still go awry.

"If we offer you the position, we expect you to graduate on time in May," he said with a solemn face.

I thought for a split second about my final project, which I had to present to graduate. All was going well with my topic on the construction of the Walt Whitman and Chesapeake Bay Bridges. There was no real reason for concern there.

"Of course. I understand."

39.

Back in Philadelphia, I sat on my couch with my laptop on my coffee table on a Tuesday evening. My presentation loomed ten days away. Afterward, I had one more week of classes to take exams in my electives. These exams wouldn't be difficult—it was my presentation that worried me the most.

The material wasn't hard to comprehend, but the task of standing in front of my entire class and faculty weighed on my mind. I was no natural-born orator. Being the center of attention at a podium wasn't my idea of fun. Just the thought of everyone's eyes on me made me jittery.

I recalled previous times when I had to speak in front of a classroom full of peers in college. My hands had shaken. My voice had quivered. I'd feared meeting everyone's eyes. It was always a painful experience.

I continued my work when my phone rang. At 10:00 p.m., I didn't expect any calls, even from Claudia. It was my mother; I knew something must be wrong. She never called me at this hour.

"Something's happened to your father. He started slurring his speech and then collapsed. I'm with him at the hospital now. They're running some tests…"

It was a shock to hear this. My father was so strong. He'd hardly been sick a day in his life since I could remember.

"Are you all right?" I asked her.

"I'm so worried. He was in such good health. Apart from his cocktails and cigars, he didn't have any unhealthy habits. I can only guess that it was a stroke."

"A stroke! This doesn't sound good." I thought for a few seconds. "I'm coming to Atlanta. I'll get an early start and drive down tomorrow."

"There's nothing you can do, Hank. You don't want to miss too much school and not graduate. You can't afford that now with your job lined up."

"I can miss a few days. I'll see you tomorrow night."

The next day, during the long drive, I wondered if my father wanted to see me. It had been almost two years since we'd seen each other. But there was no hesitation for me. I needed to be with him and my mother at this critical time. There was no way I'd sit in Philadelphia with my father teetering on his deathbed.

Will he even recognize me in the first place?

His brain might have suffered so much damage that he wouldn't. If that were so, my last forced conversations over the phone for the past two years would be my last interactions with him. That made me especially sad. To know that I never reconciled my differences with my father before he died. To know he never accepted my career ambitions and my girlfriend.

My mother had given me little information. Apparently, the doctors still needed to evaluate him. *Will he die before I even arrive?* Chrissy was in town and knew just as much as my mother. I wondered about Zach being all the way on the West Coast, if he could make it to Atlanta soon.

After making the fourteen-hour car ride, I arrived at the dimly lit mansion. My mother greeted me at the front door. Her eyes were bloodshot, with deep circles under them. Chrissy's car was in the driveway.

I embraced her, and she began sobbing and trembling.

"How's Dad?" I asked after her emotions had subsided.

"Not good. The doctors weren't able to reopen the blood vessel that clotted in his brain until after some damage occurred. His prognosis is poor. After he woke and the doctors told him he might not live, he kept saying, 'I want to die at home. I want to die at home, not in a hospital.'"

I didn't know what to say. I held my mother while she continued to cry. Grateful now that I'd made the long drive, I continued with more questions. "Does Zach know the prognosis?"

"Yes. He's flying in tomorrow. It...it may not be long for your father now. We've arranged transportation for him from the hospital to rest more comfortably here. And a nurse to take care of him before he..."

Chrissy came to the door with hot chocolate for my mother and me. I embraced Chrissy, who had a grim look on her face.

"Is he awake?" I continued.

"He was conscious but uncomfortable and in pain. There's no sense in you going to see him now. He's resting, and the doctors said they'd call if anything changed overnight. You'll see him in the morning," said Chrissy.

I was shocked, not able to begin to imagine life without my father even though we were estranged.

I guided my mother to the kitchen. Chrissy followed. We sat at the dinner table. At first, silence dominated. Then Chrissy broke it. "You know, Dad asked for you today," she said, directing her eyes to me.

"That's right. He kept asking, 'Where's Hank? Where's Hank?'" chimed my mother.

"He asked for me?" I asked.

"He was very agitated—said he wanted to see you before he died." Chrissy's eyes welled with tears now. "It's like he's refusing to go before he sees you."

"Me? What about Zach?"

"Of course he wants to see Zach, but he wants to see you the most," said my mother. "He kept mumbling today, 'Hank and his rockets, Hank and his rockets…'"

That night I didn't sleep much. Instead, I anticipated my visit to my father the following day. *What does it mean, him wanting to see me above everyone else in the family? Will he even be in his right mind by tomorrow? Had he been in his right mind today when he called for me?* I still feared what he'd say to me after all this time despite what I'd learned from my mother and Chrissy. *Will he tell me off once and for all before he dies?* Finally, a few hours before dawn, I dozed off and awoke to my alarm the next morning.

· · · · ·

At the hospital, my father's eyes lit up, and a faint smile came to his mouth when he saw me standing at his side in the intensive care unit. He remained silent, gazed into my eyes, and put his hand on mine, which rested on the bed rail.

My emotions choked me, but I managed to say, "Hi, Dad." When I saw the medical equipment around my father and his body so debilitated, I had to fight back my grim feelings. Even though Chrissy had already briefed me, I could tell from this sight that his condition was serious.

I held my breath and waited for him to say something. I didn't want to fill the void with meaningless conversation. Besides, he strained to speak; I didn't interrupt his effort.

"Hank," he said. His voice was strange, so strange, as if he were developmentally challenged. "I'm so proud of you."

He hadn't said this to me in years, since I graduated with my finance degree. I was speechless. My mother wiped away some saliva that had come down his cheek as he spoke.

"You had the guts to go after your passion in life," he continued, barely comprehensible and still looking into my eyes with such happiness. "Me…" His smile faded, and he looked away, as if contemplating something in the past, long ago. "I wasn't as brave."

I stood motionless, waiting for more, unable to speak.

"My passion was literature, Hank. I wanted to be a professor, but…" He gulped and exhaled, gathering the energy to say more, I supposed. "But I let my father convince me otherwise." He directed his eyes back to me. "I was envious of you for having the courage to become an engineer for a long time. But now…" He paused again. "Now all I feel is pride of what you've accomplished, despite your illness.

"I want you to look after your mother. I know I could've been a better husband and father. I failed both of you in that way. I'm at God's mercy now, though. He's to decide my fate." He gave my hand a squeeze. "I love you, son."

My father's eyes closed. He seemed to fall asleep all of a sudden, at peace. An alarm from one of the monitors sounded, and a nurse sitting outside the room dismissed us. She closed the door and drew the curtains along the glass wall. Another nurse arrived and directed us to the waiting room, beyond the entrance to the unit.

Then Zach arrived straight from the airport. He'd taken a red-eye flight from Los Angeles. After filling him in on the latest about my father, we all sat in the waiting room in a stunned silence.

Zach and I moved to go to the cafeteria to get coffee. In the otherwise empty elevator, Zach said, "Look, I know you and I don't talk too often, but I wanted to tell you that Dad had been talking about you a lot lately when I spoke with him over the phone before his stroke."

"What's he been saying?" I braced myself for negative comments about me, my career, and my girlfriend, despite what he'd just told me in his patient bed.

"He kept asking what Claudia was like, whether she treated you right. How your studies were going. After your NASA interview, he told me to call him as soon as I had talked to you about it. He seemed real interested in your life."

We left the elevator and headed to the cafeteria on the ground floor. "Why didn't he talk to me directly?" I asked. "He could've called."

"He mentioned something once about you being angry with him and about not wanting to cause a bigger rift than there already was."

Shocked, I said nothing. I'd always thought my father didn't care about me, but now I saw that he cared a lot more than he let on.

Zach continued. "He has a soft spot for you. I think deep down he really wants you to succeed in engineering. Just be careful what you say to him if these are his last few days. Don't regret not granting him his last wishes."

I was lost in thought. "What are they?" I finally asked.

"I don't know. We'll have to wait and see."

Two days passed. As my father had instructed, he was moved from the hospital to the mansion, where a nurse tended to him in his spacious master bedroom. Jocelyn cooked his favorite meals, though he couldn't eat much. Instead, the nurse gave nutrition intravenously.

But his health declined. He struggled more and more to speak, and his frustration at not being able to communicate was evident. His face turned a deep red before he managed a few words, which reminded me of how he looked before one of his temper tantrums.

Except there were no more tirades. He was at peace, despite his physical troubles. Each time I sat by his bed, his eyes glowed with pride. Finally, one evening, after he'd slept for hours, he woke and asked for me.

After I'd taken a seat beside him, he stuttered some incomprehensible words. He spat and turned his head back and forth, unable to speak.

"H-Hank. I'm s-sorry." Tears rolled down the sides of his cheeks. "You s-suffered more th-than anybody in the f-family. Forgive me."

His eyes pleaded with me in the midst of his anguish. It was a look I'd never forget.

I wiped the tears from his face. "I forgive you."

That was the last I saw of my father alive. He passed within a few hours.

．　．　．　．　．

The funeral was three days later. Many attended—golfing buddies, old coworkers from my father's bank, family, and friends. The minister who gave the service gave a lovely sermon about passing into God's kingdom, though I didn't remember all of what he said. At the reception afterward, I tried to smile and stood with my mother in the mansion.

The whole week, from the time I got my mother's phone call to the day I returned to Philadelphia, was a blur. Three days remained before I presented my project.

40.

The night before my presentation, I willed myself to review my notes one more time. Fatigue dulled my senses. My apartment offered nothing but silence and the odor of stale coffee at the late hour. I dozed but woke when my head hit the keyboard. *That never happened before!* Surprised, I rose from my couch and paced back and forth in my living room to wake up. The wooden floor creaked, and soon, my neighbor from below pounded on his ceiling for quiet. I ceased and sat down again.

I had been back for three days after my father's funeral, had been losing sleep, and felt the pressure to present the following day. I had seen Claudia twice since my return, but she was working this night. She'd mentioned sleeping more to me. I hadn't been able to mourn my father's death completely yet, and my mind kept going back to his last words.

It had all come down to this. Eight years of studying, doing blue-collar work, and battling my mental illness. Now I had reached the pinnacle of an engineering student's life and had to perform and perform well the next morning. I couldn't let my nerves get the best of me.

On the other side of the horizon lay my NASA job. I hadn't even begun yet but had sacrificed so much to get hired. Just the thought of working my dream occupation made me giddy. I just had to finish my presentation and the last week of exams.

My phone rang. The cable television box read 12:30 a.m. *Who is it at this hour?* The area code was unfamiliar, the location in California. I let the call go to voice mail and waited, tense, staring at the display. Finally, a beep. Holding the phone to my ear, I played the message and listened to three minutes of silence. The sound of my breath, coming harder now, was audible. *What is the meaning of the call? Is someone threatening me?*

Breathe in, breathe out. I had to concentrate on this action. I couldn't erase the thought that someone was out to harm me by crank calling. I sat holding my head in my hands, squeezing it as if to stop my train of thought. But the thoughts kept coming, like a runaway truck.

I couldn't stand the thought of being in danger again. I had to calm myself—maybe by talking on the phone with someone—or my madness might overtake me! It was only 9:30 p.m. in California. *Tom will be awake.* I held my phone but stopped short of dialing him. *What will I say? What will he say? He'll probably tell me to go to the ER. I can't do that now!* I thought of calling Claudia, but that wouldn't help. *She'll probably end up doing the same thing, telling me to go to the hospital.*

I leaned back and stared at the ceiling, regrouping. *The call must have been a mistake. That's all. Nothing to be afraid of.*

Then another call! The same California number appeared! I sent the call to voice mail and tossed my phone on the chipped coffee table in front of me. This time there was no message.

"Oh God," I whispered, closing my eyes. My chest heaved with deep breaths, my bare foot tapping the floor. Opening my eyes, I focused now on my phone again. My psychiatrist's emergency number came to mind. *He will certainly send me to the hospital, dashing my hopes of graduating on time and taking the job at NASA. I'll even be dismissed from Premier permanently as well.*

I was on my own if I was to present my project the next day. All the stress in my life and recent lost sleep had pushed me to a breaking point, even though I'd been taking my medicine. I remembered the coping mechanisms I had learned over the years. Control my breathing, analyze thought processes, and keep calm. Moving to my bed and reciting a few prayers, I lay down and closed my eyes.

I remembered a bottle of rum in my kitchen cabinet. *Maybe a shot or two will calm me down? No! I have to stay sharp for my presentation.* I put the idea of drinking myself to sleep out of my mind.

Minutes passed like hours. *The calls were a random event—no reason to worry. Don't get so anxious!* I shut off the lamp on the night table in my bedroom. The overhead light from the living room crept into the doorway, illuminating my room as when I was a child. My mind drifted to the fear that overtook me while I listened to my father yell at my mother. *Don't let the fear take control!*

. . . . .

Realizing instantly that my alarm didn't sound, I woke with a start. In my distress, I'd forgotten to set it. Light filtered through the bedroom blinds, and I heard the sounds of car tires moving over the pavement outside. *Did I oversleep?* The clock read 7:30 a.m. Presentations began at eight sharp.

I didn't bother showering. Racing to the bathroom, I combed my crew cut and washed my face. Dodging cars and pedestrians alike on my bike, I made it to the engineering building.

Claudia, who had come to see me present, approached me with a concerned look on her face. "You look tired. Are you all right?"

"Fine. I didn't sleep well last night—that's all."

"Again?" She lowered her voice. "Are you getting sick from your illness?"

"I'll be fine."

I sat in the third row, waiting for my turn, with Claudia and Chrissy. My foot tapped the floor inaudibly. I found myself running my hand through my hair. *Calm down!*

Then one of the professors announced my name. I walked up to the podium and accustomed my eyes to the glare of the light beaming down from above. A few students rustled in their seats, but otherwise everyone's eyes, including Claudia's and Chrissy's, focused on me.

I took a deep breath and began my introduction. "The opening of the Chesapeake Bay Bridge, which spans the Chesapeake Bay and connects the State of Maryland's eastern and western shores, took place in 1952. The so-called Bay Bridge was over four miles long and a feat for its time. The Walt Whitman Bridge, which spans the Delaware River and connects the city of Philadelphia, Pennsylvania to the state of New Jersey, was completed in the same decade, in 1957."

My voice was strong and my hands steady, despite my fatigue and sorrow. I glanced up at my audience to find everyone attentive, clicked the laptop to change slides, took another deep breath, and continued.

"While the Walt Whitman is a suspension bridge, one of many in the United States, the eastern-bound stretch of the Bay Bridge is a cantilever bridge, a relatively new technique of construction for major bridges that was only about fifty years old at the time of the Bay Bridge's completion. The cantilever enabled engineers to build across a longer distance without the need for ground support. In this manner, it was easily able to span between the two shores with minimal anchoring from the bottom of the Chesapeake Bay during construction.

"The westbound path's construction of the Bay Bridge used the more complicated through-arch suspension bridge method, in which the deck, or roadway in this case, intersects with the supporting arches, leaving part of the arch below the deck and part above it. Here is a photo of the westbound through-arch design…"

On I went, clicking through all of my slides on the laptop and finishing the presentation in about ten minutes.

I sucked in another deep breath to stay calm. Now came the potentially difficult part—questions from fellow students and faculty. First up was my academic advisor, Edith. "Describe to me, Hank, shearing as it pertains to bridges."

I gulped. "Shearing?"

"Yes. Shearing."

I tried to gather myself. As usual, Edith caught me off guard, and I struggled to remember this concept in my research. *Hurry, Hank! Think!* Then it came to me. "Shearing is a cutting or slicing action on a structure. Most often, an external load, such as a heavy truck or even a car moving across the deck, causes shearing. Shear force is the name for the force resisting this external load. For the structure to be sound and the deck of the bridge to stay intact, the shear force must be greater than the external load causing the shearing."

"Was shearing involved in the collapse of the Tacoma Narrows Bridge?" she continued.

I couldn't tell if she already knew the answer and was testing my knowledge or if she was truly curious about the subject. "That bridge failure was caused by high winds, which created strong resonance in the structure. Resonance is a different force from shearing."

"Thank you," replied Edith with a nod.

Relief flooded through me. Answering Edith's questions was a big hurdle toward finishing my presentation.

Another hand. It was the hot shot in the class who always boasted of his excellent grades. "What are some other examples of suspension bridges in the

United States?"

"The most famous suspension bridge is the Brooklyn Bridge in New York City because it was the longest one of this type when it was built. Its construction completed in 1883, and it was the first suspension bridge to use steel cables. Steel was a relatively new material used in bridges in this period. The John A. Roebling Bridge, which connects Ohio and Kentucky and spans the Ohio River, is also an example of a suspension bridge."

"What kind of bridge is the Golden Gate in San Francisco?" he continued.

The mention of this bridge, which was involved in my first psychotic episode, sent a shiver through me. I squeezed the front of the podium with both hands. "The Golden Gate is also an excellent example of a suspension bridge." I forced a smile.

The student leaned back into his seat, apparently satisfied.

"Any other questions?" I asked the audience. Hands continued to go up!

I directed my eyes to my project advisor, Dr. Hill. "Yes, Dr. Hill."

"Your presentation was very interesting, Hank. Very interesting. Could you tell us briefly how much of an impact differential calculus has had in the construction of bridges?"

Another difficult concept! I paused to gather my thoughts and then took a stab at it. "Newton and Leibnitz developed differential equations from their theories in calculus in the mid-seventeenth century to describe the forces in bridges as accelerations. Their theories helped suspension bridges to be stable because mathematical formulas could account for stresses moving through the structures.

"The only drawback to these differential equations was that they didn't account for wear and tear, especially over long periods of time."

Dr. Hill raised his eyebrows. "What type of wear and tear?"

"Vibration is an example. It's a force that is caused by external loads, and it only lasts seconds. Deterioration, the main cause of which is corrosion, takes place over years and even decades and is another example. These days bridge materials such as steel and concrete are more durable, so bridges are lasting longer—with the help of these differential equations, of course."

Dr. Hill, with his signature look of his index finger on his cheek and his thumb below his chin, said, "Thank you."

"Other questions?" I asked.

One more hand went up. It was the same hot shot student again! *Is he trying to confuse or stump me with his questions?* "Yes."

"Could you go into a little more detail on how a cantilever bridge works?"

I had this! "So the cantilever acts like a diving board, basically. There are three parts. The anchor arm is the short part that juts out away from the pool. It counters the weight of the long arm, called the cantilever arm, which extends out over the pool. Finally, the suspended span would be the part attached to the cantilever arm if it were to connect to the long arm of another cantilever from the opposite end of the pool."

"So which type is better—cantilever or suspension?" asked the student.

He was annoying me now. Nevertheless it was a good question. "Suspension bridges carry heavier loads and require less building material than cantilever bridges, so they are more effective structures."

He sat back again in his seat. I looked for more hands but saw none.

The professor who directed the order of the presentations stood and approached the podium. I stepped aside.

"Thank you, Hank," he said and began applauding. The rest of my class, the faculty, and visitors clapped. I met Claudia's eyes and saw nothing but pride and joy. I stepped off the stage and returned to my seat next to Claudia. She squeezed my hand and smiled broadly. Chrissy's eyes welled with tears as she stood and applauded.

Then everybody stood and continued to clap! This was unexpected, as most only acknowledged the presentations with applause. And they didn't stop until I stood again and bowed with appreciation. My smile beamed as I took my seat once more. Only I knew the ordeal from the night before, that this time my illness hadn't gotten the best of me.

Epilogue

After graduation, I signed on officially with NASA and moved into an apartment in San Jose with Claudia.

On the Fourth of July, Claudia, Tom's family, and I visited Fisherman's Wharf in San Francisco to watch the fireworks display. I held Claudia close as we watched them fly high and light up the dark sky when they exploded. As always, they captivated me.

My mother had put the mansion up for sale and moved into a retirement community, where she was making friends. My worries of her coping with my father's absence dissipated slowly. Jocelyn moved on to another job, though I held her dear in my memories.

Chrissy was now engaged and continued her work as a surgeon in Atlanta.

Zach continued on at his bank in Los Angeles, and by now his wife was expecting another baby. All was well with him. Even with his work and family responsibilities, he talked of visiting me in the near future.

Though my father was gone, I often thought about him. In an indirect way, he had made me into a man—someone who took responsibility for his actions, who took the initiative when life took a turn for the worse, and who stood up for the woman he loved. Yes, he was a despot, and I learned what not to do in life from him more than what to do. Despite his flaws, though, he had shaped me into who I was, and I was thankful.

The End

CPSIA information can be obtained
at www.ICGtesting.com
Printed in the USA
FSHW020601230219
55870FS

9 781684 330089